THE
RESTING
PLACE

ALSO BY CAMILLA STEN

The Lost Village

THE RESTING PLACE

•

CAMILLA STEN

MINOTAUR BOOKS
NEW YORK

First published in the United States by Minotaur Books,
an imprint of St. Martin's Publishing Group

THE RESTING PLACE. Copyright © 2020 by Camilla Sten.
English translation copyright © 2021 by Alex Fleming. All rights reserved.
Printed in the United States of America. For information, address
St. Martin's Publishing Group, 120 Broadway, New York, NY 10271.

www.minotaurbooks.com

Design by Jonathan Bennett

Library of Congress Cataloging-in-Publication Data

Names: Sten, Camilla, 1992– author. | Fleming, Alex (Translator), translator.
Title: The resting place / Camilla Sten ; translated by Alex Fleming.
Other titles: Arvtagaren. English
Description: First U.S. edition. | New York : Minotaur Books, 2022.
Identifiers: LCCN 2021047616 | ISBN 9781250249272 (hardcover) |
    ISBN 9781250859471 (Canadian) | ISBN 9781250249289 (ebook)
Subjects: LCGFT: Thrillers (Fiction)
Classification: LCC PT9877.29.T39 A8813 2022 | DDC 839.73/8—dc23/
    eng/20211018
LC record available at https://lccn.loc.gov/2021047616

Our books may be purchased in bulk for promotional, educational,
or business use. Please contact your local bookseller or the Macmillan
Corporate and Premium Sales Department at 1-800-221-7945, extension 5442,
or by email at MacmillanSpecialMarkets@macmillan.com.

Originally published in Sweden in 2020 by
Norstedts ingår i Norstedts Förlagsgrupp AB

Published by agreement with Nordin Agency, Sweden.

First U.S. Edition: 2022
First Canadian Edition: 2022

10 9 8 7 6 5 4 3 2 1

To Rasmus the Cat,
You were a little ray of light.
I'm so glad I got to have you with me,
Even though our time together was all too short.
I miss you every day.

·

SUNDAY, SEPTEMBER 15
FIVE HOURS LATER

·

· ELEANOR ·

The light in the small room is cold, the stark, white glare of an eco-friendly bulb. I'm sure it's meant to be reassuringly normal, just like the anonymous chair I'm sitting on, and the smooth, light-wood table in front of me.

When I look at my hands I can still see the blood, even though I scrubbed them red and raw with the antiseptic soap in the bare white bathroom.

The door opens and I give a start. The man who steps into the room is wearing a police uniform. He has short blond hair and is carrying a portable recording device in his hand.

He puts the recording device down on the table between us. It's small, gray, and efficient, but it clinks heavily against the wood.

"Is it all right if I record our conversation, Victoria?" he asks.

Victoria, as if we knew each other.

Everything is spinning. I'm so tired, so cold. I close my eyes just to make it stop.

"Victoria?" he repeats, in that same artificially soft goddamn voice.

"Eleanor," I say as I open my eyes, my tongue dry and rough. "My name's Victoria Eleanor, but nobody calls me Victoria. Only Vivianne."

"OK," he says. "Can I tape our conversation, Eleanor?"

I nod.

"Can you tell me what happened when you arrived at your grandma's?" he asks.

"Please, don't call her Grandma. She hates it. Her name's—her name was Vivianne."

"OK," he says amenably. "Can you tell me what happened when you arrived at Vivianne's apartment?"

He has bright blue eyes, so even in color that they look unreal. Easy to remember. A good marker.

Does he know? I find myself wondering. *Has anyone said the word* prosopagnosia *to him yet? Explained to him what it means?*

I'm good at explaining it. Which isn't surprising, given how often I have to.

Prosopagnosia, face blindness. It means my brain doesn't process human faces the same way others' do. I can't recognize faces, so have to memorize distinguishing features instead.

Nope, it's not so handy for parties. Yeah, it's a good excuse, only it's not an excuse. It's my life. I can't recognize a n y b o d y, not even myself in the mirror.

"I don't know what happened," I say.

He says nothing, forces me to fill the silence.

"I was going to her place for dinner. We have dinner together every Sunday; that's our agreement. She won't drop by our place or show up at my office or call me twenty-eight times in a row until I pick up, but in return I have to eat dinner with her every Sunday. And I always do. So I was just on my way there when . . ."

I stare at him. The words fail me.

"It doesn't have to be perfect," he says. "Just tell me what you remember."

So that's what I do.

·

FIVE HOURS AND
FIVE MINUTES EARLIER

·

· ELEANOR ·

My footsteps echoed in the stairwell. I would always hang back on those last few steps up to Vivianne's apartment, the place that had been my "home" for sixteen years. If it were up to me I would never go back.

The Sunday dinners were a compromise. Two hours, once a week, when Vivianne got to mutter and pontificate to her heart's content, foist light sherry onto me in small, delicate glasses, and pick me apart with a fine-tooth comb. It was my therapist Carina's idea, and the arrangement had worked well for almost four years. It was a compromise.

I didn't want to cut all ties with Vivianne. She was my grandmother in theory, my mother in practice. Impossible to live with, impossible to live without.

Still, her phone calls that oppressively hot September week had breached our agreement. She wasn't supposed to call me unless it was an emergency. I never picked up, but that didn't stop her from leaving voicemail after voicemail: four on Tuesday, six on Thursday. One more late Friday night:

"I can hear them in the walls: they're whispering to me."

That last one had made my skin crawl.

I was used to Vivianne calling me drunk and angry, drunk and sad, or even drunk and manic, but this was different. It felt wrong to think of her as old—she was just *Vivianne*, ageless—but she was almost eighty. Had she started to lose her grip on reality?

I stopped by the front door to her apartment. *V. Fälth* glistened on the well-polished nameplate, concise and precise.

I braced myself.

Why was it always so stuffy in that damn building? I was already missing my airy apartment. Sebastian's arm around my shoulders, our well-used Ikea couch, our way-too-expensive TV. I wished I could spend my Sunday nights binge-watching Netflix like everybody else.

I knocked at the door.

A few seconds passed. One, two.

The door opened.

I arranged my face into something resembling a smile and made to step over the threshold, but then I stopped. Something was wrong. The figure in the doorway didn't fit.

I stared at the person in front of me, searching for Vivianne's markers, but all I could find was a thick, knitted black hat where her shiny, meticulously coiffed hair should have been.

My eyes quickly dropped to their hands.

They weren't Vivianne's. Her long, red nails were missing, as was the bulky topaz ring she usually wore on her right index finger. And they were flecked with something that looked like rust.

"Who . . . ," I began, but the person had already pushed past me and scurried off down the stairs. I watched them go in confusion, then turned back to the door.

Vivianne was lying in the middle of the hallway. Something beside her on the patterned, slate-blue rug flashed in the light of the small chandelier. I opened my mouth to ask something, but then the smell hit me like a ton of bricks.

It was sweet and heavy—iron and meat and perfume—and it made my stomach turn.

A pair of scissors gaped on the rug before me, the blades spread. I had never seen them like that before. They had always been closed, untouchable: a beautiful, meticulously polished object that sat alongside her matching ornate hand mirror and tobacco pot on the sideboard in the dining room.

But this time they weren't polished. This time they would stain.

Vivianne reached out for them with thin, splayed fingers.

Strange, my drowsy, sluggish brain thought in that split-second moment of stillness. *What does she want the scissors for? And why doesn't she just sit up and take them?*

And then something broke my paralysis, and I realized it wasn't the scissors she was reaching for, but me; that the wet, bubbling whimper I could hear was coming from her, was her attempt to call my name; that the patterned blouse she was wearing wasn't patterned so much as punctured, repeatedly, by the scissors that lay glistening on the rug just a few feet from me.

I crossed the hallway in two steps and knelt down beside her, heard my voice babbling, as though far away:

"What is it, what's happened, what should I do? What do you want me to do?"

She always knew the right thing to do.

So I kept on asking her, again and again, even though I could see the inside of her throat, red and moist. The flesh beneath the skin.

With her outstretched hand she grabbed my wrist, an echo of all the times she had grabbed it before, and clenched it so hard that our bones chafed, as though I were a lifeline and she drowning. Which in a way she was: I could tell from her strained, rattling breaths that the reddish-black stickiness that was gushing all the slower from her neck, onto her yellow silk blouse and her antique Persian rug, was also making its way down into her lungs.

I did the only thing I could think of.

I pressed my free hand to the gap in her neck.

·

NOW

·

· ELEANOR ·

Can you remember what the person who opened the door looked like?" the police officer asks. "Can you describe their face? Was it a man or a woman? Do you remember how old they were?"

I shake my head slowly. Meet his shiny blue doll's eyes as my taut lips say:

"No."

PART ONE

FIVE MONTHS LATER
WEDNESDAY,
FEBRUARY 19

· ELEANOR ·

It's too hot in the car for my liking, but I keep my thoughts to myself. This winter has been unusually gray, and the passing fields lie pale, desolate, and frosty beneath a heavy sky, only a thin dusting of snow to shelter them from the wind. It's enough to make anyone feel chilled to the bone.

Besides, it's Sebastian's car, and Sebastian's driving, so it only feels fair that he should choose the temperature.

"Thanks for driving," I say.

He gives a faint smile, keeps his eyes on the road.

"No problem. I like driving out here. It's only in town that I get a little shaky."

I put my hand on his knee because I know it's the right thing to do, then give it a gentle squeeze. Even though we have been together six years, this type of gesture still doesn't come entirely naturally to me.

For a few minutes neither of us says anything. Then Sebastian says:

"I wonder if the house is in a bad state or something. If that's why your grandmother never mentioned it, I mean."

"I don't know," I reply.

When Vivianne's lawyer first mentioned Solhöga I assumed it was some sort of mistake. It was back when I was fresh out of the hospital, still unsure of how I would cope in the real world.

The lawyer was very matter-of-fact. He didn't offer any condolences, which came as a relief.

First and foremost we should discuss Solhöga. That was how he opened the meeting.

He kept it brief. Said that Vivianne had documents relating to a property registered in her name, an old manor house with woodland and private hunting grounds around an hour and a half's drive north of Stockholm. She had inherited it from her deceased husband. My grandfather.

"I think my grandfather died around Christmas," I say to Sebastian. "From what I've heard they used to celebrate Christmas at Solhöga, so it might have happened there. That could be why she never went back."

I see Sebastian's brow furrow slightly.

"How did he die, again?" he asks. "Sorry, I'm sure you've told me."

"I haven't," I say. "I'm not actually sure myself. She never talked about it—she didn't like to talk about him in general. I've always assumed it was a heart attack or something. I don't get the impression he was sick for long—it must have been pretty sudden."

Out here the houses are fewer and farther between, the homely rural villas replaced by farmsteads, in turn replaced by isolated old cottages with bowed walls and broken windowpanes. The icy smattering of snow lies untouched on last year's yellow grass. The entire landscape looks deserted. It's easy to imagine that we're alone out here.

I look out of the window and chew at my thumbnail, an ugly childhood habit I never quite managed to kick. For months at a time I'll be able to keep my fingers out of my mouth, but then something will happen and I'll fall back into it again. Ever since that night I've given up trying to stop. My nails are all stumps, squat and ragged, and my cuticles are constantly raw and inflamed.

The GPS impassively instructs us to turn right. Sebastian turns onto a forest-lined road.

The road to Solhöga.

· ANUSHKA ·
JUNE 18, 1965

Before I left home Mama told me this place would be nothing but cold, cold cold, that I had to get used to being freezing all the time. She made me pack thick sweaters, and even gave me her warm winter coat to wear on top of my own threadbare one.

But this house is so hot that I'm dripping with sweat. I feel too big for my skin, heavy and swollen.

We've been out here in the countryside for four days now, and I don't know how I'll make it through summer. I can't even open the windows—someone's painted the frames shut with big, long brush-strokes. Pointless as it is, whenever Ma'am and Sir are down at the lake I find myself tugging away hopelessly at the handles, resting my forehead on the hot glass, leaving greasy marks on the panes.

I always wipe them off before Ma'am and Sir get back, so that she won't find them.

Sir keeps on saying it's the hottest summer ever, and this seems to please him somehow—even when he's having to fan himself with the newspaper at breakfast. I never reply; I just smile. I know he thinks I don't understand, but the truth is I just don't know how to respond.

At first I kept quiet out of shame at how awkwardly the words sat in my mouth, how ugly and plodding my sentences were. I've always been sharp—that's what our neighbors used to say when I was little. *She may not be a looker, but she's bright*, they said to Mama. *You can count yourself lucky to have such a quick daughter. Quick-witted and quick-footed.*

But I don't feel sharp anymore, not since I came here.

I'm not funny here. No one laughs at my jokes, and no one is impressed by what I have to say. They don't even care. If I say nothing they think I don't understand, but if I speak they just hear my mangled words and assume I'm stupid.

This wasn't the new life Mama wanted for me. This isn't a new chance.

I've only been in this country four months, and I know I just have to keep at it—but God, Mama, I just want to come home.

How I wish I could just go home.

· ELEANOR ·

"There," says Sebastian, snapping me out of my thoughts. I give a start and look up.

After passing seemingly endless fields, the narrow, private road led us through a stretch of dense woodland, and now the tall, frost-dappled tree trunks open up to reveal a cluster of buildings. A sloping gravel drive leads down to the main house—a beautiful, well-kept two-story manor with white plastered walls and rows of dark windows that stare out at us blankly. Behind it I can see other, smaller buildings, and a small lake lined by frozen reeds. The ice lies perfect, blue and unbroken.

"Wow, some place you've got here," says Sebastian.

"Yeah . . . I mean, the lawyer did call it a mansion, but this . . ." I shake my head.

"What are the other buildings?" he asks.

I try to scan my surroundings. Some of the smaller buildings aren't really so small; one of them is almost half the size of the main house. I imagine it's a stable or barn of some sort, as it's set back slightly from the other buildings, nestled in at the forest's edge.

"You tell me," I say. "I have no idea."

To my surprise there are two cars waiting for us on the drive, one an anonymous gray Volvo, the other . . .

"I thought it was just going to be us and the lawyer?" Sebastian asks as he pulls up and parks.

I shake my head.

"So did I."

As the words leave my mouth, I spot my aunt. Dressed in one of her innumerable black coats, she's leaning against the wall, a cigarette hanging out of her mouth. I find myself saying—with a sharpness that's unlike me but sounds eerily Vivianne:

"Typical Veronika."

Neither of us makes any move to get out of the car.

"I thought she wasn't coming," says Sebastian, and I can hear the worry in his voice even though he's trying to hide it. Sebastian has only met Veronika once, but that was more than enough. It is for most people.

"So did I. She said she wasn't."

Her exact words were *I wouldn't come if the old battle-ax paid me to*, though in a way that's exactly what this is: Solhöga has to be surveyed and valued before Veronika can get her hands on her inheritance.

I have no close relationship with Veronika; I don't know if anyone does. When I was little she would often come over with gifts, a stale but glamorous stench of cigarette smoke wafting around her loose black clothes like a cloud. But then her visits stopped. Now I only see her at Christmas every year, for a long, excruciating lunch of saddle of venison, red-currant jelly, and potato gratin, where she and Vivianne try to size each other up from opposite ends of the table, while I try to maintain some semblance of festivity.

Or we used to. Never again. Not the three of us. Not Vivianne.

Veronika eyes up Sebastian's car with the same sort of idle, mild disgust she might show some roadkill at the side of the road. Her oversized black coat hangs like a pair of drooping wings, and her straight, black bob creates a razor-sharp frame around her narrow face.

Veronika's hair has always been her best marker. Sometimes I'll flinch if I see someone on the street with a straight, black bob like hers. I'll look up at her with my pulse racing, and only dare to exhale when she looks away blankly.

Sebastian turns off the engine.

"It's OK," he says. "It's just a few days. I'm sure she'll get bored and go home tomorrow."

Ever the optimist.

"That must be the lawyer," Sebastian says just as my eyes land on him.

If Veronika looks like a crow over by the wall, then the probate law-yer looks like a cardboard cutout of the stereotypical legal eagle. He's wearing a gray overcoat that matches his Volvo—so much so that I can't help but wonder if it's deliberate—and his hair is neatly combed to the left in a meticulous part. His black leather gloves are perfectly coordi-nated with the leather briefcase at his feet, on the top step leading up to the front door.

"Hello," I say as I climb out of the car and close the door behind me. After the stuffiness of the drive, the February air feels nice on my face.

"Victoria?" he asks, with the sort of upper-class Stockholm accent that must make it hard for him to spend any lengthy amount of time elsewhere. "We spoke on the phone, no? I'm Rickard. From Lindqvist's."

It was Rickard who contacted me a few weeks ago to suggest we visit Solhöga to compile an inventory of assets. He's younger than I initially thought—late forties, I'd say, from the lines around his eyes and the streaks of silver in his thick, dark hair. It was another, older lawyer who was taking care of the will.

"Eleanor," I correct him, smiling so as not to seem unfriendly. "I pre-fer 'Eleanor.'"

"Oh," he says. "Nice to finally meet you, Eleanor."

His handshake is firm and warm. I let go a little too soon. My pulse has quickened, a fluttering in my veins.

He's just the lawyer helping us with the inventory. He isn't dangerous. You have spoken to him on the phone, remember?

I look away to stop myself from staring at him, and my eyes land on Veronika. She drops her cigarette to the ground, puts it out brutally and efficiently with a stamp of her high heel, and looks up at me.

Neither of us says anything for a few seconds. She's waiting me out—one of Vivianne's old tricks, though Veronika would be furious if I pointed that out.

"How nice of you to come," I say eventually.

She smirks. Just the one side of her mouth—the left.

When I was a child I thought it was intentional. Back then I was still mesmerized by my aunt, who showered me in spurts of absentminded attention as if I were a little puppy. Her attention span lasted longer than Vivianne's, but her moods swung faster. And I idolized her all the more for it.

It was only when I was a teenager and Veronika's intensity had started to calcify to aggression that Vivianne told me in venomous confidence that Veronika's lopsided smile was the result of a temporary facial paralysis that had happened before I was born. *Probably a blessing, all things considered*, Vivianne had said, with her perfectly symmetrical grin. *I mean, she did always look like her father. At least the paralysis gave her face a little character.*

"I changed my mind," says Veronika. She hasn't even looked at Sebastian yet, let alone said hello. "I haven't been here since I was a child. I couldn't miss this," she goes on.

She raises her eyebrow slightly, throws a glance Sebastian's way.

"Aha. The boyfriend, I see."

Sebastian gives her a big smile, as though she greeted him politely.

"Good to see you again, Veronika."

Nicely done.

Veronika stares at him for a few seconds, then nods curtly and turns to the lawyer.

"And you are?" she asks, as though until this moment she has been blanking him entirely. I have no doubt that's exactly what has happened.

He looks at her the same way you would look at a snarling dog.

"Rickard Snäll," he says. "Probate lawyer. I'm here to assist with the inventory of assets and property valuation. You have the key, don't you?" he asks, turning back to me.

"Yes." I nod, avoiding his eyes as I step up to the front door. I reach into my pocket and fumble around for the key with sweaty fingertips. "It was in the envelope we found in Vivianne's apartment. With this address, and Bengtsson's phone number. I don't know if it works for any of the other buildings. The other locks may need different keys, but presumably Bengtsson will have those. He's—"

"The groundskeeper, yes," Rickard finishes my sentence. "I've tried to reach him at the number you gave me, but haven't been able to get through."

"Me neither," I say.

I have been trying to call the groundskeeper for weeks now, but my calls just go straight to an anonymous voicemail recording. According to the first lawyer, Vivianne's will specified that Bengtsson's salary should continue to be paid from her estate until it had been distributed.

"Perhaps he's moved on," says Rickard.

Still avoiding his eyes, I put the key in the lock and try to turn it. It's stiff, but it turns, and the door glides open on silent, well-oiled hinges.

So this is Solhöga, the secret Vivianne kept from me my whole life.

· ELEANOR ·

The hallway we enter is big and airy, with a faded Oriental rug on the beautiful wooden floor. The ceiling is high—at least ten feet—and the light that floods in through the windows on either side of the door fills every corner of the room.

It certainly doesn't look abandoned. A little dusty, yes, but there are no cobwebs in the corners, and the windows are more or less clean. A big mirror hangs on the wall to our left, and beneath it stands a small table with curlicued gold legs and a speckled marble top that serves no real purpose other than giving the eye something to land on. The surface is clean enough to glisten in the afternoon light.

Even if Bengtsson hasn't been taking my calls, it's clear he has been looking after the place. That or somebody else has.

"Is that her?" Sebastian asks.

It's only now that I see the painting. The light bouncing off the mirror opposite it both catches the eye and dazzles, but even so I can't believe the painting wasn't the first thing I saw. It's enormous—at least five feet tall and seven feet wide—and so dark and saturated that the paint seems to want to drip from the canvas.

It's a family portrait: a man, a woman, and two small girls against a dark-gray background. The man is seated in an armchair, the woman on one of its arms, her legs crossed demurely. The younger of the girls is standing next to the woman, a doll under her arm. She can hardly be

more than two years old. The older girl—five, six maybe—is sitting at her father's feet, wearing a red dress with white ribbons. Her face is an anonymous white oval, her eyes big and dark and indistinct, her hair tied in two neat, black braids.

"God," says Veronika, drawing that single syllable into a full, contemptuous sentence.

"Yes," I reply to Sebastian, then swallow. "That must be Vivianne. And Evert, and the girls—"

"Me," Veronika cuts in, pointing at her two-year-old self. It's impossible to reconcile the chubby cheeks, soft, dark ringlets, and rosebud mouth of the girl in the painting with the spindly woman with thin, arched eyebrows standing beside me.

"And . . . Vendela," she adds, her voice slightly softer as she points at my mother.

I so desperately wish I could see something of my mother in that little girl in the painting—in her neat braids or straight eyebrows, her dainty hands or carefully curled-up legs—but my memories of Mom are fleeting. I was three years and four months old when she died. Vivianne never told me the date it happened; otherwise I would have counted the weeks and the days, too.

What does it matter what day it was, Victoria? Vivianne's venomous voice rings in my head, exactly as it used to sound when she was alive: her haughty, blue-blooded Stockholm accent, the almost imperceptible speech impediment that she never quite overcame. It was as if certain sounds just landed in the wrong place. I always wondered if she had lisped as a child, or had a cleft palate that was operated on at an early age, but I never dared to ask.

She's dead. I'll never find out.

The small fragments I do remember of Mom are not of her face, but of how she smelled, how it felt to nuzzle my face into the base of her neck, the sound of her laugh, and her voice when she was angry. The clearest memory I have of her is of her shouting at me because I almost stepped out into traffic, and of how she then took me in her arms when I started crying and hugged me tight tight tight to make all my sadness disappear.

I have no memories of my father. Vivianne said he was a good-for-nothing who didn't deserve my beautiful mother, and who took off as

soon as he found out she was pregnant. Just after I turned eighteen I found his name on my birth certificate, looked him up on Facebook, and sent him a message. No reply. So on that count at least it seems that Vivianne was right.

Sebastian puts his arm around my shoulders. At first I think it's because he can somehow sense from the look on my face the short, sharp, shapeless pang of loss bellowing within me, but then he says:

"She really was . . . hmm."

Clearly it isn't my mother he's looking at, but Vivianne. Always Vivianne.

I know what Sebastian's *hmms* mean, and it annoys me even though it shouldn't: Vivianne was, in all truth, a great beauty. Even into her seventies she was beautiful, though then in an almost alarming way: white skin artificially tautened, aggressively feminine makeup, unexpectedly soft hair. She fought time furiously, like a personal affront. Vivianne didn't believe in not taking things personally; everything was personal to her, even aging. Especially when it was a fight that she started to lose.

Sometimes a beautiful face is all one has, Victoria.

Put on a little lipstick, won't you? God knows you aren't smart enough to give up on your looks.

In the painting she must have been around thirty, and Evert closer to forty, though with her in the frame it's impossible to focus on him. She's wearing a blue cardigan and a dove-gray pencil skirt—Vivianne never was a fan of color, except for on her lips and nails. Her hair falls in soft, raven-black curls that are layered around her face, her skin has a creamy white hue that almost matches the pearls hanging from her earlobes, and her plump, pillar-box lips are rounded in a perfectly balanced, enigmatic smile. One of her long, slender hands is placed on Evert's shoulder, while the other rests in her lap.

Am I imagining it, or is she painted with more detail and luster than the others? Even the little scar on her chin is there—a thin white line that only enhances the impression of harmony in the rest of her face. Is it just the way I see her, or was the painter besotted by her, too? How can it be that a woman in a painting from almost fifty years ago—her face, hair, and clothes all so unfamiliar to me—can still be so obviously, unmistakably Vivianne?

"Yes, she really was," I say, unable to wipe the tension from my voice.
I look around, and my eyes meet Veronika's.

For a split second her eyes look like they are welling up, but then she blinks, and the tears are gone.

· ELEANOR ·

I had only envisioned taking a quick look around the house to choose our bedrooms, but the improvised tour takes longer than expected. It's like traveling back in time, though not so much to the seventies—which must have been the last time anyone lived here—as to the turn of the century. The house is long and narrow, with the rooms arranged in a row. On one side of the hall we find a splendid dining room and a large working kitchen, both linked by a service passage. The dining table is so dark and glossy that I'm struck by a sudden, disconcerting urge to lick it. The other side of the house is devoted to a magnificent living room, or drawing room, as Vivianne would have called it. The rooms are all big and airy, the well-scrubbed floorboards are decked with beautiful rugs, and all the furniture appears to be antique.

Upstairs, there are four bedrooms, two bathrooms, and a combined library and study with a desk that smells of leather and wood oil. The bedroom doors are all ajar, their windows facing east.

Three of the bedrooms look identical: a square room with a wide, four-poster bed, a closet, an ornate chest of drawers, and a dainty desk by the window. The only things to distinguish them are their colors.

The fourth bedroom is bigger. I realize it must have been Vivianne's bedroom, quickly close the door, and turn away. We can all sleep elsewhere.

But beside that door we find another one. It's covered in wallpaper, as though to make it blend in with the wall. I probably wouldn't even have noticed it if Sebastian hadn't pointed it out.

"What's that?" he asks.

There's no door handle, but I poke my index finger into the lock and pull. After some initial resistance, the door gives in and swings open.

The hinge creaks, and it strikes me that this is the first time I've heard anything in the house make so much as a sound. Nothing else has groaned or scratched: everything appears to be greased, oiled, dried, and well maintained. Everything except this little door.

Outside the dusk is falling fast, but that makes no difference to the room before us: it has no windows. It's so dark inside that Sebastian pulls out his phone and turns on the flashlight, and the sterile white light reveals a small but neat bedroom. A narrow bed without sheets or blankets stands by the wall, a single, bare pillow lying on the stripped mattress.

Apart from the bed there's hardly any furniture in the room: a Windsor chair at the end of the bed, and a pewter bowl on the floor.

"What's this?" Sebastian asks.

"It was for the help," Veronika says from behind us.

I turn around. Veronika is leaning against the bannisters on the landing.

"No one ever slept in there when I was a child, but Daddy said it was a maid's room. Or had been. When we were here the help would always stay in the cottages. Mother didn't like to have them in the house overnight. She never wanted anyone sleeping in there," she says, looking at the door.

"I think that's why she wallpapered over the door. When I was really small you could barely even tell it was there, but then one afternoon Vendela and I sneaked up here and cut the wallpaper to take a peek inside." She purses her lips.

"After that Mother gave us such a beating that even Daddy kicked up a fuss, and that's saying something."

I can tell Sebastian's getting uncomfortable, that he doesn't know what to say. Part of me feels sorry for him, but another feels a sudden sting of irritation, unfair as I know it is. As I am.

It isn't Sebastian's fault he grew up with parents who wouldn't even contemplate yanking his hair so hard his feet practically left the ground. It isn't his fault that the mere thought of hitting a child puts him on edge.

That's a good thing.

It doesn't make him weak or spoiled. Just healthy.

I know that.

Deep down, I do.

"I'm guessing no one wants to sleep here, at least?" I say, looking from Sebastian to Veronika to the lawyer, who has also stopped by the door.

The smell of dry dust from the room is mixing with the faint aroma of artificial leather from Veronika's coat.

"I'll take the green room," she says. "You can fight over the cubbyhole if you want."

Sebastian rolls his eyes at me discreetly. I smile and lean in to him, just to feel the warmth radiating through his thick knitted sweater.

"I'll go get our bags," he says. "Shall I put them in the blue bedroom?" he asks. Then, turning to Rickard: "Looks like the yellow room's yours."

Rickard nods.

"Excellent."

"Great," I say as Sebastian disappears downstairs.

I stand there on the landing for a few seconds, staring at the door without quite knowing why. The raggedy line where my mom sliced open the wallpaper. The small, dark bedroom within.

Trying to shake the sudden uneasiness that sinks over me, I turn and go.

Trying to shake the feeling that the walls are watching me.

· ANUSHKA ·
JUNE 29, 1965

Their guests left this morning. I stood by the window in the hall and watched their shiny car drive down the road, getting smaller and smaller until it disappeared.

They were here for one week. Six and a half days. There were four guests in all, two men and two women, and the women were like little birds with their fluttering hands and short, colorful dresses. Their voices were chirpy and affected, but their eyes said things their mouths didn't.

Neither of the women actually wanted to be here. They thanked Ma'am profusely for the invitation, but their eyes were cold and hard, and I know that Ma'am saw it, too. I even think she enjoyed it. From what I could see, she relished their envy more than their partners' stolen glances, or the feasts the cook and I prepared every evening (so lavish we ended up having to throw away just as much as they ate), or the liquor they drank from their tall, thin glasses.

One evening I was alone in the kitchen—the cook had gone for the night after the food had been served. I could hear their tipsy, high-spirited, puffed-up chatter from the dining room, like overgrown children. My hands were red and dry, and I had blisters on my palms from where I had handled the big, hot cast-iron Dutch oven.

I had cleared the half-empty bottles of aquavit from the dining room when we served the cognac and whisky, and they were standing on the kitchen table beside me. Without thinking, I pulled out one of the stoppers and took a big swig, let the alcohol burn the whole way down my throat.

It was only then that I heard the chuckle.

I spun around to find one of their guests standing there, one of the men. He had the sort of face that had clearly been attractive at some point, but it was already starting to sag and puff, with the inklings of a red mesh of broken veins over his nose. His eyes were cloudy, of a washed-out blue that matched his pocket square exactly.

"Not so innocent after all, eh?" he said, and I felt the liquor and the nausea simmer down to a single, viscous mass in my belly.

"Forgive me," I replied hastily, looking down at the floor as the shame burned in my cheeks. "I didn't mean . . ."

I didn't know what to say. The words didn't come.

He just laughed again and took a few steps toward me. Sensing danger, I froze—like the mouse I have become, not the ferret I once was.

At first he did nothing, just picked up the bottle and read the label. My heart was pounding in my chest.

Then he said something I didn't understand, but whether that was because he was slurring his words or speaking too fast I couldn't say. Something about the bottle.

He put it down again and looked at me. Even though he hadn't moved, all of a sudden he was way too close.

He said:

"Not so bad either, now I get a better look at you."

He touched my cheek, and I felt my scalp start to tingle, felt the blisters on my palms throb and sting. His hand disgusted me. It was soft and sweaty, like a rotting mushroom.

Then suddenly his hand fell to my breast, as if landing there by chance. His thumb ran over my nipple, and I hated myself for not moving.

But then I heard a cough, and his hand was gone as quickly as it had appeared. It was Ma'am. She was standing there with her hands on her slender hips, a scornful, raging smile on her scarlet lips.

"Klaes."

The way she said his name, clipped at both ends. It made him flinch like a slap in the face.

"I–" he started, but Ma'am let him go no further.

"I must say," she said, the smooth skin around her eyes contorted into an ugly smirk, "I did think you had better taste than *that*, Klaes."

The seconds ticked past—one, two. He looked down at his feet.

He didn't say a word, just slunk past Ma'am and out into the dining room. But she didn't move. Her expensive dress fell in perfect folds around her knees, and her petite, dainty shoes were the same shade of red as her lipstick.

And then, in a voice a whole world away from the lilting Swedish she usually speaks, a voice with its very own hard melody, she said:

"Careful, Cousin. To him you're nothing but a cheap piece of furniture."

Then she turned on her heels and said in Swedish over her shoulder, like an afterthought:

"To me too, for that matter."

· ELEANOR ·

We turned on the fridge and freezer when we brought the food in this afternoon, grateful to find they worked. Although there's still no sign of Bengtsson, it seems like he's made sure we have electricity and water in the main house, which is a relief. If not we would have had to do a food run for meals that don't need to be cooked. Now I can make lentil soup for dinner as planned.

We'll be staying out here till Sunday, if needed, but the lawyer said it probably won't take that long. We have to compile an inventory of the different buildings on the land, with their rough square footage and function in case we do decide to sell, and a separate list of the furniture, paintings, and other movables in the house. There were shelves of binders in the study upstairs, and the lawyer hoped he would be able to find most of what he needed in there. He also said it might be good for Veronika and me to consider what we want to keep. When he said it Veronika rolled her eyes, but I wasn't sure how I was supposed to feel. I have no memories of this place. Nothing here feels like it belongs to me.

The faint hum of the ancient fridge has rocked me into a dreamlike state. There's no clock in the kitchen, and I've been so lost in thought while stirring the soup that it's only now I realize Sebastian has been gone awhile.

I look up from the black cast-iron Dutch oven and see the baguettes lying white and half thawed on the counter by the stove, and the kitchen window behind them.

It's pitch-black outside—so dark that it looks like a soft, black, velvet curtain is draped on the other side of the window.

I shift the pot to one side so the soup won't burn and walk through the service passage to the hallway. The passage is so narrow that it feels like my shoulders could skim both sides, and its nondescript white wallpaper has started to peel back at the seams.

He can't have been gone more than twenty minutes, max. He's prob-ably just gotten carried away in his quest for the perfect sticks for the masonry heater, meticulously handpicking branches that aren't too thin or too thick or too wet from the snow or starting to rot. . . . That's ex-actly the sort of thing that Sebastian could get excited about.

Everything's all right. Nothing has happened.

Are you quite positive about that, Victoria?

Surely you know better than to feel safe?

I try to shake Vivianne's voice from my head.

I'm better now. Not cured, because there is no cure, but better. That's what my therapist Carina says, the mantra we've been working on since I started seeing her eight years ago. Even more so now, since Vivianne, since I came home from the hospital.

A little better every day.

I quickly pull on my boots and jacket and zip it up, then open the door and step out into the snow.

The air out here is biting, the sort of cold that feels like a dry, crack-ling tongue just lapping at your skin, and I wish I had a scarf to pull up over my nose. The temperature must have dropped by twenty degrees since we arrived. When I checked the weather report for the weekend it said there was a risk of strong winds and a little snow before Saturday, but I don't remember seeing anything about such low temperatures.

In the darkness the other buildings are nothing more than murky outlines, and the forest looms around me like a wall. It's hard not to feel very alone out here.

I'm not an outdoorsy person. Vivianne would sometimes joke that our ancestors invented the indoors to save us from the so-called great outdoors, and that it would be disrespectful to go against their wishes.

Then she would give that ringing laugh that sounded like glasses clinking, and as soon as I heard it any anger or disappointment I was feeling toward her would seep out of me.

She knew that, of course—it was often why she chose to laugh.

My breath comes out in strained white puffs, and I squint at the ground to try to see where Sebastian's footprints lead. It's impossible to tell: we've been going in and out of the house all afternoon with bags and food from the car, and the snow outside the front door has frozen over, an icy sludge peppered with gravel.

"Sebastian!" I try calling.

I will him to respond but hear nothing more than resounding silence.

A little gust of air blows straight through my flimsy jacket, and my teeth start to chatter. I press my arms against my body, unable to escape the thought that it can't be good for Sebastian to have been out in this weather for—how long can it be? Almost half an hour?

Anxiety starts to gnaw at me from the inside out.

Everything's all right, I tell myself.

Nothing has happened. What could even have happened? We're in the middle of nowhere. There's no one out here to hurt him.

There's no one out here but Sebastian and me. "Sebastian!" I shout again, and start walking around the house. The gravel and ice crunch under my boots, and I hunch my shoulders against the cold.

There's no one here.

We're in the middle of nowhere.

No one is watching me from the trees.

My goose bumps are just the cold, nothing else.

"Sebastian!" I shout for the third time, as I round the corner to the back of the house.

I must be outside the dining room now, because the lights are off. It's so dark I can't even see where I'm putting my feet. I look up at the horizon and stop for a second.

The stars are twinkling in a band across the sky, so bright in the frozen air that they look burnished. They gleam like freshly polished silver.

Like scissors on a rug.

I turn around but freeze mid-step. My breath catches in my throat.

What was that?

It sounded like ice crunching underfoot.

"Sebastian, is that you?" I call out, but my voice sounds brittle and unfamiliar, as though it's coming from far away.

The feeling that I'm being watched is now so strong it's almost physical. I focus on what Carina has told me before, about having to keep my breathing under control: it's the body that panics first, the brain that follows. If I can just keep my breaths slow and force myself to relax then I can trick my mind into calm.

I look away from the house. Nothing but shadow upon shadow, in shades of gray and the deepest of blues.

But then the cloud bank moves across the sky, and for a moment the moon peeks out from between the gap.

There.

By one of the cottages, the one by the lake with the slanted black roof.

The scream catches in my throat.

There's someone standing there, a few feet from the cottage door. A tall, slim, black silhouette, seemingly genderless and featureless, just black contours and long, dark limbs.

Then the moon disappears back behind the cloud, and the darkness takes over.

I don't think. I start running back to the side of the house, my blood pounding in my ears. I'm slipping and sliding on the icy surface, but I don't stop. With every breath the cold air grates at my throat, but I can't stop.

It's when I round the corner that it happens.

I turn slightly too fast and lose my footing. I feel the impact in my wrists first; then my chin hits the ground and I give a short, stifled cry of pain as the skin breaks. The fall leaves me seeing stars, and I lie there on the ground, in a temporary paralysis of shock and pain.

The fear is still pulsing through my veins, but my thoughts have scattered. I no longer remember what I'm scared of: I know I need to get away, but not what from or why.

The footsteps approach, quick and purposeful, shoes crunching on the frozen ground.

Before me I see the blank, expressionless face and black hat, Vivianne's body sprawled on the rug, the blood-spattered scissor blades like obscenely splayed legs. I start to scuttle backward over the snow and ice but slip again, and when my right wrist hits the ground a jolt of pain runs up my arm. But then I hear a familiar voice.

"Eleanor? Ellie, what are you doing? What is it?"

Sebastian's voice breaks through my fog of fear. I blink into the light being pointed at my face and see a hand reach out.

I grab his right hand with my left and let him pull me up, my knees still shaking. I wrap my arms around him and squeeze him so tight that he gasps and lets out a little laugh before hugging me back.

"Are you OK?" he asks in my ear. "What is it?"

It's only when I let out a few cold, dry sobs into his jacket that his tone changes.

"Hey." He steps back a little. "Hello? Eleanor? What is it?"

In the blueish glare of the light from his phone I can see that his eyebrows are furrowed. He holds the phone up to my face and whistles when he sees my chin.

"Ouch," he says, touching my jaw with his thumb. "You hit yourself pretty hard there, no wonder you're upset."

I shake my head and look over my shoulder, but the light of his phone has blinded me to what little I could make out before.

"I saw someone," I say, turning back to him, my hand still on his sleeve.

"What?"

"Over by the lake," I say. "I saw someone standing by that cottage. There was somebody there."

He shakes his head, but I see his eyes pass over my shoulder to the cottage.

"Are you sure?" he asks. "It's pretty dark."

"I'm sure."

Even as I say so I start to wonder if it's true.

Carina's calm, reassuring voice echoes in my ears.

Your fear is valid, but that doesn't make it real. The fear may be true, but it doesn't have to be your truth.

This wouldn't be the first time I have seen something that wasn't what I thought it was, the first time I have let the fear take over. And I was alone, and out in the dark. . . .

Sebastian rubs my arm.

"Look," he says, his voice calm and soft. "I get that you were scared. I know this isn't easy for you. Just say the word and we'll leave here, OK? We can let the lawyer take care of everything."

I take a deep breath and shake my head.

"No, you're right. I was just scared. I didn't know where you were, and it was dark and I started to . . . see things."

Sebastian puts his arms around my shoulders, and I lean my head against his chest.

"Shall we go inside and take a look at that?" he asks. "It's bleeding quite a lot."

Now that Sebastian's here with me, with his cell-phone flashlight and reassuring voice and Sebastian smell, my breathing finally starts to settle.

"What were you doing out here, by the way?" he asks as we round the corner to the cars and the front door.

"You were gone so long, I wondered where you were."

"Oh, I'm sorry, honey," he says. "I was just trying to see if there was a woodshed or something out here. All the sticks on the ground were frozen."

Before I can reply Sebastian stops short. He points the flashlight up ahead of him.

The little cone of light sweeps over his car, bouncing off the red paintwork. The gap in the open door on the passenger side is only a few inches wide, but it looks like a gaping mouth.

Sebastian says nothing.

"Did you get something out of the car?" I ask.

I'm willing him to say yes, but I already know that he won't.

"Maybe it opened when we were getting the food out of the trunk," he says. He lets go of my hand, walks over to the car, opens the door a little farther, and slams it shut with a clap that makes me flinch.

He turns back to me and smiles. At least I think it's a smile. In the winter darkness it's hard to be sure.

"Come on, let's go patch you up and get some food in you. Sound good?"

He takes my hand again, squeezes my cold fingers with his warm ones. I follow him up the front steps.

Just as I'm stepping through the door I think I hear it again. A footstep, just a few yards away. Snow crunching underfoot.

There's nothing there.

But I don't turn around to make sure.

·

THURSDAY, FEBRUARY 20

·

· ELEANOR ·

I've been trying to get to sleep for hours.

Sebastian is snoring gently beside me, but that isn't what's keeping me awake. From a young age I learned to fall asleep to the sounds of clinking glasses and ringing laughter in the next room, so noise doesn't bother me. When I did get to sleep it would always be deep and dreamless.

Would be.

I've been prescribed sleeping pills, but I try to only take them if I have to. They leave me tired and sluggish the next day, make my limbs feel heavy and unwieldy and uncoordinated.

And they don't stop the nightmares.

I rarely ever remember them the next morning; it's more of a feeling, an impression. A flash of silver, sticky blood on my fingers, dying, rattling breaths. Blank faces all around me, staring.

I know I'll have nightmares if I fall asleep now: the fear still hasn't left me. I always knew that terror lay in the body; I grew up with fears that crept under my skin, flowed through my veins, and bubbled away in my stomach, just biding their time for the chance to break loose. But that evening in September the fear took root deep within me, became my constant companion.

Carina says it will always be that way, that it's natural. She says that wounds can leave scars on our souls just like on our bodies, and that we have to learn to live with them rather than try to rid ourselves of them completely.

After that night in September I tried to ignore it at first, pretended it was nothing. Sure, I would wake up kicking and screaming every night and Sebastian had to take time off work because I couldn't handle being alone, but still, I ploughed on. I ate regularly and exercised every morning, running until the adrenaline made my mouth taste of thunder and my eyes would sting with sweat. I could even relax, briefly, when Sebastian was there and the door was locked.

But when I got that call from the police station it all fell apart:

It's fairly common with this type of crime . . . a robbery that escalated . . . the victim's almost always chosen at random . . . of course we'll keep our eyes open, sometimes new lines of inquiry can open up after years. . . .

When I found out that they were closing the investigation, it was like that little thread that was holding everything together snapped. The hope that they would find whoever did it.

I stopped going to work. Stopped running. Eventually I stopped going out at all.

It was all the people. I couldn't handle them—all those faces I couldn't tell apart.

Any one of them could have been the person in the doorway.

Sebastian was right; I know he was. I was seeing things. He has told me that in the days before I was admitted to the hospital I was seeing and hearing things all the time. Footsteps in the hallway outside. Faces in the windows.

Stress-induced hallucinations, they called them. When I was discharged the doctors said the risk of them coming back was very small. It was a trauma-induced reaction.

Tonight was no hallucination. It was just a shadow in the night. I was seeing things. An optical illusion, nothing more.

Right?

The faint light casts subtle shadows across the old wallpaper—the moon must have broken through the clouds again. My ears are pricked, though I know I should let it go. I'm listening out for twigs cracking down on the ground. Heavy shoes on frozen snow.

Stop, Victoria.

Enough with all of this.

Why must you always be so hysterical? I don't know where you get it from. Not from your mother, in any case.

The comforter suddenly feels heavy and oppressive. I carefully peel it back, feel the cool air against my bare legs.

I'll just check the front door is locked. If I know it's locked then maybe I'll be able to scrape together a few measly hours' sleep, enough to get me through tomorrow.

The floor is icy against my bare feet, and I tiptoe out of the room so as not to wake Sebastian. My wrist is still hurting from where I landed on it, and I massage it gently with my other hand.

I step out onto the landing and head toward the stairs. Then I stop.

The moonlight doesn't reach here: the darkness is pressing down on my bare arms. And something is wrong.

I'm not alone.

The hairs on the back of my neck are standing on end, and my breaths are quick and shallow.

I want to whisper "hello?" but can't. I know there's someone here. Someone with a blank, white face and a black hat.

He's here.

Hide, Victoria.

Scream. Run.

I turn around, slowly. Listen. My heart is fluttering in my chest.

Don't let him see you.

Vivianne's voice is hoarse and rasping and scratchy in my head. I can practically feel her hot breaths on my ear. On my neck.

No—not hers. Someone else's.

Short, strained breaths at the end of the row of doors—breaths echoing my own, half a heartbeat behind. My feet move as though by themselves. I have to see what's hiding behind that invisible, half-open door, in that little room that Vivianne tried to conceal from the world.

See who's hiding in there.

You know who it is, Victoria!

Don't go in there! Run, you idiot!

I don't want to run. I've been running for months. I have to find out.

I pad silently down the hall, the runner caressing the soles of my feet. None of the floorboards creak.

As though hypnotized, I see my fingers reach for the small, wall-papered door and pull.

Someone is lying in the bed.

Curled up, their back to me.

The hinge screeches.

The figure in the bed jerks and sits up, so suddenly that I recoil. The rug slides under my feet.

It's the murderer, the person from the doorway. They turn toward me, their features blank and flattened, and they've found me—I don't know how, but here they are, at Solhöga, here to finish off what they started.

He's still sitting up in the bed. Neither of us moves.

I see the outline of dark, tousled hair and a white face, then hear a voice say:

"I couldn't sleep."

Veronika.

It's Veronika's voice.

For a second I can't shake the vision of the monster in the darkness, the shadow from my nightmares, but then she sweeps the hair off her face with a typical Veronika flick and in an instant it all clicks into place.

When I last saw her at dinner a few hours ago she seemed normal—sharp, abrasive, and sullen as usual. Now she looks almost shaken. Confused.

"I couldn't sleep in my room, it was too close . . . too close to the study, and I thought I might stop thinking about it if I slept somewhere else, but I dreamed . . ."

She trails off.

She sounds embarrassed.

I swallow. Find my voice again.

"It's OK. You can sleep wherever you want."

She shakes her head—that much I can see in the darkness.

I should do something, I know. Sit down next to her, ask her about her dream, put my arm around her.

But we aren't that kind of family.

"Sorry I woke you," I say instead.

She doesn't reply.

I make to shut the door and go, but then she says, so quietly and so softly that it doesn't sound at all like her:

"Don't shut the door, please. I can't take closed doors. Not at Sol-höga."

· ELEANOR ·

The house looks different in the ethereal morning light.

I can't lie here thinking any longer. The soft pink glow of sunrise seems to unspool across the floor, casting a gentle shimmer on the old wallpapers and slightly faded rugs as I tiptoe out of the bedroom and downstairs to the kitchen.

There's no toaster, so I turn on the stove and toast two slices of dry bread in a frying pan while gazing out the window. An airy shroud of mist is perched over the frozen lake, drifting slowly across the glinting, impenetrable ice as the sun fights its way up over the horizon.

You could really fall in love with this place.

I can't take closed doors. Not at Solhöga.

What did she mean by that?

I have so many questions, and last night and yesterday have only left me with more.

Why did Vivianne leave Solhöga? What happened here? And where is Bengtsson? It feels like as the groundskeeper, he should have been here to greet us, show us around, and give us the relevant documents about the buildings, forest, and grounds. Not too much to ask, surely, if he lives here on the property.

Would Vivianne have let a stranger live here, in the mansion she kept so secret? My gut feeling says no. She must have known him.

Vivianne had stipulated in her will that Bengtsson should continue to receive a salary from her estate until it had been distributed. His employment didn't end with her death. So where is he?

Was it him I saw last night?

No. You were just seeing things.

I start to smell burning bread, take the toast out of the pan, and put it on a small plate that's so old-fashioned it's almost trendy again: white porcelain with delicate blue flowers and a worn gold border trim.

It's when I set it down on the table in the dining room that I hear the voice.

Barely more than a whisper, quick and muffled, coming from the drawing room.

The big white doors on the other side of the hall are ajar.

I sneak over and prod them with my fingertips to open them a little more. I don't know what I was expecting, but what I find is Rickard the lawyer, wearing the same trousers and white shirt as yesterday. He's standing with his back to me, muttering into a cell phone.

"No, I haven't found anything yet. . . . I'll let you know as soon as I have any leads. But I would really prefer to communicate by email going forward, as agreed. The signal here is bad, and we wouldn't want anyone to overhear."

He pauses.

Perhaps I make a sound, or perhaps he just gets that prickling sensation you feel at the nape of your neck when someone is watching you, because suddenly he turns around. His eyes widen for a split second, and he lowers the phone from his ear.

Then he rearranges his face into a smile, and ends the call without looking at the screen.

"Good morning," he says to me, his voice composed and correct. "I hope I didn't wake you."

I shake my head.

"No," I say. "Not at all. I was already up."

I wait for him to say something, but he doesn't oblige.

"Sleep well?" I ask.

"Yes, very," he says. "The rooms are very well insulated. I didn't hear a peep from outside."

This strikes me as a weird thing to say. What would he be expecting to hear? Or who? But maybe I'm just a little off-kilter; finding him here has caught me off guard.

Still, when I sit back down at the dining table and take a bite of my now-cold toast, I can't help but wonder. Not about his words, but about the way he looked. About those milliseconds before he composed himself, when he didn't look so much surprised as . . . caught.

· ANUSHKA ·
JULY 11, 1965

M a'am is angry again.

She's been angry for days now—and I don't mean her usual condescending remarks or narrowed eyes. Last night, after Sir left for the hunting lodge to smoke a cigar, she took her coffee all alone in the drawing room, and when I bent over to top off her cup she grabbed my hair and yanked it so hard it made my eyes water. Then, with that rough, ugly voice she uses when it's just her and me, she hissed in our language:

"Has no one taught you to pour coffee from the right, you filthy little swine?"

My scalp is still sore today. I could barely tie my hair up the way she tells me to, because it hurt so much.

Since I arrived Ma'am has had her occasional bouts of anger, but only today did I realize what it's about.

It happened this morning, when I was upstairs fetching the laundry. They rarely have guests out here midweek, so today it was just the two of them. I thought they would be down at the lake by that hour: in the morning it gets unbearably hot upstairs.

My fingertips had just touched the handle of the bedroom door when I heard something inside.

My first instinct was that they were . . . well, together. I'm the one who washes their bedsheets and underwear, so I know they do it, and quite often, too. Sometimes I can hear them through the wall between their bedroom and my cubby.

I froze with my hand on the handle, too scared to even breathe: if I stepped away the floor might decide to creak, and then they might hear me.

But as I stood there locking my breath in behind clenched teeth, I heard the moans more clearly, heard them hacking and catching, again and again.

It didn't sound like pleasure. They sounded like sobs.

Then Ma'am spoke, in that studied Swedish she uses with Sir, only broken and despondent:

"You don't know how it feels, Evert. You don't; you couldn't."

Then more sobs. They weren't loud; they sounded more like the whimpers of a very young child without hope or solace.

I hate Ma'am; I'm not going to lie. So many nights I've lain awake, fantasizing about taking the heavy black frying pan from the kitchen and hitting her with it again and again, until her perfectly coiffed skull is as flat as the pancakes she forces the cook to make but then refuses to eat because of her figure. Still, it was impossible to hear those sobs and not pity the one making them.

For the very first time I felt some sort of kinship with her, for in that moment, through that heavy door, she sounded just as melancholy as I have felt since I arrived.

"Vivianne, we'll keep trying. There's no hurry." A short pause, then Sir's voice again, hesitant: "We could make you an appointment with a doctor, if you want. Just to see if there's anything they can do."

Her reply was instantaneous, sharp as a gasp:

"No!"

Silence.

Then I heard the bed creak as if someone was standing up, and footsteps heading toward the door.

I turned tail and ran, with such quick, light steps that I was behind the locked door of the bathroom before I could even breathe. I sat there on the cold, porcelain toilet lid until my heart stopped pounding. I have no idea how long that took.

I can't say that I've wondered why they don't have any children yet, seeing as Ma'am's only five or six years older than me and they haven't been married all that long. But I have heard the odd jibe from one or two of their guests, asking if they don't long for the pitter-patter of tiny feet, or if they aren't thinking of trading in their city apartment for something more child friendly.

Still, I never gave any of that a second thought, until now.

When I ventured into their bedroom to fetch the laundry half an hour later and my suspicions were confirmed by the reddish-brown marks in Ma'am's underwear in the laundry basket, I can't deny I actually felt sorry for her.

· ELEANOR ·

Sebastian and I have put on our jackets and boots and are standing in the hallway while I make the call. The signal's OK, two bars out of four, but when I tap on Bengtsson's number I go straight to the same anonymous voicemail greeting as before.

"Nothing," I sigh, and hang up, then put my phone in my jacket pocket.

"OK," says Sebastian, with a cheeriness that sounds a little forced. "Then we'll just have to try to find him!"

I smile almost in spite of myself, and open the front door.

We've agreed that Rickard and Veronika will go through the binders in the study and try to find any papers relating to the property, while Sebastian and I take a look around the grounds and try to track down Bengtsson. Rickard thought that might be a good starting point. He didn't seem all too enthusiastic about letting Veronika help out, and even though I get it, I still can't shake the feeling I've had inside me since the phone call I overheard this morning.

I can't quite articulate what it was that bothered me about it. Besides that last part:

We wouldn't want anyone to overhear.

But that doesn't have to mean anything. It's probably just about another case, or another estate. Those things are normally confidential, aren't they?

I wish I could talk to Sebastian about it, but after all that to-do with the shadowy figure by the cottage last night I don't quite dare. I don't want him to look at me that way again.

I know he doesn't mean anything by it, that he's still just worried about me. I don't remember much of the run-up to when he finally called the ambulance to take me to the hospital, after I barricaded myself in our bedroom while ranting and raving about faceless murderers with silver scissors.

He tried to talk to me about it when I was discharged, but I didn't want to. I was too ashamed.

Still, it hurts me when he looks at me like I'm made of glass; when he touches me with cautious fingers; when he asks if I'm completely sure of what I saw.

No, I'm not sure. But some part of me wishes he could just see me as Eleanor again. Not poor, weak, defenseless Eleanor, traumatized Eleanor, Eleanor who has such a vivid imagination and is always *seeing things*.

When we step out into the daylight I close my eyes for a second to let them adjust. The shrouds of night have dispersed, the sun is climbing up to its zenith, and there isn't a cloud in the sky.

After a few steps in silence, Sebastian clears his throat and says:

"What if Bengtsson's moved? I mean, we don't *know* he lives here. Maybe he just comes here periodically when something needs taking care of?"

"I've checked Bengtsson's phone number, and it's registered to this address," I say. "I just looked it up at breakfast. So it seems like he does live here. Not in the big house, clearly, but I guess in one of the cottages."

"Just seems weird that we haven't seen him yet," says Sebastian.

"Maybe he's a loner," I say. "Being the groundskeeper of an estate in the middle of nowhere isn't exactly a job for somebody who likes company."

"You're smart, you know that?" he says, squinting at me in the sunlight. I smile.

Sebastian gets small, fine lines around his eyes when he squints. He's one of those people who will get deep laughter lines, fine white creases on a tanned face. That and his eyebrows will make a good marker one day. If he sticks around long enough, that is. If he can put up with me year after year.

The snow isn't all that deep—even the drifts are no more than eight inches—but it's so hard and icy that we have to tread carefully. The gash on my chin is still stinging enough to remind me to watch wherever I step.

We reach the first little cottage. It's hardly more than a shed, with falu-red walls and a black roof—an outhouse of some sort, perhaps? I walk up to the door and give the heavy, black, cast-iron ring on it a tug. Locked.

Sebastian stands on his tiptoes to peer through the small window on one of the side walls.

"Oh, I wish I'd found this last night," he says dryly. "It's a woodshed. Would have saved me running around in the forest for half an hour."

"And here I thought running around in forests was just your thing, you Boy Scout."

Foraging for mushrooms and berries every fall; hiking in the forest; sailing in the archipelago every summer with his family or the tight group of friends he's kept in touch with since college: I never have understood Sebastian's penchant for the great outdoors. I went along with him a couple of times, in that first, heady rush of love when everything about him seemed new and amazing, when there was nothing I wanted more than to be like him. But after that first year I had to admit it wasn't my thing.

"I prefer *outdoorsman*, if you don't mind," he says with a laugh. "And it's more enjoyable when you actually have some equipment, a group of people, hot cocoa by a campfire, that sort of thing."

The sorts of things he did as a child. I can't even imagine it.

"A woodshed's pretty handy," I say. "Would be even more handy if it wasn't locked."

"As soon as we find this mysterious Bengtsson we can ask him to unlock it," says Sebastian the Eternal Optimist.

"Well, we know he isn't in here, at least. Could you take a picture and make a note?"

Sebastian takes a quick snapshot of the woodshed and notes down what it is, and we go on toward the lake.

When we're about 150 feet away from the main house I turn around and take in the scenery. A little shiver of premonition runs through me as I look up at the back of the house, at the corner where I hit my chin yesterday.

I'm sure it was nothing. But if I *did* see someone, they would have been standing pretty close to where we are now.

The next cottage we reach is bigger than the woodshed and looks more like a house. I can see lace curtains in the windows, all closed so we can't see inside.

Sebastian strides around the house and shouts:

"Hello-o? Anybody home?"

Nothing. Silence. I can't even hear Sebastian's footsteps anymore.

I follow him around the corner and find him staring down at the ground.

Three unpainted wooden steps lead up from the snow to a small front deck and a neat, black front door. Faint mud and gravel footprints lead up and down the steps. I can see them going in and out of the door, over to the corner of the deck—where you can see up to the main house—and then down to the rocky lakeshore, where the ground gets too hard and the footprints disappear.

"Looks like there was somebody here yesterday after all," Sebastian says, and looks up at me. I struggle to read the look in his eyes.

I make an effort to keep my voice breezy when I say:

"Guess I wasn't seeing things, after all."

Even I can hear the sharpness sneaking into my tone.

Neither of us says anything. Sebastian stares at the footprints thoughtfully.

"So Bengtsson must be here," I say. "It's a relief, if nothing else. Now we just have to find him."

Sebastian walks up the steps, grabs the handle, and tests it. The door swings open.

"Well, look what we have here," he says, and steps inside.

"Sebastian!" I say, shocked. "Stop, you can't go into his house!"

"Technically it's your house now," I hear him say from inside.

I seesaw for a moment; then my curiosity wins out and I follow him through the door.

· ELEANOR ·

It's a small, sweet, strangely anonymous house that looks like it has been plucked straight from a catalog of Swedish summer cottages. The only color in the décor is a well-trodden rag rug that's slightly too small for the space. The cottage can't be more than 160 square feet in size, with a kitchenette, a door that must lead to a bathroom, and a window on each of the long walls, both fitted with creamy white lace curtains. They lend the light that filters in a dreamy, warm, sepia tone, in contrast to the crystal-clear day outside.

Sebastian is already taking off his boots, and I whisper:

"Come on, Sebastian, leave it. He obviously lives here; we can't just go snooping around."

"He hasn't picked up the phone in two weeks," Sebastian replies. "And you own the house. Technically you're his landlord and his boss. If he's refusing to respond to your attempts to contact him, you have every right to go inside and see what's happening."

Sebastian uses his lawyer voice to sound more convincing. He's good at his job, but I'm not entirely sure if his argument holds up, legally.

Though I can't deny I am curious.

It's cold in here, barely warmer than outside, and when I squat down to look at the little heater on the wall I find it's switched off. I stand up again as Sebastian walks over to the tightly made bed, then pulls out the top drawer of the pale chest of drawers next to it.

"Hey, cut that out; you can't go poking around in his underwear," I say. Sebastian flits his hand without turning around.

"I'm not poking," he says. "Besides, it's not even underwear."

I roll my eyes even though he isn't looking. After taking a few aimless steps around the room I stop at the desk by the wall facing the main house. It's the only thing in the cottage with any personality, a sturdy table in a shiny dark wood with brass details. It looks like it belongs in a dark and serious study, not this little timber guesthouse. The chair tucked under the desk doesn't match it at all; its style is more in line with the narrow bed frame and the light chest of drawers.

I slide the chair aside and pull out the desk's lone, shallow drawer. It glides open smoothly and evenly, as though it has just been oiled. Inside it lie a lined notepad and a pen.

The notepad is filled with names, dates, and sums of money. It only takes me a few seconds to realize these are the accounts for the property. The entries are mainly bookings for hunting parties, but there's also the odd note like *Delivery—timber to sawmill*, with the relevant sums. The hunting party bookings are more detailed. The name of the person who booked is neatly logged, along with the size of the party, what they were hunting, how long they booked the grounds for, how many animals were shot, the date the invoice was sent, and the date the payment arrived. Any late payments are noted with a little cross, and when I flick through the pages I see a few bookings with two crosses next to them, and a fastidious note: *Repeated late payment*.

Two bookings have three crosses next to them. There the note reads: *Payment not received. Party blacklisted.*

For something so analog it's a fairly well-kept account. The first booking in the notepad is from 2009. I flick through the pages faster and faster.

"What's that?" Sebastian asks. I give a start and straighten up.

"It's all the bookings for hunts."

I look down at the notepad. I'm now up to last fall.

I turn a few more pages.

There. A note about a timber delivery, and then, two days later, the last entry. I take a quick look at the subsequent pages to make sure I haven't missed anything. They're blank.

The last person to book a hunt was someone called August Hansson. A party of six. They planned to shoot wild boar, but there's no indication of how many animals they shot. Nothing about invoicing, payment, or late payment either; it looks like the accounts have just been abandoned.

Sebastian has been standing quietly behind me as I read. His voice is different, more subdued than before, when he says:

"Isn't that . . ." He doesn't need to point or finish his sentence. I know what he's saying.

The date is the day before Vivianne died.

"Yes," I say quietly. "It is."

We stand staring silently at the notepad for a few seconds, but then I flip it shut and put it back in the drawer.

"I guess he didn't take any more bookings after she died," I say.

I feel a prickliness on the back of my neck. Suddenly I'm all too aware of how low the ceiling is, the closeness of the walls.

"Let's go," I say to Sebastian. "Bengtsson obviously isn't here. We'd better keep on looking; he may be out on the grounds."

I hastily jumped down the front steps in two hops, and look over at the lake.

I hear Sebastian close the door behind himself and come down the steps.

"Didn't you say Vivianne never mentioned him? Not ever?"

"Never," I say. "I mean, I never even knew this place existed, but I hadn't heard his name in any other context either."

"And the lawyer hasn't spoken to him?"

"No. He only got through to voicemail, like us."

"So he can't have called Bengtsson when Vivianne died."

"No."

The sick feeling in my stomach is back, and I start to see where Sebastian is going with this.

"So if nobody called him," he says slowly, "then how could he know that Vivianne was dead?"

· ANUSHKA ·
AUGUST 7, 1965

Just a few days left till we leave this house for the summer.

I'm not sure how I feel about it. The apartment in town is smaller and stuffier—dark, expensive, and stale—but it feels like the furniture has all been passed down through the generations, old but well kept, in a way that reminds me of home.

When I first got here I found it strange that people with so much money would want such old things. If I were rich, everything in my house would be shiny and new, bright and untouched. Rugs so plush your feet sink into them.

Once, at the start—before I realized Ma'am wasn't my friend, in those first few days when I turned to her as I would to a friend or a sister—I told her she had a beautiful home. I said it in the clumsy Swedish I had tried to drill into my head back home, and when I saw her mouth curl in contempt my first thought was that I had said something wrong, made a hash of the words.

"Do you dream of an apartment like this for yourself?" she asked me listlessly, and the seconds ticked past as I tried to decipher the foreign words. I had to mouth them back to myself, and I could feel my cheeks starting to flush as her faint smile grew.

"Yes," I said eventually, and then added, in our language: "I hope I can get an apartment like this so I can bring Mama and Pavel here."

Her smile disappeared just as abruptly as it had come.

"You're a filthy little half-wit who can't even speak properly," she said, and her skin seemed to tighten over the bones in her face. "So pray, do tell, how do you think you'll come to be anything more than hired help?"

She swept her index finger across one of those ugly little tables that are dotted seemingly at random around the apartment.

"Incompetent help, at that," she added. "I won't have you taking lunch until you've dusted the entire drawing room again. Properly, this time."

That was the first time I felt that I hated her.

The flash of pleasure in her eyes when she saw me flinch at her words.

Still, with hindsight, I can see there was some truth to what she said. She's a cruel woman, yes, but not stupid—that much I have seen. And in the months that have passed I have learned a thing or two myself. I have learned that the old mirrors and furniture were left to Sir by his parents, and that they're worth more than anything new. I have learned to pluck the stray dark hairs between my eyebrows, and to speak slowly and deliberately like Ma'am does so my accent is less obvious. Hers seems to have vanished completely. Her Swedish is crisp and clear and lilting, and it sounds just as natural and fluid as her well-oiled walk and her dainty, feminine gestures.

I can see why she would have found me ugly, coarse, and embarrassing when I first arrived. In that much she was right. But I'm no half-wit. In that little detail she was wrong.

I'm the *ferret*—small, lightning quick, inconspicuous. And I can learn.

A week from now we'll be back in the apartment in town. But this time I'll be able to appreciate it.

Once upon a time she too was a little Polish girl with unrefined manners and incorrectly stressed words. Now she's a Swedish trophy wife. One with a secret.

I don't know how she did it, but I can learn.

Someday I'll have an apartment like theirs, too. But mine will be big, light, and spotless.

I'll never let myself get swallowed up by this country like she has.

· ELEANOR ·

We find no other traces of Bengtsson, but we do get a better idea of the property, and take photographs and notes to match. Besides the main house, the woodshed, and Bengtsson's cottage there is also a barn—resoundingly empty and full of dust—a smaller cottage that we agree must have been for the servants or guests, a smokehouse, and a stable.

There isn't a single piece of straw to be found in the stable, but the equipment still hangs from hooks on the walls: saddles in a hard, shiny leather that has split from years of exposure to the cold; bridles; and other equipment that I don't recognize.

Did Vivianne ride, in spite of the smell? Did she enjoy spending time here?

If it weren't for the angle of the sunlight through the window, the way it falls only in February, when the light is sharp, but the sun is low, I would never have noticed it, but the sun's rays pick out a small mark on the wall in the corner. I step inside the stall and crouch down for a better look.

Two letters have been carved into the hard wood:

$A + M$

"What are you doing?" Sebastian asks from behind me.

"Look," I say, pointing at them.

He bends over me.

"Sweet. Must have been some staff who sneaked out here for a roll in the hay."

I stand up and stretch my back. The bones crack.

"Should we head back?" I ask. "I don't think we'll find him in here either."

Sebastian nods.

He pulls his hat down over his head as we step out of the stable.

"Damn it's cold," he says. "And the wind will be picking up soon. There were supposed to be gales tonight."

I rub my ears for warmth as we head back to the main house.

"Where do you think Bengtsson is?" I ask.

I look around us—at the small buildings, the treetops stretching skyward in the distance, the ice-topped lake powdered with snow. It looks like a postcard: still, perfect, and frozen. As though nothing ominous could ever happen here.

So why is my stomach churning?

Sebastian strokes his chin, trying to formulate a reply. I hear his glove scratch at his stubble.

"I don't know," he says. "Maybe he went to buy groceries. Or see his family. Maybe he didn't get any of your messages."

When he stops talking it becomes clear just how absurd it all sounds. We both know that I have called the man time and again, done everything I could to find other ways of contacting him. There are none. As far as I can tell, Bengtsson lives alone. No one else was registered at this address.

"But if it *was* him I saw yesterday—" I say, just thinking aloud, but Sebastian cuts me off:

"I'm sure that was just the shadows playing tricks on you. And the footprints could have been a couple of days old. There's nothing weird about that."

His words come out as short, sharp puffs of vapor in the chilly air.

"Plus we haven't even been here a day," he adds, trying to sound chipper. "I'm sure he'll turn up."

I nod but say nothing.

As we walk up the front steps to the house I clap my hands for some warmth, but then I stop in front of the door and frown.

"Do you hear . . . ?" I begin, but I can't finish the question before the raised voice inside the house turns to a scream.

Sebastian tears open the door.

· ELEANOR ·

The commotion is coming from upstairs. I take the steps two at a time without even kicking off my boots, leaving a trail of snow and slush on the glossy wooden boards behind me.

I find Rickard and Veronika standing eye to eye on the landing. Rickard is positioned with his back to the study and has a watchful look about him, his arms crossed, his mouth frozen in a sharp line. Veronika's face is red with fury, and her finger is pointed at the lawyer.

"Where the fuck are they?" she barks.

"What's going on?" I ask.

Rickard looks at me, but Veronika doesn't deign to throw me a glance. Her eyes are still glued to the lawyer, as though he might vanish into thin air if she so much as glances away.

"Veronika seems to have got it into her head that I've been in her room," he says dismissively.

"Did you tell him to do it?" Veronika asks, and when she looks at me I wish she would look anywhere else.

"I haven't done anything!" is all I can splutter.

"You little bitch," she snarls, flinging the words at me quickly and instinctively, in the same offhand way she might call me a brunette or an economist.

"I should have known you'd do something like this. You're just like her," she hisses.

"What is it that you think she's done, Veronika?" Sebastian asks with a studied calm.

Veronika's eyes whip around to him.

"Her pet lawyer has gone through my bags and taken Daddy's letters," she says.

"What letters?" I say, finally finding my voice now that her rage is temporarily channeled elsewhere.

"Daddy's letters." Now it's Veronika's voice that falters, if briefly. "He wrote letters to Vendela and me. I brought them with me. I went out to smoke and when I came back somebody had been in my room and taken them."

"Why would anybody want your letters?" I ask.

For a second she looks like she's at a loss for words. I can't remember ever seeing her like that before. Something glints in her eyes.

Then her face hardens again.

"You tell me," she says. "You and your little lawyer—if that's even what he is. How the fuck should I know? Maybe you want Solhöga all for yourself. Maybe you asked him to find anything you can use against me."

"Are you insane?" Sebastian steps in. "Eleanor would never do anything like that."

The stress is making my palms itch. I have to defuse the situation, get everybody to calm down.

I look at the lawyer, whose arms are still crossed.

"You haven't done anything with her letters, have you?" I ask him.

He rolls his eyes.

"Of course not," he replies coolly. Of the three of us, he looks the least flustered. Perhaps he's used to having to deal with irate clients.

"See, Veronika?" I say, trying to stop my voice from shaking. My whole body just wants to curl up in the fetal position. It's what I would do whenever Vivianne was angry.

Look at me when I'm speaking to you, Victoria!

"I haven't touched your bags, I promise," I say. "And Rickard says he hasn't either."

"Oh well, if he *says* so!" Veronika sneers, her eyes like a snake's.

"We didn't even know you had any letters. Rickard's just trying to do his job. Are you sure you haven't misplaced them?" Sebastian tries.

"I haven't lost anything," Veronika snaps. "They were there. Now they're gone. We're the only ones here. Seems pretty fucking simple to me."

"Veronika, I don't even know what you're talking about." My voice sounds thin. "Come on, we're all just here to do the inventory. No one wants to make this any harder than it needs to be. I can help you look for them, if you want?"

Veronika's eyes are glittering points in a hard mask. Any trace of the softness I thought I saw in that little maid's cubby last night is gone.

"No matter how much you try to smooth things out, Eleanor, it doesn't change the fact that somebody has been in my room and gone through my bag."

"Can you show us?" asks Sebastian.

Veronika's nostrils flare slightly. At first she shakes her head, but then she sighs and throws up her arms in capitulation.

She opens the door to the green bedroom, the one she chose yesterday before sneaking into the maid's cubby in the middle of the night. She steps inside, and I follow.

The bed is unmade, the green bedspread dangling off the side. Her black sports bag is lying on the small green mat beside it, with a swell of black clothes and a small, shabby plastic toiletry bag on top of it. Still, it doesn't look any messier than I would have expected of Veronika.

"The bag was closed when I left it," says Veronika. "The letters were in a folder at the bottom."

She lifts the bag onto the bed and carelessly tosses the clothes out of it until they are strewn all over the covers and pillows. She shows us the empty bag.

"See? Nothing."

"How did you know the letters were gone?" asks Sebastian, who is standing next to me in the doorway.

"I came back in to put my cigarettes away, and saw that somebody had been poking around. So I reached inside and lo and behold they were gone."

She looks at Sebastian and me with contempt.

"When did you last see them?" Sebastian asks, still with that same calm voice. I'm probably the only one who can hear how much her vitriol is wearing him down.

Veronika rolls her eyes.

"Thanks, Starsky, but there's no need to pull this shit with me. I know somebody took them, OK? And I know who it was."

Veronika looks at me again.

"This is so fucking low. I genuinely didn't expect this of you. Though I suppose you were raised by *her*, so more the fool me, I guess. Just tell your shitty little lawyer to give me back my letters, OK? I don't care what little game you think you're playing, but they're mine. They were the last words my father wrote to me." Her voice trembles again, but only for a second. Then the flintiness returns.

"Give me the letters. Or else, I swear, I'll give you hell."

· ELEANOR ·

Only once Veronika has stormed out of the room and down the stairs do I feel like I can breathe again.

I look at Sebastian and gulp.

"Should we go . . . look for them? The letters, I mean?" I ask hesitantly.

Sebastian shakes his head. His mouth is drawn, and there's a crease between his eyebrows. He doesn't like conflict, hates it when people lose their cool or raise their voices. Shouting is unheard-of in Sebastian's family—just like drinking too much, or taking a gap year before college.

"Why should we? It's not like we'll find anything. If the letters even exist, I'm sure they're back in her apartment in Stockholm. She just forgot them. She's not exactly . . ." He clears his throat. "I mean, from what you've said, she has trouble remembering things when she's been drinking."

"Sebastian!" I say quickly, looking back at the lawyer.

This doesn't leave the family, Victoria, you hear?

It's no one's business but ours.

Vivianne's voice sounds so clear in my head that she could just as well be standing in this room.

I do the only thing I feel I can do.

"I'm so sorry," I say to the lawyer. "I think it's hard for Veronika to be here. After what happened to Vivianne."

The lawyer's eyes are inscrutable. He shakes his head quickly.

"I understand. This can be a very . . . fraught process," he says. His words sound strangely rehearsed.

I bite my lower lip and turn to Sebastian.

"I think it might be good for us to look, anyway. She could have taken them into the maid's room—she slept there last night." I pause. "We can just look. Quickly."

I can see that he's about to refuse, but then he glances at the lawyer and sighs. The knot in my belly loosens a little.

I walk into the maid's room, Sebastian's footsteps behind me. When he closes the door I sit down on the bare, stripped mattress and run my fingers through my hair. The coolness of the room feels nice on my hot face.

"Sorry," I say to Sebastian.

"It's fine; it won't take long. Just a quick look."

"No, I mean about Veronika. I know she's . . . difficult."

"Do you have any idea why she thinks someone would want to steal her letters? What could be in them?" he asks.

I've been asking myself the same thing.

"She gave you a weird look when you asked why anyone would have taken them," he adds.

"Yeah," I say. "I saw that, too."

I can't take closed doors. Not at Solhöga.

I sigh.

"I think she just finds it hard to be here. I don't think she even meant what she said. I mean, why would I want to cheat her out of this place? It's not like I've been here before; I have no emotional ties here. And if it was about the money, well, she probably needs it more than me."

"What's even weirder is why she would think the lawyer would have taken them," says Sebastian, shrugging. "What would he do with old letters? It's not like they're going to help with the inventory."

I pause.

For a few seconds I weigh up whether to tell Sebastian about the phone call I overheard this morning. About Rickard's strange turn of phrase, and his evasive look when he realized I had heard him.

But after Veronika's bizarre, wild-eyed accusations, it suddenly feels ridiculous to start insinuating about the well-ironed, freshly shaven lawyer.

"You're right," I say. "She probably just brought them in here last night and forgot. If we find them maybe that'll get her to calm down a little, at least."

"She's not your responsibility, Eleanor," Sebastian says, slightly more softly now, and I hear an echo of my therapist's voice in his. Carina's calm, well-modulated tone.

You can't save Veronika, Eleanor.

You couldn't have saved your grandmother, Eleanor.

You didn't kill her, Eleanor. It wasn't your fault.

(But if I had just gotten there a few minutes earlier, if I had called her back the day before, if I had been a better granddaughter, if I hadn't—if I had . . .)

I shake my head.

"Come on. Let's see if there's anything here. If not we can give up. It's time for lunch, anyway."

Sebastian nods, kneels down by the bed, and peers under it. I stand up, lift up the mattress, and feel between the slats.

I can't find anything, and Sebastian doesn't seem to have any luck either. He picks up the small pewter bowl that I suspect is a chamber pot, looks under the Windsor chair at the end of the bed, and shuffles over toward the far wall. The room is so bare that it's hard to imagine anyone being able to lose something in here.

I turn to ask if we should give up and head downstairs, only to see Sebastian pressing his fingertips to the floor.

"What are you doing?" I ask, puzzled.

Sebastian pushes the floorboard again.

"I was just getting up when I noticed this plank is springy."

"Do you think it's rotting?" I say.

Sebastian doesn't reply. He just presses the plank again, harder this time.

"Sebastian?"

He wedges his fingertips into the gap at the end of the plank and carefully pulls it up. It comes out like a piece in a jigsaw puzzle.

I look on as he reaches into the hole and pulls out a small notebook.

"What the . . . ," I begin, but he whistles quietly.

"Look at this."

I sit down on the floor next to him and peer over his shoulder as he flicks through the brittle pages.

"Those aren't letters," I say, stating the obvious, when Sebastian stops on one page. The book is clearly old, and the pages are swollen with damp. They are filled with neat, blue handwriting and at first I think it's the damp that's making the words unreadable, but when I lean in a little closer I realize the characters are entirely legible; I just can't understand the words.

"I think it's Russian or something," says Sebastian.

"No, Russian doesn't use the Latin alphabet," I say.

"Oh yeah. Another language then. Not Swedish, at least."

He flicks back a few pages.

"Wait!"

He stops flicking.

"Look," I say, and point.

Sebastian reads the sentence I'm pointing at aloud.

"'I must say, I did think you had better taste than *that*, Klaes.'"

He looks at me.

"Do you know who Klaes is?" he asks.

"Not a clue," I say. "But that's definitely Swedish."

Sebastian looks back down at the notebook.

"What do you think this is?" he asks, an audible hint of curiosity in his voice.

"Not a clue," I say again.

I reach over and take the notebook, close it, and check the cover. It looks anonymous, a green, bound notebook that once had glossy, lined pages.

Instinctively I open it to the very first page. There, down in the corner. In the same blue ink as the rest of the book. Crossed out but legible.

"'An—,'" I try to read, squinting. "I think that says 'Anushka. *Anushka*, 1964.'"

Sebastian stares at the small, carefully inscribed name on the first, blank page of the book.

"Who's Anushka?" he asks.

"I don't know," I reply.

But as I'm saying it I think of those two small letters in the stable.

$A + M$

· ANUSHKA ·
OCTOBER 9, 1965

How can it have been two months?

Sometimes I wonder if I'm losing myself.

Not losing my mind: losing myself. Losing Anushka. Losing sight of that little ferret, burying her rather than hiding her. I'm becoming Annika. The name they have given me.

It has been so long since I was called Anushka that even the name has started to feel strange in my mouth. "Annika" is all I hear. When Ma'am calls for me, when she needs something, when she berates me. "Annika!" "Annika!" "Annika!"

I have come to hate every one of those three syllables. They make my head stoop, my chin nod, my eyes sink submissively to the floor.

Annika is the stupid, contemptible girl they see. But Anushka is the voice in my head. And she—*I*—am fading.

Something about this dark, stuffy apartment makes it all the worse. In the country house it wasn't so bad. Out there at least there was some sky beyond the window, sunlight bouncing off the lake, a breeze that swept through the open doors, carrying on it the scent of summer. And there were people there too—people like me, people with uniforms and bowed heads. People I could talk to. The cook who helped me with my pronunciation in those long, hot afternoons, the stableboy who showed me how to pet the horses.

Not to mention—empty spaces to hide in. Nooks and crannies. Places where I could be myself for a little while every now and then.

Here I have nowhere to disappear.

Last week, while I was dusting the bookcase, I paused for a few seconds to look at one of the books. I didn't take it out, just brushed it with my fingertips, but then I heard Sir say my name softly behind me:

"Annika."

I jumped, spun around, and started to apologize.

"Sorry, sorry," I said, grabbing my feather duster, "I am so sorry; I beg pardon; I—no." My cheeks burned.

"I beg *your* pardon," I whispered. "Forgive me."

"You don't need to apologize." He chuckled, but his eyes were sad. "You are welcome to look at the books."

I swallowed.

"I just . . . ," I started. "I wonder if this book is maybe for child."

"*A* child," he corrected me, but his voice wasn't sharp or contemptuous like Ma'am's usually is. It was kind. Like he wanted to help.

He walked over to me, reached out, and pulled the book from the shelf. He inspected the cover and then looked at me.

"Would you like to read it?" he asked.

I stared into his eyes, searching for the trap, something to suggest what he might want in return for that tempting little book, a book I might actually be able to read. The first of many.

"I have much work," I said, tentatively. "I must work first."

He smiled at me then, or half smiled, like he understood what I had left unsaid. Of course he did. He has lived with her for years, after all.

"You needn't worry," he said. "You're very capable, Annika. I just know you can keep up with both."

He placed the book in my hand, paused for a moment with his index finger on the spine, then nodded at me and left the room.

Just before I fell asleep that night I thought:

I want my name back.

No. That wasn't what I thought, not really.

What I thought was:

I want Sir to call me by my real name.

· ELEANOR ·

As I step inside the master bedroom, I barely dare breathe.
Vivianne never let me set foot inside her bedroom in the apartment in town, and although no one has slept in this room for over forty years, my brain still files it neatly under the heading "Vivianne's room"—a forbidden place, out of sight and out of reach.

It's much bigger than the other bedrooms—it must be the same size as the dining room downstairs. The bed is enormous and looks antique, its canopy resting on four carved posts that tower in spiraling dark wood. The bedspread is made of a creamy white silk that stands out beautifully against the thick, expansive Oriental rug on the floor.

Under the window there is a dainty couch in a pale pink satin, and in the far corner stands a masonry heater with hatches in polished brass.

There is even an en suite bathroom. The door is shut, and I'm just on my way to it when the dressing table catches my eye.

It looks like something out of a doll's house, enlarged to human scale: ornate and gold, with a matching chair and a round, gilded mirror that flings my own unfamiliar face back at me. A single tube of lipstick stands, lonely and deserted, on the table, and I can't resist picking it up and pulling off the lid.

It's impossible to see what color it once was: time has left it hardened and black. I hold it under my nose and inhale. It smells of dust and oil. No hint of Vivianne's scent, her heavy perfume, Chanel No. 5—always

Chanel No. 5. *The smell of luxury*, as she would say, though to me it just smelled strong and musty. Even when I couldn't recognize Vivianne's face, I could always recognize her scent.

I want to shatter this stupid, pointless mirror; I want to take one of the sharp knives from the kitchen and run it straight through the beautiful face in the portrait in the hall. I want to scream at that face: *You broke me! You never loved me; you treated me like a pet, like a lapdog. You told me I was stupid and worthless and ugly, that it was my fault Mom got cancer, my fault my father left her, and that you were the only person who could ever love me.*

You told me never to leave you.

But then you left me. You left me, and now I'm alone.

I wipe my cheek with the back of my hand. I had hardly noticed I was crying.

Carina said that it can all be true at the same time: that I can love Vivianne as much as I hate her, that can I miss her so much my body aches, while also enjoying those first few hints of a shameful freedom. In one session Carina pulled off her glasses, dried her eyes, and told me that she was mourning Vivianne, too. Carina had known Vivianne a long time, but Vivianne had stopped speaking to her when she started treating me. All my healthcare contacts came from Vivianne's circle of friends: my family doctor, dentist, gynecologist . . .

Carina was something of a departure. Vivianne usually despised psychologists. Not in her social circle, of course—psychologists were more than refined enough to qualify for Vivianne's dinner parties, so long as they came from the right background. But she loathed the prospect of therapy. When I told Vivianne my high-school teacher had suggested I "talk to someone," at first I thought she was going to slap me. She looked disgusted, her nostrils flared, and her pupils constricted, and I saw her slender, white fingers twitch.

She said they went digging around in matters that didn't concern them.

Like what, Vivianne? Like this house?

What really happened out here that made you abandon this place over forty years ago?

My gaze sweeps along the walls. They are completely bare. Not one painting, not one photograph, just that little mirror above the dressing table. There is nothing at all on the walls—except a little handle on the wall opposite the bed.

Is it some sort of built-in closet? The door is pretty big, at least three feet by three feet. I take the small metal ring and pull.

The door glides open without a sound.

Behind it there is a small recess, completely empty. It would be big enough to fit a grown person in, if she was curled up. I bend over and stick my head inside, squint into the darkness.

I see two chains running along the back wall.

I hesitate for a second, then lean farther in to get a better look.

There isn't much space, but if I perch on my knees on the edge of the hatch I can get my cell phone out and see what's back there.

This is stupid, I think. *What does it matter what it is? It was probably a liquor cabinet. I'm sure they must have had them in bedrooms in those days. That wasn't unheard-of back then.*

My phone is slipping between my sweaty, clammy fingers, but I adjust my grip and point it up at the chains.

Suddenly I feel a hard shove from behind. My feet fly into the recess and the door slams shut behind them.

The chains start to rattle, and the walls begin to move.

I try to sit up, but there's not enough space: my head smacks straight into the ceiling, so hard it leaves me seeing stars. My phone drops and bounces on the surface beneath me. The beam of light disappears.

I lie curled up in the small space, my feet pressed up against a wall that wasn't there just a few seconds ago. It's pitch-black now; what little daylight there was is gone.

The closet has transformed into a small, enclosed box with no opening. A coffin.

My breaths start to quicken. In the small space they sound amplified, seem to bounce off the narrow walls.

"Hello?" I say, my voice weak and pathetic.

Nothing.

I try to kick the door, but there's barely any space to move my legs. Whichever way I move I only have a few inches to work with. I can't roll over or move my arms.

I gulp. The first inklings of panic start to slither into my bloodstream. What happened? Did the door hit me? Did it shut by itself?

I kick again, harder this time. The door won't budge, but something happens. The closet starts to *sink*.

Now I scream, loud and hard, my voice cracking with fear. I can't keep it in, or make myself stop. With my arms and legs constricted I'm helpless, and the dread makes my mouth taste of blood and iron.

I start to wrench and kick with my entire body, try to turn around in the small space. All I want is to get out of here—even if it means bringing the whole house down in the process.

It's only when I stop that I hear the faint voices, so muffled that I think I'm hallucinating.

Now I've really lost my mind.

But somewhere in the muffled words I hear my name.

"Hello?" I cry. It doesn't come out as loud as I would have wanted—with my arms pressed up against my chest I can't get much air into my lungs—but I cry out again, as loud as I can.

"Eleanor!" I hear now, again, louder and clearer. "Where are you?"

The voice sounds like Sebastian's. It's coming from below, from under me.

"*I don't know!*" I shout. I have to work to take in enough air to yell: "I climbed into a closet and fell! I think it collapsed!"

Nothing; nothing. For what feels like an eternity I hear nothing, though it's probably no more than ten seconds. My knees are starting to ache.

I hear something click beneath me. Then the voice calls again, still muffled and far away.

"Eleanor! You're in the dumbwaiter! But don't get scared, OK? It's nothing to worry about. The hatch in the kitchen is stuck, but we'll try to get it open!"

Dumbwaiter? What the fuck is a dumbwaiter? I try to focus on his words—*it's nothing to worry about*—but then the box starts to judder, and my breath catches in my throat as I picture the inevitable crash, every major bone shattering at once, my face being crushed by the wall.

But the fall doesn't come. Just that single judder, then stillness.

Something near me creaks. I try not to think about what it could be.

Buried. Like in a coffin.

Vivianne was cremated. They put her tiny, bloodless body in a wooden box just like this one and burned it until there was nothing left of her.

Don't think like that.

But I can't help myself.

If there was anything of her left in that body, it must have felt like I do now. If there is such a thing as a soul and it remains in the body, it must have been pressed up against the sides of the coffin just like I'm pressed up against these walls. Too big for the space. Desperate to get out.

The box judders again, and I feel the nausea somersaulting in my belly. But then I start moving *up*, not down, and I blink in surprise.

"Eleanor, what did you do?" Sebastian shouts from below.

"Nothing!" I croak. "I didn't do anything."

Mumbling voices below me.

The elevator is rising slowly but steadily. Up, back up, and I can't breathe.

"What are you doing?" I call down to them.

No response.

The box stops again, and everything goes silent. All I can hear is the pounding of my heart and the air I'm sucking in through my constricted throat.

But then it comes.

Not from below, but above. Clear and close—all too close. A strangely familiar voice that makes my blood run cold.

"Just lie still."

It isn't Veronika. Or Sebastian, or the lawyer. It's another voice, one that doesn't belong here.

But you do recognize it, don't you, Victoria?

I lie unmoving for what feels like an eternity, but then the box creaks again, and I start moving upward again. Up toward the voice, the one I know and also don't.

When the box stops yet again a whole lifetime passes in two heartbeats—one, two—but then the door opens and suddenly I see space. Hands grab one of my feet and pull it firmly, and I hit the floor with a jolt that briefly knocks the wind out of me.

The person who grabbed me throws his arms around me and I may be too panicked to recognize his face, but the smell and the sound and the feel of him are familiar enough for me to know.

"Oh God, Eleanor," Sebastian says. "It's OK; you're out now."

He hugs me tightly, tightly, and I wrap my arms around him and squeeze him too, but my eyes are still wide open. I don't dare close them.

Over his shoulder I see the door to the small en suite. The one that was shut. Only now it's hanging ajar.

Like someone has gone inside.

Or sneaked out.

· ELEANOR ·

Sebastian has sat me down in the drawing room with a blanket over my shoulders and a cup of tea in front of me. The tea was steaming when I got it, but it has had some time to cool. I stare at the cup on the dusty lacquered coffee table. No coaster. Vivianne would have been furious.

Rickard has explained to me what a dumbwaiter is. Had I known before, I would probably have thought better of perching inside that would-be closet.

When the door to the drawing room opens I look up. Sebastian's dark-blond hair and thick eyebrows appear in the doorway.

Once I was out of the dumbwaiter he asked me how it had happened, how I had managed to end up inside it. I hesitated for a second, then tried to explain that I just wanted to see what was in it, and that I got shoved inside just as it started to move.

He sits down next to me slowly.

"How are you feeling?" he asks.

"OK," I reply, and sit up a little, run my fingers through my hair. "Where's the lawyer?"

"He had to make a phone call."

Sebastian places his hand on my knee—gingerly, as though his fingers could bruise me at a single touch. We used to do more than just touch. But not anymore.

Not since Vivianne died.

I turn to look at him.

"Do you think it could it have been Bengtsson?" I ask.

"What?" he asks.

"Who pushed me into the dumbwaiter. Could he have been in the house? I mean, he has the keys—he has to; he's the groundskeeper. And if he's the one I saw by the cottage, then it's really weird that he wouldn't come to say hi. I'm wondering if he's not quite all there, or something? Or maybe he's been skimming money from the hunting income, or something else he doesn't want us to find out? He could have come into the house to try to hide something, and if I went into the bedroom while he was there then maybe he shoved me into the dumbwaiter so he could get out unseen."

Sebastian says nothing.

"Come on," I say. "You must have had the same thought. He has to be somewhere. We don't know anything about this guy. The simplest explanation for why he's dropped off the face of the earth is that something isn't right."

Sebastian takes a deep breath.

"OK, Eleanor, don't take this the wrong way," he begins, and I already know what's coming.

"I don't want to go home," I cut him off.

"Look, I'm not trying to tell you what to do," he says. "I'm here for you. I just want you to feel all right."

I clench my teeth.

"I know you didn't want to come here," I say. Now he's the one who interrupts me:

"It's not that I didn't want to come; it's just I didn't want you taking on too much. You haven't been home from the hospital all that long, and I'm just trying to look out for you. It feels like this environment might not be good for you. At least not in your current state."

Are you going to let him speak to you like that, Victoria?

No.

"You know what I mean, Eleanor," he says. He doesn't look me in the eye. "All that stuff with Albin . . ."

"That was the first night after I came home, Sebastian."

"Yeah, and when our neighbor knocked on the door for some milk, you hid in the bathroom with a knife!" he exclaims. "He's lived there three years, and you've met him a thousand times, but still you thought he was some . . . some kind of . . ."

"Murderer?" I say. "Yes. OK. I saw my grandmother get murdered. I'm sure you think you would have handled it *so* much better than me, Mr. fucking Rationality, but you don't know what it's like! You have no idea. I didn't recognize him. I don't work the way you do. I have to look for markers and listen to voices and remember haircuts and try to place each and every person in some sort of context I know. So excuse me if I couldn't do that the night I got home from the psych ward!"

"I can't talk to you when you're like this," he says, getting to his feet.

"Don't you dare leave this room!" I say, getting up.

He shakes his head.

"I'm so sick and tired of being treated like I'm about to fall apart!" I say. "'Poor little crazy Eleanor, she can't go back to work because she can't take the *stress;* she can't go to the funeral because she just *can't face it;* she can't do the inventory because she's so *broken* and *damaged* and *weak!*'"

Sebastian says nothing. He just turns and leaves.

I sink back down onto the couch. My eyes feel big and burning. I'm breathing in short, sharp stabs.

The first sob makes my chest ache. I put my hand over my mouth to try to stifle it, but I can't stop the next one from rising.

Why did I do that? Why must I destroy everything?

You must have known you would destroy this sooner or later. He's too good for you. He deserves better. Someone who's healthy, and whole, like he is. You'll only end up hurting him. Better to push him away now, before you destroy him, too.

The tears are stinging in my eyes. I wipe them away sloppily with the back of my hand.

Now it's Vivianne's voice I hear in my head, crisp and clear as a bell:

Don't cry, Victoria. It doesn't become you. A woman must never cry in public. It makes her appear weak, and God knows you can't afford that.

For a second I can almost feel her fingers on my cheek, wiping away my tears with an unexpected tenderness, her long nails carefully turned in so as not to scratch.

She didn't always wipe away my tears, but when she did she always did it with her soft, white finger-knuckles. So as not to hurt me.

I consider going after Sebastian, but I know better than that. I need to give him some space. This isn't the first fight we've had, or the first time I've pushed him away like this.

I always hate myself. Afterwards.

But then I hear a noise from upstairs. A creak.

Sebastian. Or Veronika, or the lawyer.

It has to be. Right?

I can't bring myself to believe it.

Instead I tiptoe into the kitchen and take a knife out of the top drawer. It's blunt, but it will have to do.

I have to find out once and for all if we're the only ones in this house.

· ELEANOR ·

I grip the knife tightly with clammy fingers as I walk through the downstairs rooms, my shoulders so tense that my hands are shaking. The wind has started to pick up outside. It whistles through the cracks in the façade like an ominous lullaby.

Relax. Everything's fine.

Solhöga is a strange place. I can feel traces of coziness and homeliness—of late dinners and cocktails in twinkling crystal glasses, of the pitter-patter of children's feet on soft rugs—but even in spite of its cleanliness and polish, you can still feel the silence that has reigned in this house for decades. It has been a long time since anyone lived here. We are just visitors. The beautiful furnishings contrast sharply with the bare walls and yellowing wallpapers, and the tall, clear windows look out on the cold outside.

A house that stands in wait.

Once I have checked every nook and cranny downstairs, I make my way up the staircase, every creak of the floorboard echoing through my ears. I wish I were soundless—that I could move through the house like a shadow, glide through the rooms until I was sure that no one was lurking behind the closed doors. No one who shouldn't be here.

Sebastian and Veronika are outside. When I look out the window on the upstairs landing, I see them both smoking by the cars, Sebastian's eyes fixed on the horizon. He must have bummed a cigarette off Veron-

ika. Sebastian only smokes when he's stressed. In theory he quit years
ago.

I don't want to think about Sebastian or his stress right now, even
though I feel the sting of anger and guilt within me.

Still, doubt rears its ugly head.

Is he right?

Is it all in my head? Could the dumbwaiter hatch have shut by itself? Was I wrong about the bathroom door? Was the figure by the
cottage just a figment of my imagination, the footprints days old?

Maybe. I hope so. I hope this is all just my afflicted brain trying to
transform shadows into flesh and blood.

But I have to find out. I have to make sure we're alone, put my mind
at ease that there's no one here who wants to hurt me. Or him.

Sebastian's world view has never cracked. He has never seen anyone
he loves bleed out right there in front of him. He doesn't know how it
feels, doesn't know that it changes you. He doesn't understand it, because he can't.

So I open every closet. I go into the green bedroom that Veronika
had picked out, lift up anything I can, look for any traces. Nothing.

Reluctant as I am to go back into Vivianne's bedroom, I force myself
to. A mild wave of nausea washes over me when I see the dumbwaiter
hatch staring at me blackly. I cross the room slowly, my eyes darting
back and forth between it and the bathroom door.

I don't want to go into the en suite but steel myself and step inside. It's
empty. A showerhead is dangling into the rounded bathtub on its hose.

I scan the floor, searching for mud and gravel, some sort of footprints.

The floor tiles sparkle, innocently white.

Clack.

I whip around.

"Anybody there?" I ask, but it comes out as a whisper.

I heard something; I know I did.

Was it in the bedroom?

My eyes sweep back across the bathroom floor and through the half-
open door, the knife handle hard and slippery in my hand. It should feel
reassuring, but I have never, ever felt so small. So vulnerable.

Would Sebastian hear me if I screamed?

My blood is swooshing through my ears when my eyes land on the big, luxurious bed. On the darkness beneath it.

I walk toward it, my ears pricked.

Silence.

I try to take a deep breath, but my chest feels tight and constricted, like someone has a knee on my rib cage.

Have to know.

I have to know.

In one short, sharp movement I drop to my belly and look under the bed.

Nothing.

Barring the odd dust bunny, it's completely empty.

No one lying there in wait, silver scissors in their hand.

Nothing.

Feeling stupid, I get up again and brush off my sweater with my free hand. When I step back onto the landing I see that the bathroom door next to the study is locked. I must have heard Rickard going to the bathroom.

What an idiot.

I don't think there are any closets in the study, but it's the only room I haven't checked. After that I should be able to relax. I step inside.

There's a different kind of stillness in here—something about the big, well-filled bookshelves, the leather armchair by the window, and the light masonry heater in the corner. This is a room to kick back in at the end of a long day, nestle up in a thick blanket, and read some Ibsen.

The desk, so clean and tidy the last time I saw it, is now laden with papers. There are two open binders on the desktop, and Rickard has taken the documents out of both. When I get closer I see a small, inconspicuous notepad lying open, half hidden by the documents. Only one word is visible:

Evert.

I pull it out.

Evert buried?

Receipts—pharmacy?

Original will burned?

When I hear the bathroom door I jump, shove the notepad back under the papers, and walk back toward the doorway. Rickard steps out of the bathroom and raises his eyebrows when he sees me. His neat white shirtsleeves are rolled up to his elbows, revealing pale, almost hairless forearms.

"Eleanor," he says, a statement. He smiles. Just as practiced as before.

"Feeling better now?" he asks politely.

"Yeah, uh . . . I just wanted . . . Do you know where Veronika is?"

He shakes his head.

"I was just wondering where she was."

I see his eyes drop to my hand. The one holding the knife.

I gulp.

"Oh God," I say. "I must look like a lunatic. Sorry. I guess I'm a little, uh . . . shaky."

Rickard steps over to me and lays a heavy hand on my shoulder.

"I understand this isn't easy. Of course you're feeling nervous and anxious. Anyone who's been through what you have would feel unsafe. I'm impressed you can even stomach being here." He gives a wry smile:

"But maybe you should put that knife back before you get startled and jump someone by mistake."

I laugh, embarrassed, and Rickard walks past me and sits back down at the desk.

"Dinner in a few hours?" he asks. "I just want to get through the inventory of the movables. I've found a lot of information on the furniture that I'd like to take a closer look at."

"Sounds good," I say.

I leave the room and pull the door closed behind me. Just before the door meets the doorpost, my eyes land on the desk.

The notepad is gone.

· ELEANOR ·

Dusk is starting to fall as I flop back down on the couch in the draw-ing room. I have combed the whole house, so why don't I feel any calmer?

Sebastian is right. He must be. Christ, I've been sneaking around this house wielding a knife! It's pure luck that Rickard is so understanding. The mere sight of me standing there could have been enough to send him running, ending the entire job.

But the notebook...

It's his job to make notes, I tell myself firmly. There's nothing weird about that. Of course he wants to find all the documents he needs. That's his job.

Original will burned?

As much as it niggles, I try to push the thought aside. I have to let this go, now. I just have to find something to do. Occupy my mind with something else.

Maybe I should book an emergency appointment with Carina for when we get back to town?

The couch in the drawing room is so firm and unyielding that I'm struggling to sit comfortably. It's only when I shift position slightly that I realize there's something hard and bumpy in my back pocket.

I pull the small, worn notebook out of the pocket, open it, and flick through the swollen, incomprehensible pages. Then I get my phone out.

It doesn't take much to find out that the language is Polish; I just google the first sentence. I have only just enough signal to get online: it's slow, but it works. Google Translate for Polish to Swedish is anything but flawless, especially as the Polish seems a little offhand, with what must be slang and abbreviations strewn throughout. Still, slowly but surely I muddle my way through one page after another, and I manage to make some headway.

When I look up the room is bathed in lavender-blue shadow, a seamless haze that blurs the details, softens the edges. In the dusky darkness the taxidermy fox looks alive, as though at any second it might stick its nose up into the air, sniff around, and dive under the couch for cover. I scan through my translation. Read it back from the beginning, let the images take shape in my mind while my stomach ties itself in knots.

I stop at:

And then, in a voice that was a whole world away from the lilting Swedish that she usually speaks, a voice with its very own hard melody, she said:

"Careful, Cousin. To him you're nothing but a cheap piece of furniture."

Then she turned on her heels and said in Swedish over her shoulder, like an afterthought:

"To me too, for that matter."

I read that again.

Careful, Cousin.

Cousin.

It's a diary; that much is clear. And that it was written by a young girl from Poland, who came to Sweden to work as some sort of domestic worker. And that she worked for my grandparents. And that the lady of the house was her cousin. *Vivianne* was her cousin.

I lean back on the hard couch. It creaks under me.

I can't count how many times I asked Vivianne about our family as a child. From a very young age I learned never to ask about my dad—*just a good-for-nothing chump who knocked up your mother and then refused to step up, I don't want to hear another word about him; Victoria, you're giving me a migraine; you don't need him; I'm the only one you need, understand?*—but that didn't stop me from being curious about her family. Our family.

What little I did manage to tease out of her over the years I eventually pieced together into a somewhat coherent background: she was born in Stockholm, to well-to-do parents who traveled regularly, and who died before she met my grandfather at college. Once she said her father was a shipping magnate, another time that he owned a fishing company; I inferred that it must have had something to do with the sea, even if she couldn't remember the specifics. Vivianne never was all that painstaking with the details, especially not when it came to the truth.

The last time I asked her about it was after she had come home from a long night with a man I only later realized must have been her lover. I had met his wife a few times at Vivianne's dinner parties. She was short and plump, with sorrowful blue eyes but a smile on her lips. That smile was the marker I learned to recognize her by—a big smile to match her husband's wolfish grin. And his grin was never wider than when he looked at Vivianne.

That night he had dropped Vivianne off at the apartment in the early hours of the morning. I had been woken up by the noise of her coming in, and when I tiptoed into the kitchen on cold, bare feet in my oversized nightdress I found her sitting at the table in only one of her stilettos, an unlit cigarette hanging from the side of her mouth. She was holding her forehead in one of her hands, and the little scar on her chin—normally no more than a pale line—was furiously red, as it tended to get whenever she drank.

When she looked up at me her eyes were cloudy, though I couldn't tell if it was from liquor or tears.

Go back to bed, Victoria, she said.

I'm thirsty, I said, and it was true.

Vivianne gestured at the sink with her hand.

So take a glass of water then. And go back to bed.

But before I could do it she stood up. She wobbled on her one high heel, yet somehow still managed to make it look deliberate, like she was pretending to be drunker than she was.

Actually, no, she said. *Sit down. My mother—I always wished she . . . I'll get some water for you.*

I sat down at the kitchen table, and Vivianne placed a wineglass full of water in front of me.

What do you say, Vendela? she said, and I felt my stomach drop.

I wanted to say: *I'm not Vendela. Mom's dead.*

But instead I just said:

Thank you.

Vivianne sat back down across from me and watched me intently while I drank.

When I put down the glass she said:

Have I ever told you that you look a little like my cousin?

I shook my head.

You have the same nose, she said. *And the same eyebrows. I've only just noticed.* Then she shrugged.

Or perhaps I'm just imagining it. Who knows? It was a long time ago.

I almost bit my tongue, because even by age eleven I was good at reading her moods, and I could tell she was on the brink. One single poorly chosen word on my part would mean screams or a yank of my hair.

But this was the first time I had ever heard her mention her family.

I chose to take the risk.

How old is your cousin? I asked.

Vivianne's gaze was fixed just above my shoulder, as though she wasn't seeing me at all. Then she shook her head.

Doesn't matter, she said. *She's dead now. So it doesn't matter.*

Her scarlet lips were tensed, carving deep, enraged parentheses around her mouth. But her eyes didn't look angry. They looked . . . crushed.

How did she die?

My voice was as cautious as I could make it. I was already tensed up in anticipation of seeing her face cloud over with anger.

But instead she closed her eyes. I remember the skin on her eyelids being thin—so thin that I could see the fine blue veins in the yellow light of the ceiling lamp.

It was an accident, she said. *A terrible, terrible accident.*

When she opened her eyes they were full of tears.

She shook her head, then lit her cigarette. Without looking at me she said, in a dull, toneless voice:

Bed, Victoria. It's far too late for you to be up. Don't make me tell you again.

I scurried back to bed, my heart pounding. I don't know how long I lay there awake, but I remember that she still hadn't gone to bed by the time I finally did fall asleep.

The next day I tried to ask her about her cousin, but she just snapped that she had no idea how I could get such idiotic ideas into my head, that she had no cousins and never had. She said I was too old to be making up tall tales, and that I was never to mention it again.

I put down the diary and go upstairs for a while before getting started on dinner. I lie down on the bed in our bedroom. The last light of day is no more than a hint of lilac beyond the forest outside.

Could the diary be a fake? I find that hard to believe. It was well hidden, written in Polish, and the paper was aged.

Besides, why would anybody write a false diary and hide it out here? No one has been here in decades.

No, the only logical assumption is that the diary is real.

· ANUSHKA ·
DECEMBER 2, 1965

They celebrated the start of Advent on Thursday. At the breakfast table Sir asked me if we celebrate Advent where I'm from too, and Ma'am laughed that lilting laugh she only uses when she's mad. She told him to "leave the girl in peace and let her do her job."

I don't know what got into me. But I looked at Sir and shook my head and told him we don't celebrate Advent back home.

"So how do you celebrate the approach of Christmas?" he asked, as though he genuinely wanted to know.

I glanced at Ma'am out of the corner of my eye. She was pale and steely, her perfect, painted lips a heart in the middle of her face. She was wearing her red woolen winter dress, the one I have to wash in cold water until my fingers ache. She likes red, I've noticed.

"Nothing special," I said, pronouncing the words carefully and conscientiously, the way I have heard Ma'am say them. I had spent all of the previous evening practicing saying them like her, wrapping my tongue around all the treacherous sounds.

"We just celebrate Christmas at Christmas."

This made Sir laugh, and he looked over at her.

"Well, that sounds pretty nice—what do you say, Vivianne? How about we give all those dinners and Christmas parties a miss and skip straight to the day itself?"

She smiled at him, that sudden smile that lights up her whole face. I have tried to teach myself that too, with less success.

"Oh, but I love all the dinners and Christmas parties," she said, then reached across the table and gave his hand a squeeze. "I simply *adore* them! And don't try to fool me, Evert; I know you do, too. You've been looking forward to seeing your cousins for weeks!"

It was like she had waved a magic wand. He raised her hand to his lips and kissed it, then laughed:

"Quite right, my darling," he said, his voice completely altered.

He didn't look at me once while I cleared the breakfast, and when I was back in the kitchen scrubbing the hardened egg yolk off their plates I found myself having to wipe my eyes with the back of my arm, without knowing why.

Still, I have to admit: I agree with Ma'am. Their dinner party was a symphony of fragrance and color, with deep red wine in glittering crystal and merry music on the record player. There were eight of them in all, Sir and Ma'am and three of his cousins and their wives, and they were all dressed festively in reds and greens. One of the wives was wearing an enormous gold, star-shaped brooch on the lapel of her blazer. It caught the light every time she moved, gave off sparks that seemed to hover and twinkle in the air.

I was rushed off my feet all night trying to keep up, even though they brought in another girl to help out. Her name is Märit. I was about to tell her to call me Anushka but changed my mind at the last second.

It was a long night, but not as long as it could have been. One of the cousins and his wife had to leave early, because she's heavily pregnant.

As her husband helped her to the front hall and into her jacket, I couldn't help but stare at the way her belly stuck out like an abnormal growth beneath her green maternity dress. Then he knelt down in front of her and helped her to put on her boots, one at a time, so tenderly and so carefully that you would think she was made of porcelain. It gave me a strange pang in my chest.

When I turned away to get back to clearing the coffee cups, I saw Ma'am staring at the cousin and his wife. Ma'am's eyes expressed such a naked longing that it felt like I had walked in on her undressed. But it wasn't the same longing that I felt: it wasn't the cousin she was looking at, but his wife's big belly.

In the blink of an eye the look was gone. She wasn't even looking their way anymore; she was laughing at something one of the other cousins had said, leaning over the table while he lit her cigarette.

When I collected the laundry the next morning, there was no underwear from Ma'am.

I don't know what made me look in the trash, but there they were: fine, lacy panties in a creamy-white silk, with blood in the gusset. Cut into small pieces, with the silver scissors she keeps in her bedside table.

· ELEANOR ·

E leanor?"
  I give a start and look up at the doorway.
"Why are you lying here in the dark?" Sebastian asks.
I sit up on the bed.
"You can turn on the light."
He flicks the switch and closes the bedroom door behind him.
I look at him.
"Sorry," I say eventually.
He shakes his head, walks over, and presses his lips to my forehead.
"It's OK."
I can't help but note that he doesn't say "sorry" back, but I don't have the energy to dwell on that. Instead I close my eyes and breathe in his smell, so like home.
"Where have you been?" I ask.
"I went for a walk in the forest. Just wanted to clear my head a little."
Alone? For hours? I don't ask.
Did you see anyone? I also don't ask.
"What have you been up to all afternoon?" he asks.
I hesitate, hear Vivianne's voice in my head:
He isn't family, Victoria. He won't understand.
We don't discuss such things outside the family, do we now, Victoria?
"I tried to translate that book we found," I say. "In the maid's room."

"Wow!" Sebastian says. "Any luck? What was in it?"

"It's a diary. It belonged to a maid who worked here."

"That's cool. So what did she write?"

I shrug in a way that feels unpleasantly calculated.

"Nothing special," I lie. "Just about her daily life. What it was like working here."

Sebastian walks over to his bag and starts looking for something.

"I'm sure you could donate it to a museum," he says. "There's probably a lot of interest in old diaries."

"Yeah, I'm sure."

A maid. Vivianne's cousin.

I'm about to say it out loud, but then I swallow the words.

How would it sound if I told him I'm starting to think Vivianne lied to me about who she was? That she hid so much more from me than just Solhöga?

It would sound like paranoia.

He won't listen to you, Victoria.

Sebastian stands up holding a pair of thick socks. He yawns, covering his mouth with the back of his hand.

"I'm starting to get hungry," he says. "Shall we get dinner ready?"

He starts walking to the door, and for a second I stand there, staring at his back.

It was an accident.

When we're in the hallway downstairs, I can't help but look up at the portrait of the perfect little family. I see the face that belongs to the matriarch, the lady of the house. Vivianne. Her high, smooth, white cheeks, her carefully curled hair. Big, dark eyes. The barely discernible scar on her chin, a thin, pale line.

Before me I see the eyes from the kitchen that night. Tired, drunk, and filled with heavy tears.

A terrible, terrible accident.

· ELEANOR ·

When I hear someone walk into the kitchen behind me, I assume it's Sebastian coming back from the bathroom. So I jump when I hear Veronika's voice.

"Have you been to the cellar yet?"

I spin around with the kitchen knife in my hand, and see Veronika leaning nonchalantly against the doorpost. When she sees the knife she raises her eyebrows and puts up her hands in mock alarm.

"I surrender," she says.

I immediately lower the knife.

"Where've you been all afternoon?" I ask her, as I go back to chopping the cucumber for the salad.

"Took a little stroll," she says from behind me. "Then I went back to my room. Have to keep an eye on my belongings, after all."

I don't have the energy to be polite to Veronika anymore.

"Oh, just give it a rest," I say, with a hint of Vivianne's grating sharpness. "Why would we care about your stuff? Just because you can't remember what you packed doesn't mean you have to be a bitch."

I'm expecting a quick, angry retort, or for her to storm out. Instead the silence lasts so long that I turn back around to look at her.

There's a smirk on her face, her mouth sagging ever so slightly on the side that was paralyzed.

"Yes, sir! I'll behave. Promise."

I sigh and sweep the unevenly diced cucumber into the salad bowl.

"In that case you can drop the passive-aggressive comments," I mutter, taking a tomato from the small bag of fresh vegetables. I press the dull knife into the tough skin.

"What can I say? I learned from the best," she replies.

Hard to argue with that.

With the oven on it's warmer in the kitchen than the rest of the house. It feels like the temperature in here has dropped during the afternoon, and when I glance out the window I see that snow has started to fall.

"You didn't answer the question," Veronika says.

"What question?"

"If you've been to the cellar yet."

The tomato pieces are coming out big and chunky, almost mashed under the dull knife. I wonder if there's a knife sharpener in here. It feels like there should be—isn't that the kind of thing you would usually find in an old kitchen? That being said, I'm not sure I would know how to use one if there was.

"I haven't seen any cellar door," I say.

"It's outside, around the side of the house. I remember there being a wine cellar down there."

I stop, can't help but let out a laugh.

"Aha," I say, looking up at her, "and you're hoping that the bottles are still there?"

I look up at her, and she gives me a sly half smile. It makes her look younger somehow, smooths away the bitterness in her crow's-feet.

"Exactly. Come on, *Victoria*. Don't tell me you aren't tempted by the prospect of rinsing this day down with some fifty-year-old cognac."

"Don't call me that," I say instantly.

She doesn't reply. Just waits, with that slanting little smile.

In the end I say:

"Fine, maybe I am."

Once the two big frozen pizzas are in the oven, I pull on my boots and jacket and follow Veronika out into the falling snow.

The snowfall is light, romantic: big, fluffy wads that drift idly down to the frozen ground. When Veronika isn't looking I try to catch one on my tongue but miss, and she smirks when she sees me with my tongue out.

"Are you done, or do you want to stop and have another go?" she sneers.

I quickly retract my tongue and ignore the question.

"So where is this cellar?" I ask.

Veronika leads me around the corner, and after a few steps she stops and points at a small, white door that's only about four feet tall. A door for children and hobbits—no wonder I missed it before.

She tries to open it. Locked.

"Try the front door key," she says.

I bend over, put the key in the lock, and turn. It's so stiff that I think it won't budge, but then it releases and the key turns with a click.

I pull the door open. Veronika walks down the narrow steps ahead of me. I hesitate for a moment on the top step, and can't help but throw a glance over my shoulder at the lake and the trees. The light, playful snow seems to have the whole forest holding its breath.

My eyes wander over to the small guesthouse.

There's no one there—no shadow behind the lace curtains, no figure outside the house.

Where are you, Bengtsson?

"You coming or what?" Veronika calls from down in the darkness, and I shake my head and walk down the steps.

But I close the door behind me. I still can't shake the feeling I'm being watched.

· ELEANOR ·

Down here in the darkness it smells of damp and soil. I turn on the flashlight on my cell phone and move it until I see Veronika's blinking eyes. She raises her hand to block the light.

"I should have brought mine too," she says. "Can you light up the room a little, so I can see?"

The room is square, low ceilinged, and almost completely empty, except for a couple of boxes piled up in the corner. The ground is uneven, soil that doesn't quite feel compacted enough to call it a floor.

"There," she says, and I sweep my light where her finger is pointing until it lands on another little door. It's shut, but there's no lock.

"Why is there no light down here?" I ask as I step over to the door and pull the rusty iron ring that appears to serve as a handle.

"We used to bring kerosene lamps down with us," she says. "They didn't run the wiring down here."

I cast her a quick glance while opening the door.

"How often did you come down here? You can't have been more than a baby when you stopped coming to this place?"

"I was five the last time we were here," she says, squeezing past me down another set of steps into the wine cellar. "But before that we spent every summer here. And we would come in winter too, for Christmas and a week in February, to escape the city and get some fresh air, as they say."

I follow her down the dark steps, my pathetic phone flashlight our only light. The steps are narrow and creak alarmingly under our feet, but they hold.

Yet more smells of damp and soil, a sharp whiff of cellar.

Veronika whistles and says:

"See, didn't I tell you? Jackpot."

When I point the phone past her I see what she's talking about.

Before us stand rack upon rack of dusty, untouched wine bottles, crates of thick, green tubes of champagne, and stout flasks that must contain some sort of aquavit.

"I had no idea you were here so much," I say.

Veronika's too busy inspecting the rows of bottles. I'm feeling faintly nervous: I have seen her drunk before—back before she became persona non grata in Vivianne's house—and it was never a pretty sight. Vivianne would watch her through half-closed eyes with a thin, mildly disgusted smile on her lips, as if Veronika's drunkenness confirmed everything Vivianne thought of her. Once Veronika even threw her wineglass at the wall. Vivianne didn't say a word, just watched the deep red wine soak into the wallpaper.

The stain is still there.

"Yup," says Veronika, pulling out a tall, green bottle and inspecting the label. "I loved Solhöga," she adds.

"You did?" I ask, surprised.

I can't take closed doors. Not at Solhöga.

"That was a long time ago," she says.

She holds out the bottle that she has been examining in the light.

"You do drink red, don't you?" she asks.

"Veronika, I don't know if we should be touching this stuff. Honestly, it looks like it could be worth a lot. It should probably go on the inventory."

Veronika gesticulates at the rest of the room, still with the wine bottle in her hand.

"Come on, Eleanor. How many bottles do you think there are here? Five hundred? One more or less won't make a difference. Besides, they're *our* bottles—our inheritance—they'll only be split between us. I think we're fine to uncork a few in advance."

I purse my lips. Veronika holds out two bottles to me.

"Come on, Ella Eleanora. I can't carry them all by myself."

I fold straightaway, even though I know she's just using my nickname to manipulate me. It's the name she used to call me as a child.

"OK."

Veronika turns back to the racks, pulls out another bottle.

"Vendela loved Solhöga too," she adds. "There was a slightly older girl who was the daughter of one of the workers. We weren't allowed to play with her in town—Vivianne said it wasn't appropriate for us to 'consort with the help'—but out here there weren't so many rules. Vendela was always trailing her around like a shadow. I was so jealous of them, but they would never let me play with them."

She bends down over a box and slides off the lid to reveal a solitary, rotund, clear bottle of an amber-colored liquid. Something in her face softens.

"Oh, look. Albert de Montaubert, 1935. I had hoped . . ." She goes quiet.

Veronika hands me the wine bottle in her hand and pulls the cognac out of the box.

"In answer to your previous question," she says, quieter now, "I would come down here with Daddy. Vendela hated this place, she thought it was scary, but I wanted to go wherever Daddy was. So I would come down with him when he was fetching a bottle or two. He would let me smell whatever he picked out, tell me about the aromas. Sometimes I even got to try it. Obviously it always tasted like shit to me—I was too young to appreciate the stuff—but Daddy liked it, so I wanted to try it all the same."

"He let you drink it?" I ask, not managing to keep the judgmental tone out of my voice.

"Oh, just a drop, it's not like it did me any harm," she says, throwing me a pointed look over her shoulder, a challenge. I keep my mouth zipped.

"He just liked it that I took an interest," she says quietly. "He wanted to share it with me because I idolized him. Unlike anyone else in the house, I actually listened to him." She pulls the cork out of the cognac bottle and twists it forcefully, the sinewy muscles in her bare forearms tensed. It comes out with a pop. She lifts the bottle to her nose and takes a deep breath, and I see her half-closed eyelids flutter at the smell.

"It's funny, you know. Mother only started drinking after Daddy died. Before then Daddy was the drinker. She hated it; she nagged him about it all the time. Not that alcohol ever made him aggressive or insufferable or weepy or what have you: it just seemed to calm him down. Daddy was so on edge otherwise. His hands would shake whenever he was sober. But after a glass or two they were completely steady. It was like he was more himself after a glass of cognac. Like medicine." She puts down the bottle.

"But she begrudged him even that," she says. "Even just a glass. And then, after he died, after the funeral . . . then it was her turn. She started drinking, throwing parties. Daddy was dead, and all Vendela and I could do was cry, but there she was getting drunk and living it up."

She opens her eyes and looks straight at me, and I almost shrink back from the rawness, the nakedness, of her gaze. Everything she usually hides behind her sarcasm, smirks, and venom.

"In case you ever wondered why our relationship was a little strained," she says, "that was definitely part of it."

"I don't think anyone had an easy relationship with Vivianne," I say, and then Veronika gives that same dry, cackling laugh that I remember from when I was little. It makes me feel warm inside.

I pluck up some courage.

"Hey, Veronika, I've been thinking."

Veronika raises an eyebrow.

"About what?"

"I used to ask Vivianne about her family when I was little. Our family, I should say. But she never wanted to talk about them."

"No," says Veronika. "But that isn't so strange, is it? Her being an orphan, and all."

"She never told me what happened. Do you know?"

Veronika shrugs.

"I think they died in a car crash. My grandmother and grandfather, I mean. In France."

"Not Poland?" I say.

"Why would they be in Poland?" Veronika asks dismissively. "Vivianne said they had a house on the Riviera. They spent their summers there." She pauses, before going on: "I remember Vendela being desperate to go abroad when we were in our teens. She begged and pleaded, but Mother flat out refused. She said we lived in the best country in the world, and that there was no reason to leave it. And that everyone down on the Continent was dirty and stank."

So I'm not the only one Vivianne lied to. She lied to Veronika, too. I can't ignore the diary. Unless Veronika is a better liar than Vivianne was—which she isn't—she clearly has no idea where Vivianne was really from.

"How about Grandpa Evert?" I ask. "Did he have any family?"

"Yes, but we never saw them, not even when I was little. Mother said they hated her."

"But you must have met them at some point?" I say, and Veronika shakes her head.

"Nope. Never."

"Do you know anything about them?" I ask. "How many siblings he had? Or if his parents were still alive?"

"Even if they were alive then, they certainly aren't now."

Veronika tilts her head to one side, like a predatory bird watching its prey.

"Why are you suddenly so interested in this family?"

I shake my head, trying to keep my facial muscles still.

"I don't know. With Vivianne gone, it would be nice to have some family, I guess."

Veronika laughs again, only this time it isn't so much dry and cackling as cold and cruel.

"Believe me, you should count yourself lucky not to have any more."

"I miss her," I say. "Don't you?"

I know it's stupid, but I can't help it. Some part of me is still hoping she'll say she does, too. She's the only person left who shared Vivianne with me.

She gives me a long, hard look.

"No."

I say nothing.

She pulls one of the wine bottles out of my hands, then turns and stomps up the narrow steps in the weak light of my phone.

Once I've followed her up I kick the door closed, scurrying as fast as I can on the icy ground to catch up.

"Veronika?"

She stops and waits for me. The cold wind snatches at our warm breaths.

I'm disconcertingly aware of the dark buildings brooding in the distance, the shadows between the trees.

"Did you ever meet Bengtsson when you were here? As a child, I mean?"

Veronika's eyes aren't on me, but on the gloom beyond us.

"Maybe," she says. "I can't remember. I was so young. There were always people working here. Maids, cooks, gardeners."

"Don't you wonder where he is?" I can't help but ask.

Veronika's face is half lit by the light coming from the house. The other half lies in shadow. But in the eye that I can see I think I detect something resembling pity.

"Don't worry so much, Eleanor," is all she says. "Nobody's out to get you. OK?" She looks up at the house.

"Everything that happened here is over now."

· ANUSHKA ·
FEBRUARY 19, 1966

Finally the light has started to return; for a while there I thought I was going crazy. Some days it was so dark I would wake up in the morning thinking I was in hell, the way Mama used to describe it—a land of eternal darkness and cold.

We spent this weekend out in the summer house. They took me with them, and Märit too, since their cook there works for another family in winter. They invited a few friends out there for the weekend to "escape the city and get some fresh air."

Sir drove us to the house, and Märit and I both sat in the back seat, clinging on desperately as the car bounced along the gravel road. The journey felt like it took forever, and I started to feel sick from the bumpy ride. Still, even though I could feel the acid rising in my stomach, I didn't dare ask them to stop, because I knew it would send Ma'am through the roof. So instead I bit my cheek and tried to breathe long, deep breaths while focusing on the beautiful wintry landscape outside.

I didn't expect it, but when we finally arrived and I caught sight of the house I was filled with a sense of, well, relief. The sun was higher in the sky than I had seen it in months, and the air was so crisp and so clear it was like licking an icicle.

It was only when I saw Sir looking at me that I realized I was grinning from ear to ear.

"Yes, I think we're all in for a wonderful weekend," he said to me, and

I couldn't help but nod and direct my smile at him, look into his light-blue eyes. He doesn't look like the boys we used to gawk at back home, me and the girls on my block. Still, even though he isn't what I'd call handsome, it's hard not to get lost in his eyes. They're blue like the crisp winter sky.

"Now, Evert," Ma'am said reprovingly as she stepped out of the car, her fine white gloves adjusting the thick fur draped over her shoulders, "they're here to work. Don't go getting their hopes up."

"Oh, I'm sure they'll find some time to relax too," he replied cheerfully, then looked at Märit beside me with her little bag. "Märit, do you ever ice-skate?"

"Yes, Sir," she said, nodding excitedly. "I go every winter on the lake where my parents live!"

"Then perhaps you can teach our Annika?"

Out of the corner of my eye I saw Ma'am's lips purse when he said "our Annika," just as those very same words made my stomach contract.

"You haven't done it before, have you, Annika?" he asked, his eyes back on me. Still with those light, sharply focused, blue eyes.

I shook my head and found I couldn't remember a single word of Swedish. The only thing I could choke out was:

"No, never. We never went ice-skating back home."

When I realized it was my own language that had passed my lips, I clapped my hand to my mouth. I swear I saw Ma'am's lips curl briefly in delight when she saw my embarrassment, before she said sharply:

"Annika! What have we told you? You're in Sweden, so speak Swedish. Honestly, some people . . ."

My cheeks burned, and I hated her.

"Come, my love," Sir said, putting his arm around Ma'am's shoulder and petting the thick, dark, mink fur. "We're here to have fun and relax! Why don't we go see how the new rugs look upstairs, while the girls get lunch ready for when the guests arrive?"

She allowed herself to be calmed, and I felt both grateful and disappointed, without being able to put my finger on why.

But the weekend went better than those first few minutes boded. Their guests were of the more pleasant variety, and none of them got too drunk that first night. They praised both Märit and me for the delicious food. I apologized to Märit afterwards, for taking credit for what was really her work.

But she just chuckled and stroked my cheek, so tenderly that it made me miss my mama with a sudden, crushing intensity that I haven't felt in a long time.

"Both of us made it, silly," Märit said. "Can't you see I couldn't have done it without you?"

On Saturday morning we actually got some free time after breakfast, because the whole party went for a walk in the forest. Last summer I had taken to spending what little free time I got in the stable, with the horses. The stableboy, Mats, would hold the reins while I patted them, so they wouldn't get nervous. Being there always made me feel unusually calm, but the horses aren't there over winter.

"I'm sorry," I said to Märit. "I didn't know they wouldn't be here. Obviously they can't stay here in winter! I should have known . . ."

Märit just shook her head.

"Annika, you couldn't have known," she said. "I'm sure they'll be back in summer. Who knows, if the bosses like me enough then maybe I'll get to come back!"

This made me almost breathless.

"Oh, I wish you could!" I exclaimed. "I really really hope so!"

Märit laughed, but not in the barbed, pointed way that Ma'am does to show she's laughing *at* me. No, Märit's laugh made me feel like I had made her happy, which in turn made me feel happy, too.

"My little girl would like that," she said, nodding over at the stable. "She's never met a horse before."

This shocked me, though I don't know why: Märit's a few years older than me, so it isn't strange that she should have a child. But when I cast a discreet glance at her hand I did recall that I had never seen a ring on her finger. She was wearing gloves so I couldn't see it just then, but I was almost certain.

"I didn't know you had a daughter," I said to her.

"Her name's Kicki. She's almost five."

We both went quiet. I didn't know what to say, but then Märit smiled.

"Now, Annika. Since you tried to show me the horses, it's my turn to show you something. Come, let's get out onto the ice."

· ELEANOR ·

The wine is harsh and acidic and it tastes like it's either very expensive or very bad, but the kitchen smells of freshly baked pizza and the windows have started to steam up from the heat of the oven. After two glasses, that nervous, prickly feeling I've had since my run-in with the goddamn dumbwaiter has finally passed.

I give the dumbwaiter hatch in the kitchen a tug: it is well and truly stuck.

"Not so *dumb*, really, all things considered," Veronika remarks, nodding at the hatch. "It goes down to the wine cellar, too."

"Would have been nice if the wine could load itself," I say. "Then we wouldn't have to go down to get it."

Veronika smiles her permanently lopsided grin and raises her glass in agreement.

"We used to play with it as kids," she says. "It drove Mother up the wall. I would hide behind Vendela whenever Mother was angry: Vendela was so good at talking her around. She knew exactly what to say to make her laugh and forget she was ever mad."

"Really?" I have hardly heard Veronika talk about my mom before. Hardly heard anybody talk about her, that is.

Veronika nods. There's a softness in her eyes, set off by the bluntness of her fringe.

"Vendela was really funny—razor-sharp. Though it didn't always work on Mother. Sometimes she would get mad because Vendela wasn't showing enough respect, but most of the time Vendela got away with it." She clears her throat. When she speaks again her voice is quieter.

"I still miss her, you know. I still can't believe she isn't here. Twenty years . . . or, God, it must be twenty-five now, right? Time flies." She shakes her head.

"Sometimes I still get the urge to pick up the phone and call her. She could always get me to laugh at myself. Sometimes I wonder how things might have turned out if she hadn't . . . well. Different. Probably. Maybe better."

Veronika gazes down into her wineglass. Then she looks up, a tight smile on her face.

"To your mom. And my sister. Cheers."

I clink her glass, try to swallow the sudden lump in my throat.

When Sebastian comes into the kitchen, showered and changed, we have already dug into the pizzas, eating them in messy slices with our hands. For a few seconds he and Veronika eye each other up cagily; then Veronika holds up the second bottle of wine and asks:

"Want some?"

He nods, takes the wine, and grabs a slice of pizza. I smile at him, warmth flushing through my stomach. Sebastian doesn't normally go for pizza—he's careful about what he eats, a trait he gets from his health-nut dad. But here he is, humming with satisfaction as he chews and swallows. The heat of the kitchen is making me a little sleepy, but in a nice way.

"Hey, you," I say, sneaking my arm around his waist and looking up at him. He gives me a soft, greasy-lipped kiss.

"Hey, you." We smile at each other. Then he takes a big bite of his pizza and I giggle.

It's only when the lawyer walks in that I realize I'm drunk. He stops in the doorway and stares at us with raised eyebrows: by this point we're sitting in an uneven circle on the floor, the pizzas served up on flattened packaging to save on washing up, the salad bowl full of orphaned forks that appear to change owner whenever anyone wants a bite. The kitchen has no table, just an island of sorts, and though we should really be sitting in the dining room, by some tipsy, tacit agreement we've ended up here. The dining room feels so quiet and formal. It's like eating in a room full of ghosts from dinners past.

"All done up there?" I ask. He has been going through the old binders in the study almost all day.

There are two empty wine bottles on the floor, and Veronika is uncorking the third. I ask if he would like a glass.

He hesitates for a moment, but as the cork pops out in Veronika's ever-steady hands he smiles and says:

"I never say no to red."

I've been a little wary of him since I overheard his phone call. Not to mention the incident with Veronika's letters. It's not that I really think he's shady: for all I can tell he seems to be exactly who he claims to be—a well-paid lawyer from a loaded family with some fancy lineage.

But somewhere at the back of my mind it strikes me that alcohol could get him to loosen up, so to say. That I might be able to ask him a question or two. Pry a little.

I just have to make sure I don't get too drunk myself.

The only problem is, after a few glasses the wine is starting to taste really good and I'm feeling relaxed and safe for the first time in a really long time. Despite the house, and the dumbwaiter, and Bengtsson, and Vivianne.

It's hard not to want to stay there in that feeling, just for a little while.

I'm so sick of being scared.

The lawyer joins our circle. He drains his first glass so fast I see Sebastian's eyebrows jump in surprise. The lawyer presents his empty glass to Veronika, who refills it just as efficiently.

Sebastian takes another slice of pizza, and I lean my head against his shoulder, sigh, and close my eyes for a second.

"Did you spend your summers here as a child?" I hear Rickard ask. I have to stop thinking of him as "the lawyer." He has a name. It helps to put names to faces, as poorly as that saying applies to me. But it does make it easier for me to remember their markers.

Rickard looks at Veronika, who nods.

"When I was a very little girl," she says.

I don't know if she's on her third or fourth glass of wine. It's impossible to tell by looking at her.

"We came here every summer," she goes on, "and often for a week in winter, too. She—Vivianne—insisted. Daddy never wanted to come, but she always kept pushing him. Even up until he . . ." Veronika shakes her head. I can see the muscles in her slender neck tensing.

It's Rickard who breaks the silence. His voice is soft, less prim and professional than before.

"Was this where he died?" he asks.

Veronika hesitates slightly, then downs the last of her glass with a quick, hard gulp.

"Yep. In the study."

"I'm sorry," says Rickard. "It must be hard for you to be here."

Veronika shrugs. I can tell she's trying to look nonchalant, but the movement is stiff, robotic.

"It was a long time ago," she says, with a tone of voice that makes it clear the conversation is over.

I couldn't sleep, I hear the echo of Veronika's voice in my head.

It was too close . . . too close to the study.

"Did Solhöga belong to Vivianne's family?"

Rickard directs the question at Veronika, but I can't help but cut in:

"Are you this interested in the history behind all the estates you work on?"

He looks at me and smiles.

"No," he says. "Most of them are pretty boring, to be completely honest. It's not every day you get the chance to get to work on a secret mansion, if I can call it that."

Veronika laughs, and yes, I smile, too.

A reasonable answer.

A rehearsed answer?

Stop being so paranoid, Eleanor, I tell myself. *Sebastian's right. It's all in your head.*

Not everyone is a blank-faced, scissor-wielding would-be murderer. There don't have to be horrible secrets lurking at every corner.

This is an old house with a broken dumbwaiter and a reclusive groundskeeper who probably just took the weekend off. It doesn't have to be any more complicated than that.

"To answer your question, Rickard," Veronika says. "Solhöga was from Daddy's side. It had been in his family for centuries."

"But he didn't like being here?" Rickard asks.

Veronika shakes her head. I think I see her shoulders stiffen slightly.

"No. He was more relaxed in town. Being out here made everything worse. It's not so strange when you think about it—it was his family home, and I'm guessing that family wasn't so much fun to grow up in, given that he cut all ties with them before I was born. I suspect he had his reasons. For all we know, he had bad memories of this place."

"While Vivianne appreciated Solhöga all the more?" Rickard asks.

"Yes, exactly. And nothing could get in the way of what Vivianne wanted. I guess she probably liked the idea of having a country mansion to show off to guests. So what did it matter to her that her husband couldn't stand the place and would sooner see it razed it to the ground?"

She nods at me.

"You if anyone know what she was like."

I smile; tight, stiff.

"Yes. I know."

Sebastian takes my hand, gives it a cautious squeeze.

"So you have no contact with the rest of your family at all?" Rickard asks, looking from Veronika to me.

We sit in silence for a few endless seconds. I hear the wind howl in the chimneys.

"Mother had no family," says Veronika. "No siblings, no grandparents. Her mother and father died in a car crash on vacation in France when she was young. She only met Daddy after that."

I take the wine, fill both my and Sebastian's glasses.

"How did they meet?" Rickard asks.

A wisp of his neat dark hair has fallen across his forehead. He looks like a businessman who, after a late client dinner, is about to slip his wedding ring into his pocket and buy a drink for one of the young girls at the bar.

"I think they met at college." I look at Veronika.

"Yeah, they were seated next to each other during an art history lecture."

"I didn't know she studied art history," I say.

"I only heard her mention it once or twice," says Veronika. "Vendela used to pester her about it when we were little, and eventually Mother gave in and said they met at a lecture on Swedish church murals. She seemed almost embarrassed. I guess it wasn't romantic or grandiose enough for her."

"Funny," says Rickard. "According to our records, Vivianne didn't go to college."

Veronika smiles.

"I suppose she never graduated," she says. "She got bored easily. She was probably only at college because she didn't have anything better to do, so when she found herself a husband, well . . ."

"I guess that's what people did in those days," I say. "Right?"

Rickard looks me in the eye for a few seconds, then shrugs.

"I don't know. I imagine."

Veronika holds up the last, empty, wine bottle.

"All gone."

Sebastian groans theatrically. He always gets more dramatic when he's a little drunk.

"Noo! Disaster! Wasn't there any more in the wine cellar you found?"

"Believe me," I say, "there's enough in that wine cellar to keep a hundred drunks happy for a hundred years."

"Then I say let's go get another bottle," he says. "We've earned it."

Our collective gazes turn to the window. Even with the condensation it's clear that the snow and the wind have both picked up. Just the thought of stepping outside and walking the couple of hundred feet around the corner makes me want to curl up under a little blanket and disappear.

"I think we'd better stay inside," I say. "They sent out a class-two warning a few hours ago."

"Lucky we don't need to go out, then," says Veronika, standing up. She strolls steady footed over to one of the cupboards and pulls out the bottle of cognac she had hidden inside. "So, friends," she says. "Shall we take a *digestif* in the parlor?"

A quiver runs through me.

When she says "digestif" with that affected French accent she sounds just like Vivianne.

It suddenly hits me that Vivianne's speech impediment might never have been a speech impediment after all, but the remnants of an accent.

· ANUSHKA ·
MARCH 11, 1966

She's pregnant.

When I got back from the store to find Ma'am sitting in the kitchen, positively beaming, with tears running down her cheeks and a glass of sherry in her hand, I genuinely didn't know what to make of it. All I could do was stand there and gape at her, my arms full of fish and carrots and potatoes.

Then she saw me in the doorway, raised her hand to her mouth, and giggled. Her eyes brimmed over again, sending trails of black eye makeup streaming down those perfect white cheeks.

"Anushka," she said, which only added to my shock. "Come, sit with me, please. Let's celebrate."

I don't know if it was Ma'am's unusual behavior, or the fact that she was speaking in our language, or that I noticed her dainty white hand resting on her belly, but suddenly it clicked.

"Ma'am is expecting," I said, and she giggled again, her attempts to wipe away her tears of joy only smearing the color across her cheeks.

She nodded.

"Yes," she said, "we've just come from the doctor. He said I'm in the second month."

Even with the smeared makeup, Ma'am had never been more beautiful. She seemed to glow from within. And even though I didn't want to let myself get sucked into her orbit, won over by her radiance, it proved impossible to resist.

"Anushka, please, sit with me, sit," she said again, and pulled out a chair for me. "Fetch a glass for yourself. You must celebrate with me."

I don't think Ma'am has ever so much as offered me a glass of water before—not once in the past year. As I ran to fetch a glass, I despised myself for my puppyish eagerness.

The sherry was sweet and burned in my throat, and I gave a little cough. Ma'am's eyes glistened. My bag of fish and root vegetables was still standing on the black-and-white-checked floor by my chair.

"It'll be perfect, Anushka," she said. "Now everything will be just perfect. I knew this day would come."

I was afraid to say anything, in case I said the wrong thing and broke the spell. But I couldn't just sit there in silence either, so I forced out an:

"Is Ma'am hoping for a boy or a girl?"

Ma'am stroked her still-nonexistent bump and said:

"I know Evert's hoping for a boy. But I should like a girl. At least to start with. A little girl to dress up in cute dresses and play with—wouldn't that be divine?"

"Märit has a little girl," I said, and Ma'am frowned.

"Märit?" she asked, absentmindedly. "Who's Märit?"

I cleared my throat.

"Märit who was with us at the country house," I said. "She sometimes helps out here with dinners and parties."

"Oh, the blonde," she said, waving her hand. "Yes. Well, I shan't be letting my little girl play with her. My girl is to grow up in the right circles."

My throat tightened slightly, but it released as if by magic when she leaned in and placed her hand on mine.

It dawned on me that she was probably more than a little tipsy. The sherry bottle was already half-empty, and I didn't recall us having an open bottle in the house. She must have had a glass with Sir when they came back from the doctor's—a third, used glass was still standing on the kitchen table—but even so, she must have had a good deal herself. I had never seen her drunk before.

"I'm so happy you're here," she said, confirming my suspicions. "This sort of thing should be celebrated with kin. And you are my kin, Anushka—you are."

I didn't want to believe her, didn't want to let my delight go to my head. But I did, on both counts.

"Whatever Ma'am needs, I'm here," I said, the words bubbling over like champagne poured too quickly. As it did the first time I served it for them, for which Ma'am had given my hair a swift yank.

"I'll help you with everything, Cousin."

She said nothing, and for a second I was scared—terrified—that I had stepped over the line, gone too far by calling her Cousin.

But then she smiled, and looked at me with eyes that twinkled, and her long, elegant fingers gave my hand a squeeze.

"Cousin," she repeated.

Then she let go of my hand and drained the last of her sherry glass.

"I know I haven't always been . . . ," she started. Then she shook her head so that her dark, shiny curls danced around her eyes. "Anyway," she said, and smiled again, a big, gleaming smile that was only for me. "Things are going to be different now, Anushka. You realize that, don't you? Everything is going to change."

· ELEANOR ·

The cognac is smooth and strong and sweet and I can't tell whether I like it or not, but I drink it all the same.

Rickard has sat down in one of the armchairs opposite me, his suit jacket draped over the backrest. He is holding his cognac glass as though he's in an advert for it, gazing at the liquid in the soft light of the chandelier, with a look on his face that could be either pensive or drunk.

Veronika is slowly pacing the room. She seems almost detached. Every now and then she picks up one of the small ornaments dotted around the place, studies it, and then places it back on the shelf.

"So, that groundskeeper," says Rickard, and I see Veronika look up from the little glass bird in her hands.

His voice has loosened up a little from the alcohol. It's funny: most people get more informal when they drink, whereas he actually seems to sound more refined.

"Don't you find it strange that he seems to have vanished off the face of the earth?"

My fingertips start to tingle, and I sit up a little straighter.

When I look around I see that Veronika's eyes are already on me. Maintaining eye contact, she gives a faux-nonchalant shrug before turning back to Rickard.

"Well, obviously it's strange," she says. "But nothing to get all hot and bothered about. He probably didn't know we were coming out here to poke around. For all we know he's just been out in the forest."

"For days?" I can't help but ask, though I sense I would be better off keeping my mouth shut.

"So he's visiting family, then," she says, a mild irritation in her voice. "I don't get why everyone's suddenly so obsessed with this guy."

I look away.

"Even so . . . there's a lot about this that's strange," I say tentatively. "A secret mansion out in the forest, a secret groundskeeper nobody's seen . . . For all we know there might not be any Bengtsson—it could just as well be Vivianne's pseudonym for renting out the hunting grounds."

"This isn't a 'secret mansion,' Eleanor," Veronika snaps. "I came here as a child. Just because *you* didn't know about the place doesn't mean no one did."

I bite the inside of my cheek. Even though I disagree with her, I feel somehow caught out.

Sebastian steps in.

"But somebody does live out in the guesthouse," he says. "We could see that, right? Just because none of us have met Bengtsson doesn't mean he doesn't exist. And somebody has clearly been taking care of the buildings and the forest. I can't see Vivianne dropping in every now and then to fell some trees."

"One of us might even have seen this famous Bengtsson," Veronika interrupts, throwing herself into a chair. She slides down so far she's almost horizontal, the cognac glass dangling perilously from her fingertips. Still, she doesn't seem as fuzzily relaxed as the rest of us: she seems sharp and awake, a strange look in her eyes.

"What do you mean?" Sebastian asks.

Veronika nods at me.

"It would appear my dearest niece has seen him," she says. "Isn't that so? Didn't you see someone down by the guesthouse?"

I stare at her—as does Rickard, with renewed interest.

"Are you sure you weren't seeing things?" Rickard asks, softly. "It's easy for your eyes to play tricks on you in the dark."

I turn my head slightly, glare at Sebastian out of the corner of my eye.

"Yes," I say. "It's easy to see things."

The wine is loosening my inhibitions.

"Though we did see footprints out there," I add. "In the spot where I thought I saw someone."

"But they could have been a few days old," Sebastian immediately counters, "couldn't they? We don't know that they were from yesterday. They could have been from when he left the house. To go to his car, or something."

"We don't even know if he has a car."

"He has to have a car—you couldn't live here without one."

That much is true. But still. I can't let the thought go.

"So if he was here until just a few days ago, shouldn't we see traces of his car too?" I persist.

"But we don't know where he usually parks. It's not like we've been combing the area for wheel tracks."

"Or," I say slowly, "it might just be that both the car and Bengtsson are still here."

I know I'm going to regret this tomorrow. But these thoughts have been going around and around in my head all afternoon. I can't keep them in anymore.

Veronika raises her thin, dark eyebrows so high they disappear under her fringe. She locks her dark eyes on mine.

"So what do you think is going on here, Eleanor?" she asks, her voice thick as syrup. "That he's prowling around the grounds? Or that he's here in the house with us now—creeping around the empty rooms, listening to us, waiting for us all to fall asleep? . . ."

I suddenly feel very conscious of the doors on either side of the room, of the windows behind me, of the thundering silence extending outside this room and around us.

The bathroom door hanging ajar.

"Give it a rest, Veronika," says Sebastian, uncharacteristically sharply.

Veronika cackles and sits up in her chair.

"Christ, I'm just kidding," she says. "I think he's just out there taking care of the grounds, too. Either that or he had a stroke while out shooting small game."

I swirl my cognac slowly in the glass. The silence feels heavy, loaded.

"In any case, it doesn't matter," says Sebastian. "We don't need him for the inventory, do we?"

He turns to Rickard, who shrugs.

"No, I don't think so. Though it would obviously be much easier if we could speak to someone who knows the property well."

"But we'll be finished tomorrow," says Sebastian. "You said so earlier today."

"I said it would take a day or two more," Rickard corrects him.

Veronika looks at Rickard. Narrowed eyes in a narrow face—thin shards of glass under heavy eyelids.

"How did it go with the hunting lodge, by the way?" she asks. "Was the door locked?"

"What hunting lodge?" I ask.

"Daddy's hunting lodge. In the forest."

"And you're only mentioning this now because?"

"I don't know what you do and don't know, Victoria," she says. "Mommy dearest barely let me speak to you for ten years. And it's not like you invite me around to your fancy apartment either."

"Eleanor," I say quietly. "My name is Eleanor."

"Oops, silly me," she says. She isn't smiling now. "Sorry. So easy to forget."

"You know very well that I didn't even know about Solhöga until Vivianne died," I say.

Rickard clears his throat.

"Do you know where this hunting lodge is, Veronika?" he asks. "Can you show it to us?"

Veronika gives a blasé wave of the hand, and her many rings flash in the dim light.

"Tomorrow," she says. "Tomorrow."

Sebastian looks over his shoulder and through the window to the whirling snow outside. The wind has started to kick up now, too: I can hear it whistling through the cracks in the walls, caressing its way down the chimney toward the fireplace.

"Yes," he says. "I don't think it's a great idea to head out there now, in any case."

"The house isn't built for winter," Rickard observes. "It gets cold in here fast when the temperature drops."

"They used to call this place their summer oasis, though for us kids that wasn't always the case—especially not when it was hot. I mean, we were pretty free to play around out here, but Mother never let us swim in the lake. I tried to run in once, but she caught me at the water's edge and yanked my hair so hard that my head was sore for days. She said the lake was there for decoration, not for grubby little kids to cool off in." Veronika looks down into her glass, seemingly dwelling on some memory, then goes on:

"But anyway, this was Daddy's childhood home. They lived here all year when he was little, and we used to come here in winter, too. But of course the place was at its best in summer. That's why she called it Solhöga—*Suncrest*."

"She?" I ask. "It was Vivianne who gave it that name?"

Veronika nods.

"The family just called it 'the country house,'" says Rickard.

"How would you know that?" Veronika asks.

Rickard rubs his temples with his knuckles.

"I think I heard one of my older colleagues at the firm mention it," he says eventually, "someone who had been in contact with Vivianne before."

A silence falls.

"I assumed Solhöga was an old family name," I say. "It sounds like one."

Veronika peels her gaze from Rickard.

"That's Vivianne for you. Or her and Daddy. It was something she had said when he brought her out here, just after they met. She said that the sun seemed to climb higher here than anywhere else. He said that that was when he knew he wanted to marry her." Something at the edge of her mouth softens.

"Strange she stopped coming here," says Sebastian. "Did she never say anything about why she abandoned the house?"

Veronika's eyes glisten in the mild yellow light of the lamps.

"It was after Daddy died," she says. "I never knew if she sold it or not. All I knew was that the subject was off-limits. Vendela tried a few times, but Mother just brushed it aside. After a while I assumed she'd gotten rid of it. I was surprised when it turned out she had kept it all these years." She pauses.

"Daddy hated this house," she goes on, her eyes now on the ceiling. "He hated being here. It must have been—" She breaks off, takes a swig from her glass, and clenches her teeth.

"Makes you wonder why she didn't just sell it," Sebastian says. "It must be worth a lot."

"Some things are more important than money," Rickard says, a strange quality to his voice.

Veronika raises her glass.

"Here's to Solhöga," she says. "To the house my mother prized more than her husband's peace of mind, the one she deserves, because her love never lasted longer than her whims allowed. Cheers."

She knocks back the last of her glass and slams it down on the table.

"Veronika," I say, but she isn't listening to me. She's trying to pour herself some more cognac, but the bottle is empty. She must have drunk more than I noticed.

"We need more wine," she says, looking at the front door. "I'll go."

"Veronika, no," I say, getting up. "Come on. We don't need any more to drink."

Suddenly I feel both very sober and very, very tired.

"Sit," she says. "Sit down, that's an order. You're good at taking orders, aren't you, my little lapdog?"

Sebastian has also stood up.

"I think it's time for you to go to bed, Veronika," he says.

Veronika just laughs.

"Hey, pal, I'm not my niece," she says to him. "I don't march in step just because you tell me to."

"Veronika, you can't go out in this weather," I say. It's not just that I don't want her to drink any more: if she goes out in this snow I feel like anything could happen. She's drunk enough to wander off, lose her way, get stuck in a snowdrift, and freeze to death. However tired and angry I am at her right now, I don't want her to get lost in the snow and die.

"I'll go," says Rickard, getting up. "OK, Veronika? I'll get a bottle of port; we'll have a quick nightcap, and then go to bed. How does that sound?"

Veronika gives him a long, hard look—too long—and I'm about to open my mouth when she jerks her head in assent:

"Thanks. Good boy. Fetch a little port and a cigar. Let's ring out the night with a bit of class."

Rickard nods at me.

"Thanks," I say to him, quietly. "It's unlocked, but take a good flash-light."

"Keep an eye on her," he mutters, equally quietly, before he goes. "Make sure she doesn't wander out on her own. Half a glass more and she'll be out cold on the couch."

· ELEANOR ·

"Do you think she's OK up there?" I ask Sebastian. "She's been in the bathroom awhile."

Once Rickard had gone, Veronika had tottered off up the stairs. I look over at Sebastian, who in turn looks over at the doorway, and as though by tacit agreement we both get up and head upstairs.

Sebastian pauses for a second outside the bathroom, then calls through the closed door:

"Veronika? Everything OK in there?"

His voice is breezy, unlike Veronika's, which sounds rough and wrung out:

"Yes," she replies.

Sebastian shrugs.

"I think she's OK," he says. "With any luck she's puking."

I shake my head.

"I don't think she's the type," I say. "Vivianne had a stomach of steel. I do, too."

"That doesn't mean *she* does," he says. "You aren't exactly alike."

No, maybe not. Perhaps that's why Vivianne held on to me so hard.

You and me, we're the same, Victoria. Never forget that. All we have is each other.

Sebastian looks over his shoulder at the door to the master bedroom. It's ajar.

"Mind if I take a look?" he asks. "I didn't really get the chance to look around before."

"Sure, let's go," I say. I feel the same pull toward that room as I did before. Stronger, even, now that the cognac has lowered my inhibitions.

The dumbwaiter hatch is still gaping hungrily on the wall, which sends a bolt of discomfort piercing through my fog. Sebastian closes it without a word. At least this time I've managed to come in here without a knife in my hand. . . . Some sort of progress, I guess?

Sebastian looks around at the room. When he opens the door to the en suite bathroom I'm hit by a sudden impulse to stop him, but of course there's no one inside. It's just a bathroom with a sloped ceiling and tiles on the walls and floor.

I look through the window. The character of the snow has changed. The flakes are smaller and denser now, and they seem to be flying rather than falling.

"It's very stark," Sebastian says, as his eyes scan the bare walls.

"Yeah," I say, sitting down on the bed. The mattress is unexpectedly soft, and I sink down so far I almost lose my balance.

"Maybe Vivianne took the paintings that were in here back to the city," I suggest. "I mean, she does have a lot of art in her apartment."

Strange, ill-matched paintings in different styles and from different ages cover every square inch of her apartment walls, united only by the fact that at some point Vivianne took a liking to them and paid the artist's asking price. Vivianne consumed art in the same way she consumed people, quickly and passionately and fleetingly. But unlike the many friends who had come and gone over the years, Vivianne's paintings had to resign themselves to being forgotten rather than cast out.

"Could be," says Sebastian.

He walks over to the big, heavy closet and reaches for the first door. The next thing I know, all the doors are open, revealing hanger upon hanger of stiff dresses in flashy colors.

Sebastian whistles and looks at me over his shoulder.

"I guess she didn't pack up everything!"

He starts rifling through the hangers with both hands, then pulls out what look like two summer dresses with wide skirts, and a slim evening dress in a deep red silk with a big, dramatic collar.

"It's like the wardrobe department for *Mad Men!*" he says, placing them next to me on the bed.

I can't help but laugh at him. The tension between us from the conversation in the living room seems to have dissipated. Sebastian loves beautiful clothes. His father is the same—he always thumbs my sweater sleeves and jackets, and asks me about the fabric. All of Sebastian's clothes are carefully curated, well loved, and well cared for, unlike mine, which are mostly bought offhand. He even packed carefully for this weekend: What shirt to pair with surveying one's girlfriend's inheritance?

Vivianne would have appreciated that side of Sebastian. She liked well-dressed men. She always said I had no feel for style, that it was something either you were born with or you weren't.

I touch the evening dress, rub the thick fabric between my fingers. The dresses smell strange, like a combination of mosquito spray and old flowers.

Sebastian sees me sniff and says:

"Mothballs, I think."

The fabric truly is beautiful.

He carries on shuffling through the hangers, and pulls out a three-piece checked suit.

"Groovy," he says, pawing at the big buttons.

He holds it up and looks at it.

"Do you know what size your grandpa was?" he asks.

I raise my eyebrows.

"What do you mean?" I ask.

Sebastian throws me a quick, crafty look and starts unbuttoning the suit jacket with nimble fingers.

"Oh, come on," I say, and can't help but laugh.

"I just want to try it!" he says. "It's in perfect condition! When am I going to get a chance like this again?"

I shake my head.

"Go on, you too," he says, laying the suit down on the bed and pulling his sweater over his head.

His skin is smooth and pale, so light that the fine strands of hair on his chest almost look black. I can hardly remember when I last looked at him like this.

"Try the red one," he says. His pupils are big and dark, and he has a cheeky grin on his face.

I hesitate.

Keep your dirty little mitts off my clothes, Victoria.

"I shouldn't," I say.

"Come on," he says. "Just try it." He has already pulled off his trousers and is now untangling the waistcoat from the hanger.

I stare at the red evening dress. I have never seen Vivianne in it, of course—it has been here all this time, abandoned and forgotten—but I have seen Vivianne in other red dresses. Tight and low-cut and glitzy.

I don't own anything that resembles this dress. I have never worn anything like it.

"I doubt it'll fit," I say, but I stand up and pull my sweater off all the same.

The air in the room is cold against my suddenly exposed skin. I feel self-conscious. I see Sebastian sneak a glance at me as he buttons up the waistcoat over his bare chest, feel him eyeing me up. It's like we're suddenly strangely shy around each other, like this is the first time we're seeing each other like this.

The first time in a long time, in any case. The first time since she died.

But right now I don't want to think about that night.

I unbutton my jeans and pull them down over my hips. They catch on my underwear, and my cheeks flush—either from the alcohol or from something else. I throw them onto the floor and pick up the red dress from the bed.

The fabric around the zipper has yellowed with age, and it catches twice. I have to tease it down, terrified of breaking it, but eventually I manage to get it open.

I pick up the dress and pull it over my head. The fabric is completely stiff; it has no give at all. I think it's going to get stuck around my shoulders, but a second later it glides past them and the waist slips into place.

I stop and look down at myself. I have to tug at the hem a little to take it all the way down to my knees, but the shimmering red fabric encircles my thighs and hips like a second skin. I reach back to pull up the zipper but can't get it all the way up.

"Can you help me?" I ask Sebastian quietly over my shoulder.

He says nothing, just steps over and zips me up all the way to my neck. Then he gently places his hands on my shoulders and turns me around to take me in.

"Wow," he says softly.

He looks at me for a long, long time—then up again, into my eyes. I don't think I could move, even if I wanted to; my whole body is frozen in time. All I'm aware of is the light pressure of his fingers on my bare shoulders, of his proximity.

"You have to take a look at yourself," he says after a few seconds—hours—have passed.

Out of the corner of my eye I see the dressing table, gold and gleaming. I'm almost reluctant to look in the mirror.

But in the end I do it anyway.

I never recognize myself in mirrors, not in the way I know others do. I was already a teenager by the time I realized that was something I was supposed to be able to do; I had gotten used to seeing a stranger staring back at me from the glass, a face in the crowd, like the girls in my class who all looked identical except for their hair—long and black, short and blond, bushy and red. Hair was one of the first markers I ever taught myself to look out for, and it's still one of the best markers I have. My friends now know to send me a picture of themselves if they have a new haircut to make things easier. They used to, at least. Before everything happened and I disappeared out of their lives.

The woman now reflected back at me in the gilded mirror doesn't look the way I have learned I look. I am looking for someone pale and slightly introverted, with an oblong face and shoulder-length dark hair, but the person staring back at me refuses to be a wallflower. The dress cinches in her waist and rounds out her hips. The neckline is sharp and dramatic, sweeps along her shoulders in a straight line that accentuates her collarbone. The dress is a little too big on her bust and snug on her stomach, but not so much as to cut in.

The shimmering, red, raw silk makes her skin look luminous and her eyebrows seem even darker.

When Sebastian rests his chin on my shoulder I jump.

"You're so beautiful," he says quietly into my ear.

I shake my head.

"No," I say, "it's just the dress."

He gently twirls me around so we're standing eye to eye again. The waistcoat is buttoned up over his bare chest, and the suit trousers are hanging off his hips. He must be thinner than my grandfather was.

He tucks a lock of hair behind my ear.

"It's not just the dress. It's you. You're beautiful in it."

For one long, tremulous second I dare to believe him.

The specter in my head remains silent.

He leans in, and his lips meet mine, and I close my eyes.

Then the bedroom door opens and I step back, startled, and the spell is broken.

Veronika reels a little in the doorway, staring at me wide-eyed.

"You . . . ," she begins, but then she goes quiet.

"Veronika," says Sebastian, "how are you feeling?"

She doesn't even throw him a glance. Her eyes are still on me.

Then she seems to wake up.

"Fine, fine, all good. So I see you've been going through Vivianne's closet?"

I look down at myself and then at her.

"Yeah, we just . . . ," I start, but I don't know what else to say. Instead I just shrug.

"Well, don't let me interrupt," she says, "but I was just wondering if you've seen the lawyer? Rickard?"

"No, why?"

"He hasn't come back. He isn't anywhere downstairs."

"Are you sure?" Sebastian asks.

She nods.

"I checked all the rooms."

Only now do I notice the new sharpness in her voice. She's still pretty drunk, but there's an alarm behind the buzz.

"He's been out in that blizzard for almost half an hour."

A silence sinks over us.

"Let's take another look," says Sebastian, walking to the door. "He has to be in here somewhere."

Veronika turns in the doorway to let Sebastian pass, and he disappears onto the landing.

I make to follow him, but she stops me in the doorway, eyeing me up from head to toe.

"You know," she says slowly, "in that dress for a second I thought you were Mother."

Her eyes are watery, but she doesn't look away.

"You look just like her in it."

· ANUSHKA ·
APRIL 29, 1966

I don't know why I thought that afternoon would change anything. I genuinely believed Ma'am would start to see me as her cousin, as family—that something about the child would make her look at me in a different light.

There were a few lovely, glistening weeks when the congratulations seemed to come flooding in with each passing day, brightening up all the apartment's dark corners. As the light returned to this dark, godforsaken city, Ma'am too seemed to glow all the more.

But then March became April, and overnight the honeymoon period ended.

It started when she threw up her breakfast one day. She couldn't make it to the bathroom in time, so she did it in the kitchen sink, and it was left to me to wipe up the semi-digested bits of bread that I had toasted just a few minutes before.

Sir ran his fingers over her hair and patted her cheek, and said it would soon pass. She tried to smile sweetly in response, but I could see how much she despised her own weakness. It made me feel a sudden, unexpected camaraderie with her: I too have always hated being sick, hated when my body fails me.

He thought it was just a onetime thing, and so did I. We assumed it would get better with time. But a couple of days after that she couldn't even keep water down.

After that she just stayed in bed, dark circles under her eyes, her throat convulsively, compulsively retching from the nausea.

It didn't get better. It got worse.

Sir called doctors, who came to the apartment and examined Ma'am with long, cold instruments made of shiny steel, prescribed little brown bottles filled with thick liquids, and then never returned again. But what did their medicines help when she couldn't even keep water down?

One morning a few weeks after it started, I walked into Ma'am's bedroom with a tray of water and the decoction the latest doctor had prescribed. Ma'am swiped the bottle from the tray and hurled it at the wall with such force that it shattered. A shard of thick brown glass nicked my cheek. I touched my face, looked down at my bloody fingers and then at her. She was staring me down with such loathing I almost recoiled.

"You're trying to poison me," she hissed. "You and Evert and those fake doctors, all of you. I know well enough what's making me sick. Don't you come near me."

For a second I didn't know what she was going to do. I stood frozen on the spot, not daring to move.

But then her face crumpled up and she started to cry, faint, whimpering sobs that cut right through me. I wanted nothing more than to hold her and heal her, somehow, to take her pain away.

Instead I turned and ran.

Ma'am doesn't deserve this. However much I have hated her, she doesn't deserve this. No one does.

There are no guests anymore—no one to breathe life into this apartment long into the night. Instead everything is quiet and subdued, and everyone seems to be walking on eggshells.

Ma'am is in her third month.

Six more months of this.

And then what?

· ELEANOR ·

My mind is racing. Rickard is gone.

When I called his cell phone, I heard it ringing in the study upstairs. He didn't take it with him.

"Should we go out and look for him?" I ask.

I feel sick—not the sudden nausea of too much alcohol, but the heavy, sticky kind that breaks you out in cold sweats and sends the anxiety skyrocketing.

"I've always been taught that you should never go out after someone in uncertain weather conditions," says Sebastian. "Not without the right equipment,"

"Could he have . . . gone?" I ask doubtfully. "Driven away?"

"Not without his cell. And why would he?" Sebastian asks. "Besides, he was pretty drunk. I don't think he would drive in that state."

"Just because it's illegal doesn't mean he wouldn't," I say.

"No, but there's no reason at all for him to leave," says Sebastian, running his fingers through his hair. "Maybe he couldn't find his way back in the blizzard? If he was drunk, could he have gotten disoriented in the snow?"

Everything I wish I had said is sitting on the tip of my tongue. *The phone call.* And Veronika's suspicions, and all those questions he was asking when we were drinking, how curious he had seemed . . .

And now he's gone.

But I can't get the words out, can't bring myself to accuse him of something when I have been silent all this time—especially now that he could be freezing to death in the forest for the sake of a bottle of port.

"We can check if his car is still here," I say. "Just so we know."

"She's right," says Veronika, and I look at her in surprise.

"He could have lost sight of the door but found his car, climbed inside, and fallen asleep," she goes on. "It's not so unusual for . . . people to do that when they've had too much to drink. Find whatever shelter they can and pass out. I'll go check."

I look at Sebastian and see that he's thinking the same thing as me. That little pause before "people."

It sounds like she's speaking from experience.

"I'll go with you. His car's just down the drive; it's only a few steps."

When Sebastian says nothing I go on: "We'll check the wine cellar, too. He might have fallen asleep down there. We'll be quick, in and out. He can't be anywhere else. Stay here in case he comes back."

I put my hand on Sebastian's arm. After a few seconds he purses his lips and nods.

· ANUSHKA ·
MAY 13, 1966

S he lost the baby.
  There was so much blood.
I don't know how she could survive losing so much.
I don't know how she'll get through this.
I don't know how any of us will.

· ELEANOR ·

I regret my decision as soon as we step out the door. The wind has gone from intense to lashing: it comes in hard bursts that knock me sideways, and the whirling snowflakes prickle my face and calves like needles.

I follow Veronika around Sebastian's car, and have to scrabble at the red paintwork to stop myself from falling when an especially strong gust of wind tries to sweep me off my feet. Veronika looks like she's about to fall headlong, but she catches herself just in time. Her black coat is swept up around her like a blanket, and for a second the wind lifts it so it hangs in the night like a black crow's wings.

There. Rickard's car.

I don't know if I'm relieved to see it or not.

Veronika tears open the driver's door and ducks inside. Unlocked. That's something.

I am so focused on getting out of the wind that I don't even check if the car is empty before slinging myself into the back seat and closing the door behind me. It's only when the roar of the wind turns to a faint hum and the still darkness of the car takes over from the pounding blizzard that I register that Veronika and I really are alone in here.

"So he hasn't left," I say. "And he isn't here."

"But it's unlocked," says Veronika. "So maybe he was here."

She's slurring her words again. It's cold in here, and I'm suddenly scared that she's about to do exactly what she warned us about.

"Hey, stay awake," I say. The wind is whistling through the slits in the car's body, and the windshield is covered in snow—so much so that I can't see the lights from the house. Everything is black.

"I'm not asleep," Veronika says irritably. I hear her feel around for something, and then the car is filled with light. The flashlight on her cell phone.

I don't think Rickard has been here. I think he must have left the car unlocked by mistake, or because he planned to fetch something later, or simply because we're out here alone in the forest. The gravity of the situation starts to sink in: our lawyer has disappeared, and it can't take many hours to freeze to death in this weather.

My throat starts to feel tight, so I try to take long, deep breaths to stop the panic from overcoming me. Vivianne's dress is compressing my diaphragm, preventing me from taking in much air. I try to do box breathing, a technique Carina has taught me. In: one, two, three, four. Hold: one, two, three, four. Out: one, two, three . . .

What happened? How could he just get lost in the storm?

Or did he not lose his way?

Was there somebody out there waiting for him?

My heart is fluttering in my chest.

"Veronika, I think we should get back inside," I say, trying to sound less panicked than I feel. "Back to the house."

To some kind of safety. We should be safe there. Safer, at least.

Veronika doesn't move. Her flashlight is still on, but she isn't looking at me. She is staring down at the little compartment between the driver's seat and the passenger seat.

"Veronika?" I ask. "What is it?"

She doesn't turn around, so I don't hear what she says, but I see her pull something out and look at it.

"What are you doing?" I ask. "Stop that; we can't go poking around in his stuff."

"The *little shit!*" she yells, so suddenly that I flinch.

She opens the door, letting in the wind, the snow, the cold.

"He's going to fucking pay for this!" she screams. "I'm going to find him and . . ."

I don't hear the rest: her voice is drowned out as she flings herself out of the car and into the darkness.

"Veronika!" I cry out in shock, but she doesn't reply.

I fumble around in my jacket pocket for my cell phone, turn on my flashlight with fingers stiff from the cold. My hands are shaking as I lean forward and light up the driver's seat.

It's a bundle of papers. At first I don't realize what I'm looking at, but then the first line of one of the pages catches my eye. The handwriting is so curly it's almost childish and the letters are a little scrawled, but it's easy enough to read.

Dear Veronika,
How I miss you & your sister!

My eyes automatically run down to the bottom of the page, and when I see the signature it all clicks into place.

Your father,
Evert Fälth

Veronika's missing letters.

· ELEANOR ·

I point my phone at the ground, see the heavy tracks in the freshly fallen snow, and start following them through the driving storm down toward the lake. My breaths are heavy and rattle in my throat, and the snow that has landed and melted on my calves has started to dribble down into my boots, chilling my feet even more.

The dress is so narrow I can barely run, and even when I try to I keep stumbling on the slippery ice beneath the fresh snow. The second time I stumble I feel one of the seams in the skirt give way, but at this point it's a relief. At least now I can move a little more freely.

"Veronika!" I scream into the belting wind. "Veronika, come back!"

She could be anywhere by now.

The hand holding my cell phone is so cold it's starting to turn into a numb claw. I switch hands and shove the frozen one back into my pocket, well aware that in just a few minutes the other will feel exactly the same.

How long does it take for frostbite to set in?

Veronika was right; the thought drums through my head as I run. It was Rickard. He did take her letters. He took her letters, and now he's somewhere out here in this blizzard. And so is Veronika.

And me.

All alone.

The pathetic little beam from my flashlight is enough to light up

Veronika's tracks, but it also blinds me to my surroundings. All I see around me is darkness: I have no idea how far I am from the house or the forest, or how close to the lake I am. All I can see are tracks in snow.

Why did he have the letters? Why did he take them?

Did he know Veronika had them, or did he just chance upon them? And why was he going through her stuff anyway?

What is he really doing here?

Who is he?

Where is he?

All I can hear is the wind in the trees, hear it tossing the thick trunks to and fro. I can feel it too, feel it tearing and pulling at my body, trying to fling me around. My face is so numb I can't feel my lips anymore. When I moisten them with my tongue they feel cold as ice.

I don't know if I'm crying, or if it's snow that has melted on my cheeks.

"Veronika!" I scream again.

The night is pressing down on me from every side. My numbed face feels like a mask against my skull.

A white, shiny mask.

My heart is pounding in my chest and I'm right back in the dumb-waiter; back outside the house, my eyes fixed on a shadow by the lake; back outside the door to Vivianne's apartment, before a faceless figure who shoves past me without a word.

Without a sound.

Just before I hear Vivianne's rattling breaths, I pick up the smell of sweat and blood and mortal dread.

Those rattling breaths, like the wind between the treetops.

Is that snow or blood I smell?

It isn't real. *It isn't real.*

I have to anchor myself, remind myself where I am, root myself in the now.

But in this now I'm lost in a blizzard and my aunt has disappeared into the night and my lawyer has frozen to death, and *yes, I do hear something now, something that isn't the wind or the rustle of branches or my own breaths or my skittering heart but that sounds like . . .*

Footsteps.

Not Veronika's heavy gait—quick, light steps. Running.

"Veronika?" I say. Not a call, or a question. A prayer.

I raise the phone and swing the light around me wildly, trying to catch something, anything, but it just bounces off the dense flurry of snowflakes around me, enveloping me, concealing me, and blinding me at the same time.

I whisper:

"Vivianne."

The word has passed my lips before I even realize I'm saying it. I don't want to be here. I want to be at home, in the warmth. I want my grandmother to be here. I want Vivianne to be tucking me up in bed, to brusquely pull the cover all the way up to my chin and then stroke my hair, unexpectedly gently, to kiss me on the forehead and then rub away the lipstick mark with her thumb.

I sob, my whole body shaking. I don't dare move, because then the shadow might take me; any step I take could be leading me straight into its arms. But I can't stay here either. I can't, I can't, I have to move even though I can't, because if I stay here I'm going to freeze to death. I'll freeze right here and die, all for fear of a shadow that might only exist in my head.

Go, Victoria. Get a move on. You can't stand around dillydallying all day.

Vivianne's voice is tetchy and irritated in my head, and it immediately makes me straighten my back.

That's better! Now, steady hands, steady mind. Keep your hand still so you can see her footprints. That woman stomps like an oafish longshoreman, so they shouldn't be too hard to find. Pick up the pace.

I point the light at the tracks. The snow is whirling, but the wind prevents it from settling, so I can still see Veronika's footprints.

I start to run. My whole body screams and resists, and now I'm longing for that numbed feeling, because when the blood starts coursing through my body again my frozen nerve ends come back to life, stinging and burning like someone has doused me in gas and lit a match. But I keep on running in her tracks. And then all of a sudden I'm down by the lake, and for a second my heart stops when I think the footprints are going to continue out onto the ice and disappear down into the depths.

But then I turn my head.

At first I hardly see the dark bundle on the ground. A thin layer of snow has already started to cover her, and she melts into the surrounding darkness. But the blackness of her coat is swept out over the stones on the lakeshore, and her ebony hair lies draped over a single outstretched, pale arm.

"Veronika!" I cry, and run over to her, dropping my phone in the process. I kneel down beside her and roll her onto her back. The hood of my jacket has fallen back, and the wind is whipping my hair around my face as I touch her cheeks with fingers frozen stiff.

She's so cold I think she's dead. She lies pale and still under my unfeeling fingertips.

She's dead. I was too late. She's already dead.

I am vaguely aware of my teeth chattering, of myself sweeping her hair off her face and saying her name again and again, without any hope of a response. I fumblingly run my fingertips to the side of her neck, as inwardly I see the blood gushing out, a gaping wound in a neck that isn't hers, dark, wide eyes searching for mine, gasping red lips that aren't getting any air.

But I blink and blink and that image dissolves and all that's left is Veronika, still and almost beautiful in death, and she . . .

Breathes.

It's faint, very faint, but I put my hand to her chest and feel it moving up and down: the most beautiful movement.

"Veronika," I say, and I keep on talking to her as I shake her and smack her until her eyelids start to flutter. "Come on, Veronika, we have to get back; you have to get up or you'll die. We'll die. Do you understand? Can you hear me?"

The tears and snow are blurring my vision, but I pick up my phone, clumsily pull Veronika's arm over my shoulders, and haul myself up, using all the strength I have left. My legs, my arms, and my shoulders are screaming, but I manage to get both Veronika and me to our feet.

"OK," I say. "See? Not so bad. Now just a little way back to the house. You can do it."

Veronika mutters something slurred and incoherent in response. Her head is lolling, but she is carrying the majority of her own weight.

Good girl, I hear Vivianne's approving voice in my head.

"Let's go," I say to Veronika, aiming the light of my cell phone up ahead.

I see our tracks, the ones we have to follow to get back.

But they aren't all I see. Something else imprints itself like a Polaroid in my brain, something that changes everything in the blink of an eye.

Another cluster of footprints leading away from the lake.

"Veronika, come on," I say, my voice high-pitched and shrill with desperation. "You have to hurry up now. Back where it's warm. Come on."

I half drag her up to the house with a strength I didn't know I possessed, even though the snow is still prickling, taunting, pressing us down to the ground, even though she's so unsteady on her feet that at times she's practically dangling from my shoulders, her feet dragging along the ground. I'm in pain, but I don't feel it. I'm thinking only one thing.

I have to get us back to the house.

When I see the lights in the windows, I'm so close to dropping Veronika and starting to run, but I manage to lug her up with me the whole way. When we round the side of the house I scream for Sebastian, and then he's there with me, helping us up the steps, and I scream to lock the door behind us, refuse to go any farther into the house until I hear it click behind me.

It's so bright in here that my eyes start to sting. I hear Sebastian saying things, asking things, but his face is fuzzy and the hallway is spinning and his voice is barely more than a murmur. My knees start to buckle under me, and I lean on the doorframe for support.

Veronika has collapsed in front of me onto the rug. She is slumped headfirst on her knees with her boots still on, snow and gravel on the parquet floor. Her forehead is resting on her hands.

I look at the back of her head. At the big gash in her part. At the hair that has clumped into a caked-in mass of cloying blood.

Someone has hit her in the back of the head.

PART TWO

FRIDAY, FEBRUARY 21

· ELEANOR ·

I am woken by something cold on my forehead and a voice saying my name.

"Eleanor? Eleanor, can you hear me?"

Gradually I realize I'm lying on something firm but springy.

I open my eyes and squint into the light.

Objects slowly come into focus. The light of the chandelier, the bookshelves on the walls. The couch beneath me.

I'm lying in the drawing room.

Someone is sitting next to me on the couch. The light is coming from behind his head, shrouding his face in shadow.

I sit up hastily, my eyes scouring his face, searching for something to turn the anonymous into the familiar—lips, nose, eyes, eyebrows . . . the eyebrows.

Sebastian.

The tension in my chest eases, and I can breathe again.

"Eleanor," he says, that familiar voice. When he tells me that I fainted, I can hear his voice tremble in a way I have never heard it before.

Someone has draped a blanket over me, and it slips down as I sit up. I realize I'm still wearing that goddamn red dress. Someone has pulled off my boots, and my calves are blotchy, swollen, and red. My skin is throbbing, and I quickly pull the blanket back onto my legs so that I don't have to see them.

"Where's Veronika?" I ask, looking around me. My voice is hoarse and crackly.

"I carried her upstairs. I tried to clean the wound, but it was hard. The blood was all caked into her hair." He clenches his teeth—hard—and I can see his jaw muscles tense.

Now it all comes trickling back.

The letters. The blizzard. Veronika.

The footprints.

I briefly close my eyes.

"Could I get a glass of water, please?"

Sebastian jumps up so fast he seems to almost lose balance.

"Yes, sure. Of course."

He disappears into the kitchen and comes straight back with a cloudy, full-to-the-brim glass of tap water.

I drink deeply and thirstily, feel it rinse away some of the sour film on my tongue. When I put down the glass Sebastian is sitting in the armchair opposite, his elbows on his knees and his eyes on me.

"How long were we out there?" I ask.

His eyes are shiny and his cheeks pale when he says:

"Almost half an hour. It's after midnight."

"Did Rickard come back?"

He shakes his head.

"I checked in the wine cellar," he says. "He isn't there."

I bite the inside of my cheek.

"I went out there when you didn't come back," he goes on. "When I didn't find you there I wanted to go out and look for you, but I—I didn't know where to go, and I couldn't see you with all the snow, and I . . ." He shuts his mouth. His hands are clasped so tightly that his knuckles are going white.

I close my eyes and shake my pounding head.

"I'm glad you didn't," I say, opening my eyes. "You did the right thing."

Sebastian, who has always been so strong for me, my rock. It looks like he's about to fall apart.

Between stiff, bloodless lips I say:

"There was somebody out there with us. In the storm."

Sebastian stares at me as though he doesn't understand what I'm saying.

My voice is about to buckle when I say:

"Sebastian, there's something I have to tell you."

· ELEANOR ·

Once I have told him everything there is a long silence. Sebastian is staring at me, but I can't bring myself to meet his eyes.

"So you think it was Rickard who did that to Veronika?" he asks eventually, putting words to what I haven't dared to express myself.

"I don't know," I say. "Him, or . . ."

"Bengtsson," he sighs, finishing my sentence for me.

"Yes," I say. "Bengtsson."

"What do you think is happening here, Eleanor?" he asks. "Why would either of them do something like that? Why would Rickard go out into a blizzard and wait for someone to come out so he could attack them? He wasn't even the one who wanted more wine!"

I shake my head.

"I don't know, Sebastian," I whisper, pressing my head into my hands. "I don't know. Maybe he did something, or was doing something he shouldn't have been doing, and Veronika caught him. . . . I have no good explanation for this. This sort of stuff just doesn't happen."

Oh yes it does.

I know that all too well.

Certain things just don't happen until they do. People don't get murdered in their homes until they do—until they're lying on a rug with their neck sliced open and fear in their eyes, their last, unsaid words dying on their lips.

Is this really so much more inconceivable?

These things are unimaginable, until they happen.

"Why didn't you say anything, Eleanor?" he asks eventually.

I look up at him.

"You should have said something," he goes on. "You should have told me you overheard that conversation; you should have—you had no right not to tell me."

I shake my head. It feels too heavy for my neck.

"But I did try to tell you things, Sebastian," I say, the words stinging in my throat. "Didn't I? You just didn't believe me. You thought I was being paranoid, that I was seeing things that weren't there. I couldn't tell you anything. You had explanations for everything: it was just a shadow, just my imagination, just the dumbwaiter slamming shut all by itself; there's nothing to worry about here; no one else is here with us; everything is fine; it's all just delicate, fragile Eleanor. Right?" By the end I'm spitting out the words.

Sebastian looks like he's at a loss for words.

"In the end I didn't know what to believe," I say. "I tried to believe I was just imagining it. That you were right, that there was nothing to worry about. But you were wrong." My eyes feel dry.

Sebastian runs his hand over his face, shakes his head, and looks away.

Silence.

"There has to be some kind of explanation," he says. "Veronika . . . maybe she slipped, fell on a rock, and hit her head? Are you really completely sure there was somebody out there with you?"

For a second I'm lost for words. But at the same time I understand.

Sebastian needs a logical explanation—needs to believe that Veronika just slipped, that Rickard just got lost in the snow, that everyone is behaving exactly as one might expect. He is a hairsbreadth from falling apart. This is all too far removed from his reality for him to be able to compute.

It was the same with Vivianne. He was so desperate for a logical explanation that he immediately bought what the police said. A burglary gone wrong—that much he could deal with. After all, nothing like that would ever happen to him. He would never fight back if someone tried to burgle him. He would simply give them what they wanted, and hey, presto, they would leave him alone. He who is so calm and rational and charming.

Unlike Vivianne.

"You saw her head, Sebastian," I say. "You've seen that lake. None of the rocks around there are jagged enough to make a gash like that just by landing on them. And she was facedown when I found her. If she had slipped and hit her head she would have been on her back or her side. Someone hit her. From behind."

He avoids my eyes, doesn't want to look at me. Doesn't want to take in what I'm saying.

"Anyway, it doesn't matter," I say. "Not anymore. We don't need to rake up who's done what or what all this is. We just have to call the police. And get an ambulance for Veronika."

Sebastian shakes his head. He opens his mouth for the first time in minutes:

"I've already tried, Eleanor." His voice is laden with anxiety.

"What?"

"When you fainted and I saw what had happened to Veronika, I tried to call an ambulance," he says. "There was no service. It must be the storm. None of us had a great signal to begin with. I'm guessing there's only one cell tower in the area, and it must be down."

"Shit," I say.

"You can check your cell," he says. "I hope I'm wrong and it's just my phone, but . . ."

I pull my phone out of my jacket pocket. He's right. No service.

"Fuck," I say. "Fuck. Fuck, fuck, fuck."

He nods.

"We can't drive now," I say.

"No," he says. "We've all been drinking, and in this weather . . ."

I laugh bitterly, so bitterly that my throat stings, and shake my head.

"We'll just have to wait till tomorrow," I say. "The doors are locked. Even if Rickard, or Bengtsson, or somebody else is out there, they can't get inside."

"Yeah, I guess we don't have a choice. But poor guy if he's out there in this weather. I hope Rickard's found shelter somewhere. I still can't believe he would do something like that. There's no logic to it, Eleanor. He's only here as a lawyer. He has no reason to do anything but his job—even less to try to hurt somebody."

I don't know what to say to get through to Sebastian anymore.

"Do we really know he's a lawyer?" I try. "We don't know anything about him. He just called me a few weeks ago and said it was time to do an inventory. We never checked. I never called the firm to make sure he was who he said he was. I just took him at his word. It made sense. We don't know what ulterior motives he might have. And that phone call . . . it sounded shady."

Sebastian stares at me. I know he doesn't want to hear any more, but I go on:

"He took Veronika's letters. We don't know what he wants. All we know is that there are things he hasn't told us, and that now he's disappeared in the storm, and that he probably hit Veronika and left her for dead.

"Could it have been . . ." I moisten my lips with my tongue. "I know this sounds crazy, but could he be the one who killed Vivianne?"

Sebastian shakes his head, runs his hand over his face.

"But why?" he eventually manages to get out. "It's absurd, Eleanor. Why would he kill Vivianne, pose as a lawyer, and come out here with us? Can't you hear how crazy that sounds?"

"I know," I say. "But too much about him feels shady for me not to wonder. And he seemed very interested in Solhöga. And the family. He asked so many questions." I blink my eyes shut.

"If he knew about my prosopagnosia, he would know it would be safe for him to come here, that I wouldn't recognize him. There's something about this house, Sebastian. Something happened here. I don't know what, but whatever it is—whatever Rickard wants, it has something to do with this house."

Sebastian looks at me, his face scared and open, like a child's.

"What do we do?" he asks.

I look through the window, at the flurry of snow outside.

"We leave," I say. "We wait out the blizzard, and then we go. Back to Stockholm. Whatever's going on here, it can stay in Solhöga."

· ANUSHKA ·
JUNE 4, 1966

Six days ago—two weeks after Ma'am stopped speaking—Sir decided we should all go out to the country house.

"A little fresh air and sunshine," he called it. His voice was brisk and artificial, and his eyes had that hard sheen that came when Ma'am lost the baby. They look like two icy blue marbles.

"It'll do us all good. Don't you think so, Annika?"

He caught me with his pale, shiny eyes, and all I could do was nod.

Truth is, I don't know if anything can help. Ma'am has hardly moved a muscle in almost three weeks. She must have gotten up to use the bathroom, but if that's the case I haven't seen it. Whenever I go into her bedroom she's lying there just as I left her. On her side, staring at the wall with dry, open eyes.

We leave early tomorrow. I hope it helps. Perhaps getting out of the apartment where the child bled out of her will make a difference. Even I have started to feel like the walls are closing in on me, suffocating me.

Sometimes I think I can smell it again, that thick and sweet and dreadful smell; that I can hear the echo of her shrill, prolonged wails coming from the walls.

I can only imagine how it must be for her.

· ELEANOR ·

As I lie here in the darkness of Sebastian's and my blue bedroom, I can feel the events of the past twenty-four hours inside me: a pain in my stomach, a pain in my body. The worst of the damage from the snow and the cold has passed, but my back, hips, and knees feel sore no matter how I lie.

I'm acutely aware of Sebastian's breaths, and Veronika's, fainter, in the room next door. My whole body tenses up every time I hear one of them shift in their sleep. My ears are listening out for the creak of a plank, for the whistle of the wind through a crack.

For the sound of a door opening, a window shattering.

I don't know what time it is when I finally accept I'm not going to get a wink of sleep. I carefully coax myself out of Sebastian's arms, stroke his cheek, and walk out of the bedroom.

Ridiculously enough, my pulse slows as soon as I leave the heat of the bed, the safety of numbers. Once I'm standing there alone on the landing by the stairs, listening out for something other than silence, I feel alert, yes, watchful, but not as afraid. It's liberating to stop trying to relax and sleep.

There can't be more than a few hours till dawn. Soon we'll get to leave this goddamn house and all of its secrets behind us.

My eyes have adjusted to the darkness, and I study the black contours of the staircase as it swings off down to the first floor, feel the soft fibers of the rug against my bare feet. The howl of the cold as it forces its way into the house sharpens my senses.

How does all of this fit? Rickard, the footprints down by the lake, the stolen letters. Ever-absent Bengtsson.

It feels like it has to all fit together, somehow. Even if it can't—if the mere idea is absurd.

How could Vivianne's violent murder be linked to who she was before she was Vivianne?

How could her death be linked to this mysterious Bengtsson, who somehow feels like the key to it all?

Or is that just what I want him to be?

What was he to you, Vivianne? An employee, or something else?

She trusted him enough to let him take care of this house for over forty years. The house that she kept from everyone else. The house she didn't even tell me existed.

Where is he? Is he alone in the forest? Is he here, outside, now? Was it him, not Rickard, who hit Veronika in the head and left her for dead in the blizzard? Has he attacked Rickard? Is that why Rickard hasn't come back?

Why, Vivianne? Why is all of this happening?

My feet lead me to the master bedroom. Vivianne's bedroom. The lamp is still on: at least the electricity is still running. The dresses from the closet are still lying out on the bed, and Sebastian has added the red silk dress to the pile.

It looks like it has been through the wars. When I take a closer look, I see that the seams have split over the thighs and at the waist, and that the hem is flecked with snow and mud. It must be from when I knelt down next to Veronika.

I pick it up and reach for a hanger in the closet but feel something strange in the fabric.

I look down at the dress, twist and turn the soiled red silk in my hands to see what it is I'm feeling. There seems to be something stiff *inside* the material.

It's only when my hands find the discreet pockets at the hips that I see how it could have gotten there.

I reach inside the pocket and pull out a photograph. It's flimsy, but still glossy, and even though it's a black-and-white Polaroid, the lines are still sharp. Perhaps being hidden away in a pocket has helped to preserve it, saved it from getting faded by the sun in a frame.

The photo shows two young women and a little girl. They are standing outside in the sun, and the women are wearing identical uniforms, so stereotypical that they almost look like party costumes: black, long-sleeved dresses, white aprons, white collars, and little white hats. Maids' uniforms.

One of the women has dark eyes and long, dark hair tied back in a tight braid under her white hat. Her hands are clasped in front of her hips. The other—who looks a few years older, more like twenty-five—is blond, with short, curly, bushy hair and a big smile on her face, in contrast to the younger woman's serious expression. The little girl, who is holding the smiling woman's hand, has identical blond curls.

I study them carefully before turning over the photo. There, in the bottom corner, is a short note in a fine hand.

Annika, Märit & Kicki, 1966

Annika. Anushka.

So are these the people I read about in the diary? And is the young woman with the braid the one who wrote it? Vivianne's cousin?

I study the dark-haired woman in the photo carefully, try to glean something from her face. If my brain worked the way it was supposed to I could look for similarities, something about her solemn gaze or the shape of her face that might remind me of Vivianne. But as it is, all I see is a young, serious woman, her face half in shadow and her hair pulled back too severely from her face.

When I hear the sound I jump.

It's quick and faint and it comes from downstairs. I stand stock-still, my heart pounding, but force myself to start breathing again: it wasn't the sound of a footstep, or of a door, or of a window. It was something else.

I put the dress back down on the pile on the bed, leave the photograph on top of it, and sneak downstairs. My mouth is dry, and even though I lick my lips again and again, my tongue feels sticky and doesn't seem to do any good.

I stop on the bottom step. Hold my breath. Listen.

Nothing.

I don't know how long I'm standing there—probably no more than a few minutes. My eyes scour the dim hall, listening for some sound other than the whisper of the wind outside. It's completely still. I can feel my own pulse in my earlobes, fingertips, and scalp, can feel the gazes of those four sets of eyes in the family portrait. Three of them now dead.

Just as I let out the breath I've been holding in and take that final step, I hear it again.

Two short beeps.

It's a phone—my phone. And I have just gotten a message.

I run into the drawing room, where my phone is still lying where I left it on the coffee table last night, turn on the screen, and stare at it.

No signal. Two percent battery left.

And one message, received five minutes ago:
Help humtlodge rikrd

Above those three words, the name of the contact who sent the message beams in clear, emotionless letters:
Bengtsson—Groundskeeper

Then my battery dies, and the screen flickers and goes black.

· ANUSHKA ·
JUNE 8, 1966

Märit arrived a few days ago. She has her little girl with her this time. They are staying in the small servant's cottage out by the stable. I didn't get to meet the little one for the first few days, as we were so swept off our feet getting the house in order after the winter, but today Märit brought her into the kitchen when we were preparing lunch.

It's been a long time since I've met any children, but she seemed small for her age. A fair, shy girl, she hid behind Märit's skirt and didn't want to say hello. Märit whispered to me to give her a strawberry. When I held it out to her, she snatched it and popped it into her mouth, her eyes fixed on mine. Once she had swallowed it she gave a wary smile, her lips still sticky from the juice.

It would have been a lovely moment, were it not for Sir walking into the kitchen right then. I stood up straight, and Märit said, "Good morning, Sir," but he didn't seem to hear her. He just stared at the little girl, and a muscle twitched in his temple.

Then he said, in a voice that was unexpectedly, horribly soft:

"You can't have her in the house, Märit. It's . . . Vivianne can't see her."

Märit pursed her lips and nodded.

He hung back in the doorway for a second.

"What's your name?" he asked Märit's little girl. She refused to answer, just sucked her thumb and stared up at him until Märit gave her a little nudge in the back.

"Go on, answer him," said Märit. "Tell Sir your name."

The little girl pulled her thumb out of her mouth. It was sticky from the strawberry juice that still dotted her lips.

"Kicki," she said.

"Kicki," he repeated. "What a lovely name."

He smiled serenely.

I had to look away. It hurt me to see the pain in his face, the lines that hadn't been there before.

"Don't bring her into the house, Märit," he said. "It's not good. For Vivianne."

"Yes, Sir, I understand," said Märit. "Can she go in the stable? She likes the horses, and the boy who looks after them can keep an eye on her."

"Fine," he said, and after a few seconds he gave a curt nod, turned on his heels, and went.

It was only later that afternoon on our break, when we were sitting on the steps in front of Märit's cottage, that she asked. Kicki was playing at the edge of the lake, splashing around in the warm water in only her undergarments, and Märit was playing some music on the record player she had brought with her from the city. I didn't recognize the song, but I liked it, because even though it was Swedish it reminded me a little of the music I used to listen to back home. Sir and Ma'am only listen to classical music. Sometimes it feels like the whole house belongs to a different century.

"So," Märit began. She pulled out a cigarette and offered one to me too, and I took it even though I haven't smoked since I came to Sweden. I had to take teeny-tiny puffs to stop myself from coughing, but even so, there was something so nice about sitting there on the steps in the warm sunshine, smoking as if I had every right to be there. Not just the servant, the shadow.

"What's happened to them?"

I held back a second before I replied, because in some way I didn't want to betray them. But at the same time it would be good to be able to talk about it.

"Ma'am was pregnant. But she lost it," I said.

Märit sighed. Her eyes were fixed on Kicki, and she took a long drag on her cigarette.

"I could almost tell," she said. "God. Poor woman."

"Yeah," I agreed, as I thought of Ma'am lying there in that bedroom, her eyes glued to the wall and her pale, thinning limbs hidden under layer upon layer of blankets.

"She's a witch," said Märit, "but she doesn't deserve that."

I gave a start when Märit called her that word, then gave a little titter, which the cigarette smoke turned into a cough. Märit started to laugh, and gave me a clap on the back.

"Well," she said when I had finally caught my breath, "you and me, Annika, we're going to have a nice summer all the same. You and me and Kicki."

When she said it I felt my heart swell up a little.

I do hope she's right.

· ELEANOR ·

The pale winter sun can hardly break through the thick cloud that has continued to roll in overnight. The snowfall has let up slightly, and the wind too, but I don't trust this respite. Something about the gauzy, thin light makes me think of dirty water, and it feels like the storm is simply catching its breath.

None of our phones have had a strong enough signal for us to get through to the emergency services. A few times in those last, sleepless hours of the night the signal dipped in for just a few seconds, one bar out of four. It was apparently enough to receive that message, but not enough to send one or have a conversation. Rescue just out of reach.

We're sitting in silence in the drawing room. Sebastian has his head in his hands and his elbows on his knees.

"We don't even know Bengtsson," he says. "We've never met him. And I don't trust him—if he's even the one who sent that message. I don't trust anything about this."

I can't argue with that.

I can't even think.

"We don't know what he wants, Eleanor," Sebastian says. "We don't know what this is. But that doesn't have to be our problem, OK? What-ever's happened to this Bengtsson, it isn't your fault. It isn't our respon-sibility—it *can't* be our responsibility."

I can hear the desperation in his voice. He wants someone to come and fix this for us, to take over, take care of it. Someone competent and commanding and adult.

"But if it was Rickard who hurt Veronika, and who killed Vivianne, then he could have done something to Bengtsson, too. Hurt him, or locked him up. To make sure he doesn't say something Rickard doesn't want us to know."

"We don't know if he's done anything, Eleanor," Sebastian counters. "That's just speculation."

"You're the one who's always saying that things don't happen for no reason," I say. "Do you really think all of this is just coincidence? Rickard disappears, and then we find Veronika's letters in his car, and then somebody hits Veronika over the head with a rock, and then we get a cry for help from Bengtsson. The most logical explanation is that Rickard is the one behind this. I don't know who he was talking to on the phone, but it has to have something to do with Solhöga. Whatever he wants, it has something to do with the house. He's looking for something. He needed us to get here, get into the house, so he contacted us posing as a lawyer. He spent all yesterday afternoon holed up in the study with the old files. I think he's trying to find something. And clearly he's willing to kill to get that information."

Sebastian shakes his head.

"You can't know that, Eleanor. You don't know anything for sure," he disagrees.

"We know that someone's asking us for help. That's what we know."

Silence.

"So what do you think we should do?" he asks, his voice verging on despair. "Go out into the woods and try to save him? This isn't a movie, Eleanor. In real life people call the police."

"We've tried that," I say, and he yells:

"So we get out of here! We go home and then we call the police!"

I look at my bitten-down nails and my dry, red hands. Raise them to my hot face. It feels like my skin is about to burst.

"If Bengtsson managed to send that message and Rickard found him then we might not have much time, Sebastian," I say quietly between my fingers. "Soon it might be too late. Rickard could kill him and take off."

Sebastian doesn't reply.

I drop my hands and look at him.

"He asked us for help. And I can't just drive away. OK? I can't leave him, not now. Not if Rickard's the one who killed Vivianne. I can't just leave somebody here to die."

Sebastian looks at me imploringly.

"We can just go, Eleanor," he says. "Please. Let's go. Don't ask me to do this."

I want nothing more than to give in, to sink into his arms and say that he's right. To drive back to Stockholm and away from all of this. To go home. To safety.

But if we go I know I'll never feel safe again. I won't—not if I don't find out.

"I have to, Sebastian," I say. "I can't force you to stay with me. You can go. Do it, if you want. Take Veronika with you and go. But I have to try to help him if I can."

For a single, tremulous second the air stands still between us. Then his shoulders drop.

"OK," he says.

· ELEANOR ·

The snowfall is still sparse, but above us the clouds are rolling in so fast there must be a storm up above them. Even though it's now after 8:00 am, it's still so dark that it feels like the sun has hardly crept up over the horizon, and at the edge of the forest there are deep shadows lurking between the trees.

I'm holding the map Veronika drew. She did it propped up in bed, her face scrunched up in a grimace of pain and concentration, her pallor a sharp contrast to the shadows in her face. We all seem to have aged ten years since yesterday.

Still, there was a strange sort of understanding between us when I explained the situation to her.

"You're complete fucking idiots if you go out to that lodge. You know someone's waiting for you out there, right?"

"Yes," I said, "but we have no choice."

She sighed and shook her head, grimacing when the movement seemed to make the pain in her wound worse.

"You're a great girl," she finally said, in spite of herself. "This is stupid. But brave."

Then she added:

"Just don't think I have any intention of going with you."

"Oh, believe me, Aunt Veronika," I said, my voice as bone-dry as hers, "I wouldn't even dream of it."

This had made her laugh, cackling and choppy.

I'm clutching a rusty monkey wrench Sebastian dug out of one of the kitchen drawers. Meanwhile he's carrying the biggest meat cleaver he could find. It's enormous, the sort used to cut game.

We should be feeling ridiculous. I'm sure we look like idiots, two grown adults on our way out to a little cottage in the woods, armed like we're expecting a run-in with a zombie horde. But I don't feel ridiculous. The weight of the wrench is more reassuring to me than Sebastian's presence.

All of my senses are on high alert as we cross the silent, frozen landscape in the dim winter light. This place looks different from how it did last night, when it felt like a swirling, dark hell without directions or fixed points. Most of Veronika's and my tracks have been covered, but here and there I think I can see snowdrifts and hollows that we must have left.

Us. Or somebody else.

We pass the first, tall trunks and the open expanse is consumed by forest. The bark of the trees is covered in hoarfrost, their branches heavy under the fallen snow. In just a few weeks it will start to melt away. The birds will be twittering.

I see Sebastian's face out of the corner of my eye. His lips are pursed, his eyebrows heavy and furrowed. I should feel safe when he's with me, but instead I just feel exposed. I can't protect him. I don't even know if I can protect myself.

The trees stand silent and expectant around us. The landscape looks completely untouched. Like a painting. As though no one has set foot here in a hundred years.

"Is it far?" Sebastian asks when I stop, look down at the map, and pull my cell phone out of my pocket to use as a compass. I don't know how reliable the map is, but it's the only one we have.

"Hard to say," I reply. "Veronika said it was about half a mile north from the edge of the forest behind the stable, but I don't know how far we've gone. The compass says we're going the right way, at least."

"OK," says Sebastian with a nod.

He looks at his meat cleaver with a mix of distaste and fascination.

I do the same, my gaze running along the rusty blade and the surprisingly sharp, shiny edge.

"OK," I say to him to break the trance. "We should be pretty close. Let's go."

I start walking in the direction the compass is pointing in, taking long, heavy steps to appear more confident than I feel.

Trying not to listen out for the steps I thought I heard last night.

Trying not to see blank, white faces emerging from behind the trees and merging with the snow-covered landscape, trying not to hear voices whispering in my ears.

Just lie still.

Was that voice the last thing Vivianne heard?

And why did it sound so familiar?

Was it Rickard's voice?

Maybe I'm just imagining I recognized it, but I can't shake that feeling, that echo of security I seem to associate with it. Somebody I have met. Somebody who made me feel safe.

Lie still.

Are those the words I'll hear when he attacks us from behind, grabs Sebastian's meat cleaver, stands over my helpless body, drives the blade into my exposed neck, and—

"Is that it?" Sebastian asks, breaking my train of thought, and I look to where he's pointing.

Yes, there is something over there, a little to the right of our current course. A shape too dark and angular to be something that has sprung from the ground.

"Must be," I say, trying to keep my voice steady.

We head toward the building, a low timber cottage that almost blends in with its surroundings, the windows small and the curtains drawn. There is a chimney, but you can hardly see it for the heavy blanket of snow on the roof. The simple door faces us, a cautious invitation.

Step inside.

I grip the monkey wrench, feel the beads of sweat breaking out onto my forehead and cooling off in the wind. The snowflakes are still falling around us, small and light and so fine that at times they appear to hang, weightless, in the air. The clouds seem darker now than they were just a few minutes ago.

We stop at the door. The fact that I can't hear anything doesn't make my heart pound any less.

I whisper, so quietly that my lips hardly move:

"I'll go first. You keep a lookout behind us. See if anyone's coming."

A few seconds' wait to hear if he protests. Nothing.

I put my hand on the brass door handle. It's marred by age and weather, and stiff to push. But it isn't locked.

The door glides open in front of me with a creak. It takes me just a split second to see all I need to see.

The big, open space. The moth-eaten animal heads glaring down at me from the walls through blind, glass eyes. The large Oriental rug in the middle of the floor.

The middle-aged man lying motionless on the floor.

And the body hanging from the chandelier above him.

· ANUSHKA ·
JUNE 21, 1966

I don't know what to do. I don't know what to think.

The last few days Sir hasn't wanted any dinner. He says it's too hot, but he's lost so much weight that his clothes are hanging off him, and I don't think he's eating much at all.

Kicki had been fussy during the day, so Märit asked if she could leave me alone in the kitchen that evening, in case one of them needed anything. The implication being that they probably wouldn't.

I said yes.

At first I found it boring sitting there all by myself, but then I just found it calming. In these light evenings, the sky over the treetops has a color all of its own, an impossible hue somewhere between blue and a tepid yellow. As I sat on the steps by the open kitchen door, I could smell the scents of the day changing, the heavy, metallic overtones of the heat giving way to the milder, green fragrances coming from the shadows between the trees.

When the bell in the dining room finally chimed I was so steeped in silence that I jumped. I smoothed out my apron with both hands and scurried into the dining room.

It was only Sir there, and he was sitting with his legs splayed in a way that made him take up more space than usual. The top button of his collar was undone. There was no glass on the dining table, but something about his drifting eyes made me suspect there was probably one to be found nearby—and that it had been drained more than once already that evening.

"Annika," he said, a statement. It seemed like he was waiting for me to reply.

"Would Sir like something to eat?" I asked, as Ma'am had taught me to.

He smiled. It made him look sad.

"Yes, please. But nothing heavy. Have we any of the potato salad and the roast beef left?"

"Not the roast beef," I said, "but we do have chicken cold cuts."

"Excellent," he said. "Thank you, Annika."

I had already turned to go back to the kitchen when he added:

"You can serve yourself a plate, too, Annika."

I stopped short. Just for a second. I thought:

Say you've already eaten. (I hadn't.)

Say you aren't hungry. (I was.)

Say . . .

"All right," I said over my shoulder, in a voice that was a cold, perfect imitation of Ma'am's, and carried on into the kitchen.

I took out two plates, served some cold potato salad on the shiny porcelain, and cut the chicken into thick, white slices. Outside the sun had disappeared over the horizon, but the sky wouldn't be getting dark. Perhaps it's these light nights. They make everything feel unreal. When the boundary between day and night starts to blur, you start to wonder what other boundaries might not be so immovable, what other rules can be relaxed.

We ate slowly, without talking. I didn't think the food tasted of anything. When Sir put down his knife and fork they chinked against the plate and I made to get up to clear it away, but he raised his hand and said:

"No, Annika. Sit. Stay."

I sat down again slowly.

His gaze was down in his lap, and then he sighed.

"How do you think she seems?" he asked.

I swallowed. I knew who he meant.

"I don't know," I said eventually.

He shook his head slowly but didn't look at me.

"I don't know what to do, Annika," he said. "I just want to know what I can do to help her. If I try to talk to her she says nothing. If I touch her she screams at me to leave. I haven't slept in my own bed in weeks. She won't even look at me. It's like she hates me."

This all felt far too private. It was none of my business. Part of me knew he would never have spoken to me like that if he hadn't been drunk.

"What shall I do, Annika?" he asked, and then, finally, he looked at me, his cloudy, ice-blue eyes boring into mine.

I swallowed.

"I—I don't know," I stuttered. "I wish I could help."

He had a little crease between his eyebrows, but it vanished when he started to smile. It was new; it hadn't been there last summer. I wanted to smooth it out with my thumb.

"You're kind, Annika," he said. "So kind."

We both went quiet. I swallowed again.

"Could you try to talk to her?" he asked, and my eyes widened.

"Me?"

"You're her family," he said, and my heart stopped. "You can talk to her in your language, can't you? Maybe then she would listen. Maybe she would understand it better. Because she isn't listening to me. Not now."

My heart started pounding again, pitter-pattering away in my chest. My mind was racing.

"I . . . ," I started, but I didn't know what to say. "I'm not . . . I mean . . . family isn't . . ."

He looked at me with such sadness in his eyes that I trailed off.

"I know, Annika," he said. "I've known all along. I'm not so stupid as to believe a teenage girl from Poland just showed up on our doorstep out of the blue asking for work."

I swallowed. "But . . ." But I didn't know what else to say.

"All I want is for Vivianne to be happy," he said, and the way he said it cut me to the quick. "It's all I've ever wanted. Do you understand? If my wife needs to believe that I believe she's the daughter of a wealthy Swede who grew up in France, then I'll let her believe it. If my wife wants to maintain that our maid, who looks just like her, is just some poor kid without family or prospects who turned up on our doorstep, then I'll let it be true so long as that's what she needs. But I'm not stupid. Or blind."

I opened my mouth, then closed it again.

He closed his eyes.

"Forgive me," he said. "This is inappropriate. It isn't your responsibility, Annika." He stood up, but his feet weren't as steady as they should have been.

He stopped by my chair and looked at me. It took me half an eternity to dare to raise my eyes to meet his.

"Thank you for listening, Annika," he said, stroking my cheek with the back of his hand. "It was very kind of you."

Then he pulled away as though I had singed him, and walked away.

· ELEANOR ·

I totter into the lodge, trying to figure out where to look and what to do, vaguely aware that my wrench has fallen to the floor.

"Oh God. Oh God oh God oh God," Sebastian drones, and I realize he's in shock, and, somewhere inside me, that I am too, because my knees don't buckle, and I don't scream or cry. I feel strangely removed from this entire scene.

I recognize the man on the floor—or, really, I recognize his clothes, flecked as they are with melted snow and mud. There are twigs and needles from the trees caught in them.

I kneel down next to Rickard, hear Sebastian say:

"No, Eleanor, don't; he might . . ."

"I have to check," I reply.

With a little effort I manage to roll Rickard onto his back. I'm aware of the dangling legs a foot or so from my face, but right now they don't seem to matter.

I think:

They don't smell.

When Vivianne died it smelled of blood, and sweat, and fear. Iron and urine.

But it doesn't smell in here.

It must be because it's so cold. The temperature in the lodge is hardly warmer than outside.

Rickard is cold too, I note when I place my fingers on his neck to try to find a pulse. His face is gray, his eyebrow is cut, and there's dried blood under his nose. Something that looks like thin, dried vomit has dribbled down his cheek and onto the floor. A leather glove on one hand.

Next to his other, bare hand lies an old, outdated cell phone.

I feel for a pulse on the clean side of his neck, and after a few seconds I am rewarded with weak, fluttering heartbeats that tickle my fingertips.

Once I have the pulse I look to his eyelids and see that they are twitching. His rib cage is moving, slowly and laboriously.

He's alive, I say to myself, only now registering Sebastian beside me. He's staring down at Rickard with his hand over his mouth.

"What's happened to him?" he asks.

I shake my head.

"I don't know."

I stare at him lying there, and then I say:

"Rickard."

He groans. Some of the dried flakes of blood at the edges of his mouth break off and fall onto the rug, where they blend in with the expensive dark-red woolen fibers.

I hesitate, but then I pull down the zipper in his jacket and unbutton his shirt. I start to open it but stop when I see deep, dark-purple bruises. His stomach feels swollen and rigid to my touch.

Sebastian makes a little sound at the sight.

"God," he whispers, and for the first time I feel something starting to seep through the shock—something that threatens to wash over me and sweep me away. Panic, or disgust, or something in between.

I do up the shirt.

"It looks like he's been hit by a train," I say, standing up.

"Or kicked," says Sebastian, "Hard, while he was on the floor."

There are no sounds around us.

When I look up at Sebastian I see he isn't looking at me, or at Rickard.

He is holding a piece of paper, his eyes fixed on the body hanging behind my shoulder.

"I think we might have found Bengtsson," he says quietly.

· ELEANOR ·

I finally force myself to look at the man hanging from the chandelier.

It's impossible to tell how long he has been dead. His face looks spent and shrunken, and the sagging folds of skin shift from shades of gray to purple. What little hair there is on his head is short and gray. His arms hang limp and lifeless at his sides, his hands so swollen that they look like inflated gloves. His fingers are black, the nails like small, dull jewels at their tips.

He is dressed in unpretentious clothes. An oilskin coat, a pair of thick jeans. There is a boot on one of his feet; the other lies nearby. It has landed sole down on the rug, almost as if someone has deliberately placed it there. It's a nice, light-brown leather boot with red laces. It looks expensive, and must be fairly new—perhaps a treat he bought for himself, pushing the boat out a little. A pair of really nice boots.

The man hanging from the chandelier looks like an actor made up to play a corpse. It's impossible to compute that he was once a living, breathing person just like Sebastian or me.

But that boot . . . the sight of that lonely, clean boot is too much.

I tear my eyes from it, bite the inside of my cheeks so hard I taste blood, and only then do I ask Sebastian, in a voice that almost—almost—sounds normal:

"What's that?"

Sebastian hands me the piece of paper he is holding. He isn't looking at me, but his eyes aren't focused on the hanged body either. They are fixed on a point on the rug, as though if he zones in enough on that point he can convince himself that the body and Rickard aren't here, that none of this is real.

I reach out and put my hand on his arm.

"Hey," I say quietly.

Sebastian seems to have to make an effort to tear his eyes from the rug, but he looks at me. His nostrils are flared, his teeth clenched.

I touch his cheek.

"Step back," I say, as softly as I can manage, putting all my heart into sounding like his girlfriend and not some hollow shell currently running on survival instinct alone. "Look away, OK? For me."

Sebastian stares at me for a few seconds but then closes his eyes, puts his hand on mine, and gives a curt nod.

He takes a short, jerky breath. And another. Then he turns around and takes a few steps away, gazing at the fireplace.

I look down at the piece of paper.

The paper is lined—the same sort that was in the notepad in Bengts-son's house, I realize. The same handwriting, too. Neat and slightly boxy.

> *I have kept watch for them for half a century. The burden was mine, and I promised to keep the secret, but it's over now. I don't need to anymore.*
>
> *I am tired, tired and lonely. It's no way to live.*
>
> *I kept my promise. No one can demand more of me. I have given all I could give.*
>
> *I don't know if I made the right choice. Perhaps now I will find out.*
>
> *I don't have many possessions. Let them go to the heirs with the rest of the estate. They can do as they wish with it. The place has brought me no joy, but perhaps for them it will be different.*
>
> *My will and keys are in the main kitchen. Bury me anywhere, so long as it isn't here. There is no one left to care*

*where I lie or what happens to my body. And it makes no
difference to me.*

   I am tired.

   I want to rest.

Mats Bengtsson, September 16

I read it twice. The second time I can see him hanging there out of
the corner of my eye. Just hanging there. A body that was once a person. A man who was once a boy. Mats Bengtsson? *The* Mats, the stableboy Anushka writes about in her diary? The one who worked here, for
Vivianne. Did he stay here all these years?

I don't register that I'm crying until I wipe my eyes with the back of
my hand.

I have kept watch for them for half a century.

In my head, Vivianne hisses like a memory:

I can hear them in the walls; they're whispering to me.

The last phone call.

I scrunch my eyes shut to try to silence her. Then I open them again.

"Sebastian, can I use your knife?"

Sebastian doesn't reply.

"Sebastian?" I ask, placing my hand on his shoulder. He flinches.

"Sorry," he says, straightening up; he was bent double studying the
fireplace.

"Your knife," I say.

"Here." He hands it to me. I take it, feel the smoothness of the wooden
handle, planed out by many hours of use, all too long ago.

"We have to . . . we have to cut him down," I say with a gulp. "We
can't leave him hanging there."

"We should leave him," says Sebastian, still with that awful, mono-
tone voice. "We shouldn't touch the body in case the police . . ."

"I know, but . . . we can't just leave him hanging there. We have to at
least cut him down so he can lie and rest. OK?" My voice cracks, and I
whisper:

"He says . . . he says he's tired. He says he wants to rest."

I don't know if it's because he can hear how close to breaking point

I am, or because something of the endless weariness in those small, scrupulously chosen words manages to pierce through the shock, but in the end Sebastian nods.

"OK. What do you want me to do?"

"We should probably . . . ," I start. "If I climb up and cut the rope then somebody has to catch him." I see the disgust etch itself into his face, and say:

"He's been hanging here for over five months. I don't know what'll happen to the body if it drops straight onto the floor."

He is so close to saying no. I can see that. He wants to refuse, with an aversion so strong it's physical. But I stare at him quietly, and he looks me in the eye, and then he says:

"OK."

I have probably never loved him as much as I do in that moment.

"Thank you," I say.

I look around, swallowing. There's a small footstool that has been kicked aside below the hanged man, but it looks too rickety.

I walk over to one of the velvet armchairs by the fireplace, and put the knife down on one of them. They are solid, substantial pieces, as I realize when I start dragging it over to the body. My arms are aching and I'm still sore after everything that has happened in the past few days, but I manage to get it all the way over. I pick up the knife again, feel its cool weight in my hand.

"OK, I'm going up," I say to Sebastian, my voice shaking just a little. "When I say so, grab him."

Sebastian stands right next to what was once Mats Bengtsson, just a few inches from the lonely boot.

"OK."

When I'm standing with one foot on each armrest, for a few seconds I'm afraid they'll give way under me, but they hold without so much as a groan in protest. The hard stuffing is stable under my feet, and I reach out for the rope. The blue fibers are so taut they look like they might snap at the slightest touch.

Now that I'm this close I can smell something. Not decay, exactly, but something else, frostbitten flesh, perhaps—something cold and irony that lingers on the hands, no matter how many times you wash them.

I almost vomit—I feel my stomach lurch—but manage to keep it down. I force my eyes to look at the rope, and not what is hanging from it.

"Sebastian," I say, unable to even pretend my voice is really carrying. "Now."

The silence that follows lasts an eternity, but then I hear a movement, and see the rope suddenly shift. Sebastian has taken hold of the body from behind.

I lift the knife and start cutting the rope.

The fibers break, quickly and mercifully. They are brittle and worn, and the cold has taken its toll. It takes no more than a minute for the blade to cut its way through.

Still, that minute lasts all too long.

When the last, thin strand of rope finally snaps, the muscles in my arm are screaming, and Sebastian lets out a little sound as the full weight of the body falls onto him.

He lays him down on the rug. Mats Bengtsson. More than five months after his death.

After Vivianne's.

I look at Sebastian, and then I walk over and take him in my arms, squeeze him tightly, paying no attention to the faint smell of corpse now radiating from him, too. I just hold him, because that's what he needs right now, and it's what I need, too.

Everything stands still.

And then Rickard gives a long-drawn-out groan and opens his eyes.

· ANUSHKA ·
JULY 1, 1966

The past few days it has rained nonstop. It's cool but not cold, and more than anything else it makes for a nice respite from the heat.

Yesterday I knocked on the door of what was once their room but is now Ma'am's room (Sir has started sleeping in one of the guest rooms), and found her out of bed. The sight shocked me so much I gave a start.

"G-g-good morning," I managed to stutter. She didn't turn around. She was standing by the window, gazing out at the lake. Her unwashed nightgown was hanging from her narrow shoulders, and her hair dangled down her back. Seeing it like this, and not in its carefully curled locks, I could suddenly see how similar it is to my own—rough and stubborn.

I was only in there to do some dusting and I don't know what got into me, but I asked:

"Would Ma'am like me to brush her hair?"

At first she didn't move. But then she turned around, so that her profile was lit by the light of the window, and nodded.

She sat down on the chair by the dressing table and handed me a heavy brush with a silver handle. Standing there behind her, I could smell her. It wasn't an offensive smell, necessarily, but a smell of body, one that clearly hadn't been washed in a while. Her hair was greasy at the roots, and the tangles were almost matted. I separated the strands one by one and brushed them gently, delicately, the way Mama used to brush mine when I was a child, her eyes so tired that they were almost falling asleep. I tried to make my hands as soft as my mama's.

Ma'am's face didn't move. She just stared at herself in the mirror. Without makeup on she looked both older and younger at the same time.

The rain was streaming down the windowpanes. The light outside was mild and gray, leaving no sharp edges.

When I brushed her hair out and looked at her in the mirror I saw that her eyes were closed. The deep wrinkles in her forehead that have appeared as if by magic over the past few months had softened.

"Thank you," she said quietly.

I placed the brush down carefully on the dressing table in front of her, then lingered there for a moment.

"I'm sorry," I said.

For a few seconds, the only sound to be heard was the rain pattering against the windowpanes.

"Go."

She had opened her eyes. She looked so tired.

"I . . . ," I started, but she said it again:

"Go, Annika."

And then she added, with a voice that made my stomach drop:

"Please, just go."

And so I went.

· ELEANOR ·

Rickard!" I say, and kneel down beside him.

His eyes are bleary and bloodshot and they flit around between us as he tries to sit up, but then he groans, coughs, and gives up.

"Don't move," I say. "You're . . . pretty badly hurt."

I don't want to tell him I'm afraid he could have internal bleeding or a ruptured spleen or something. The bruises on his midriff look like nothing I have ever seen before, and though I don't know enough about serious injuries to be able to tell how bad things really are, his shallow breathing and pale, sweaty skin suggest it's bad. Very bad.

Sebastian has knelt down beside him, too. Rickard's eyes dart back and forth between us. He seems to be struggling to recognize us.

"Do you remember who I am?" I ask.

He nods and shuts his eyes again.

"Do you remember messaging me?" I go on. He must have sent it from the small, black cell phone on the floor, the one I now see lying next to him.

Bengtsson's phone. How could it still be charged, after all these months? Bengtsson must have turned it off before he put the noose around his neck. That would be why I went straight to voicemail whenever I tried to call. When Rickard found it and turned it back on there must have been a little battery left.

Rickard nods again.

"Where am I?" he asks. He takes a few deep breaths, grimacing with every inhale.

"You're in the hunting lodge. Do you remember how you got here?"

He slowly shakes his head.

A sharp gust of wind makes the chimney howl. I look over my shoulder at the door. It's still shut, but that doesn't stop my heart from pounding.

"Rickard," I say, "can you look at me?"

He opens his eyes and searches for mine. I can see that even this takes some effort.

"Do you remember who did this to you?"

Nothing in his face suggests he understands the question.

"Listen to me," I say. "You have to say something, so I know you understand me. You went out to the wine cellar to get a bottle."

He nods.

"Did you go to the wine cellar? Or did you go somewhere else? Like to your car?"

"No," he says. "I went . . . to the wine cellar." The breath he takes between the words sounds strained.

I try not to hear the wet, bubbling sound in his chest.

"Then what happened?"

The silence lasts so long I don't think he's going to say anything more. His face is so drained it looks like it would feel cold to the touch.

"There was someone there," he says eventually. "I saw someone in the storm. I shouted, but he ran away. I followed him. Then I saw . . ." He raises his hand and touches his head. Frowns, as though trying to remember something.

"I saw . . . lights. Bright lights." He licks his lips. "That's all I remember."

I look at Sebastian, who raises his eyebrows but doesn't say a word. I don't understand either. It could be a false memory, from the head trauma. Or something as simple as a flashlight in a snowstorm.

But that thought seems worse.

Because who would that be? Who would be wandering around in a storm with a flashlight?

A few hours ago I would have said Bengtsson. But now I know it can't be him.

So the figure by the cottage . . .

The thought coils, cold and noxious, in the pit of my stomach.

"Do you remember what happened to you?" Sebastian asks. "Your injuries are . . . pretty serious." He swallows.

Rickard purses his lips. They are dry and pale.

"No. Maybe I fell, or . . ."

I cast a glance at Sebastian, and can tell he's thinking the same thing as me. Those injuries couldn't come from a fall. Someone has hurt him, badly, the same person who hit Veronika's head so hard the blood left thick, matted clumps in her hair.

But I don't think Rickard is trying to hide something. I believe him when he says he doesn't remember. He doesn't seem to be in any condition to be lying.

"Do you think you can stand up?" Sebastian asks Rickard, who looks at him with resignation in his eyes.

"I don't know," he says. "I can try."

Sebastian looks at me.

"We'll be right back, OK?" I put my hand on Rickard's arm, trying my best to sound warm and caring. Rickard looks at me for a long time. I don't know if he's searching for something in my face, or if I'm reading something into his look that isn't there.

With aching muscles I stand up and walk over to Sebastian by the fireplace. From above the mantel a moth-eaten elk head stares down at us haughtily, its eyes glimmering, cold and blind, in the dim light of the windows.

Sebastian opens his mouth, then shuts it again.

"I'm sorry," he says quietly. "I'm so sorry, Eleanor. I should have listened to you. I should have trusted you."

It should feel good to hear this, but I don't feel anything at all. It doesn't mean anything, not anymore. Not when I so desperately wish I were wrong.

"It doesn't matter," I say, but Sebastian shakes his head.

"No," he says, "you were right."

"Not about Rickard," I say.

"No. But about there being someone here. That you saw someone, that something wasn't right. I should have listened."

I allow myself to close my eyes, briefly, to come back to myself. Then I open them again.

"We have to get out of here."

"How are we going to take him with us?" Sebastian asks.

He is trying to muffle his voice, but the lodge is so small that Rickard can probably hear our mumblings anyway.

"He'll have to walk. We can support him, but he'll have to walk."

"I think his ribs are broken, Eleanor. If he stumbles they could puncture his lungs."

"Better that than leaving him here. All we have to do is get him back to the house. Then we can put him in a car and drive to the nearest hospital."

Sebastian runs his hand over his mouth.

"Shit, Eleanor," he says—not even a whisper anymore, barely even an exhalation. "What is this?"

I shake my head.

"I don't know. I . . ."

Then it hits me.

I walk back over to Rickard and sit down. When I speak, my soft, accommodating voice is gone.

"Rickard, look at me," I say, and he opens his eyes with visible strain. I almost relent when I see the exhaustion and pain on his face, but I steel myself.

Sometimes we have to get our hands a little dirty, Victoria. Don't let anybody push you around. Don't let anybody try to dodge your questions or lie to you. You can't play your next hand until you have all the cards.

"Rickard, I found Veronika's letters in your car."

Even through the pain in his face, I can see him suddenly go still, a new watchfulness in his eyes.

"It was you who took them, wasn't it? Don't try to deny it."

His breaths are slow, audibly rattling in his throat.

"Yes," he says eventually.

"Why?"

He is still eyeing me up with that watchful gaze. When he opens his mouth I can already tell he intends to lie.

"I mistook them for—"

"If you lie to me I'm leaving you here," I interrupt.

My voice sounds alien to my own ears.

Sebastian says, "Eleanor," in shock, but I don't look his way. I keep my eyes on Rickard, let him see that I mean what I say.

Do I?

I don't think I could leave an injured man to freeze to death, with only a corpse for company. But by this point it feels like I have been walking through a fog for months. I have to know what all of this is.

You may not be able to leave him here, but I can, my dear. Leave this to me.

For what is perhaps the first time in my life, Vivianne's voice is very welcome in my head.

I see when the shift happens in Rickard's eyes. When he makes the decision.

When he opens his mouth again, he sounds different. His voice less nasal, a touch deeper.

"I'm not a lawyer."

· ANUSHKA ·
JULY 7, 1966

Oh, help, I don't know what to do.

Part of me is annoyed at Märit, because if she hadn't said anything I wouldn't have noticed. Before she said it the thought hadn't even crossed my mind, but now I can't look at him without blushing!

It all happened yesterday at lunch. I have started taking any root vegetables that are beginning to spoil out to the stable—the horses seem to like chewing them, and Kicki loves the chance to feed them. At first she was afraid of them, but now she reaches her chubby little hand as high as she can toward their muzzles, and when the horses chomp at the carrots she feeds them she giggles herself breathless. That always makes me chuckle, too.

It was a beautiful day yesterday, with fluffy white clouds floating across the sky and a mild breeze blowing in the trees, making everything smell of pine and sunshine. When I got to the stable, the stableboy was showing Kicki how to brush the horses. He's kind and a little quiet, and Kicki seems to like him.

When I walked in he looked up and seemed to lose his train of thought, and Kicki had to tug at his arm to remind him to keep on brushing. I smiled and said hello, handed Märit the bread I had brought with me, and then gave Kicki a bunch of carrots to feed the horses with. I said hello to the stableboy, who smiled bashfully and nodded back at me.

It was only when Märit and I were sitting on the steps in the sunshine that she nudged me in my side.

"So, what do you think of him?" she asked.

"Who?" I replied, but then answered straightaway: "Oh, he's nice. I think he's just worried about his wife."

"No, not *Sir*," she said, "Mats."

"Mats?" I asked, now confused.

Märit jerked her head back. I turned around automatically to see the stableboy, who had gone on to inspecting one of the horses' hooves—the little brown one he sometimes lets Kicki sit on and walks around.

"I don't know," I said. "He's friendly?"

Märit laughed at me. She has a dimple that appears when she laughs like that, high up on her left cheek.

"Oh, Annika. You must have noticed that he's head over heels about you?"

It felt like my whole face was starting to blush, and I shook my head.

"Don't be silly! He's not at all!"

"Hey, just because you haven't noticed doesn't mean it isn't true," Märit said, turning her face up to the sun. After a few weeks out here, her freckles have started to appear. Mama always said that freckles looked dirty, but the way they look on Märit makes me wish I had them, too. I have skin like Ma'am's—so pale that I just get sunburned and pink nosed in summer.

"I think you should have a summer fling, Annika," said Märit.

I must have looked so puzzled that Märit assumed I didn't understand.

"You know, a little romance," she said. "With Mats. A beautiful young girl like you. It would do you a world of good. And he's pretty cute when you really look at him. Under all those sack-like shirts he wears, his shoulders are big and broad."

I couldn't even look at her now; I just shook my head as she laughed and put her arm around me.

I wish she hadn't said anything! Now I can't even look at the poor boy without going red as a beetroot, and he seems to have noticed too, because he won't even meet my eyes.

No, I don't want any fling with him, but how could I say that to Märit? I'm scared she would see there's something I'm not telling her.

Mats isn't the one I think about before I go to sleep. As I close my eyes on that hard little bed in my windowless cubby, his sweet brown eyes aren't what I see.

The eyes I see are a bright, light blue.

The one I think about is sleeping in the bedroom next to mine.

But I could never say that to Märit.

· ELEANOR ·

"Who are you?" I ask Rickard.

His gaze is still steady and locked on mine, but I can see that even this takes some effort. His forehead has started to get clammy, and the sweat is beading along his hairline, even in spite of the cold.

"I'm a private investigator."

Private investigator. My exhausted mind is racing so fast that for a moment I appear to lose all ability to speak.

The light in the little lodge has dimmed even more. All of the corners are in shadow. The cloud cover above us must be so thick and dark that it's completely shutting out the pale winter sun.

"Like a private detective?" I ask.

He nods weakly.

"So why did you say you were a lawyer?" Sebastian cuts in.

"I needed access to the house for an assignment. The easiest way seemed to be through you and your aunt," he says to me. "I found your phone numbers online, called, and said . . ."

"That we had to come here to compile an inventory of assets," I finish his sentence.

He nods again.

The only words I manage to utter are:

"But why?"

"My client hired me to reclaim Solhöga," he says.

have willed the house out of the family. Traditionally the house had passed to the eldest son in each generation, and she said Evert would never have wanted it to go to Vivianne. According to her, her eldest son is the rightful heir to Solhöga, and she was adamant that Evert agreed with her on that. She said there had to be documents out here. Evert died without a real will. But she believes that there was one, and that Vivianne kept it from them."

I swallow.

"And then?" I ask, repeating Sebastian's question.

I see Rickard hesitate, but it's not like he has any choice but to talk.

"And then, to try to find out if Vivianne did have something to do with Evert's death. If it really was suicide, or if Vivianne killed him for the inheritance. Pernilla Fälth said the police refused to listen to her when Evert died, but she was certain there had to be some proof out here, and that with Vivianne gone I would be able to find it."

Vivianne. My grandmother. The only one who loved me, the only one who looked after me.

A murderer?

I think of her long fingers, of her thin, sharp, red nails. The cigarette that always sat between her fingertips, or her perfectly rouged lips.

That terrible gurgle when she tried to breathe through her slit throat.

The blank, white face that is all I can see when I try to remember the figure I saw in her doorway.

Given the right circumstances even you would be capable of anything, Victoria my dear, I hear her whisper languidly in my head. *Just look at you now: you're letting a dying man lie on a cold floor until he gives you what you want.*

"So you called Veronika and me and said you were a lawyer," I say. "To get yourself here. To Solhöga."

Rickard nods.

"It's where he died," he says. "Your great-aunt said that she and the whole family had repeatedly tried to contact Vivianne to access the house, and to buy it from her, but Vivianne wouldn't even respond to their letters. That made Pernilla Fälth suspicious. She said Vivianne would have no reason to deny them access to the house, unless . . ."

"... there was something here she didn't want them to find," I say, finishing his sentence.

Or something she didn't want them to find out.

It was an accident. A terrible, terrible accident.

· ANUSHKA ·
JULY 13, 1966

I have to get out of here. I have to go home.

There's no other option.

Some things can never be undone. Once certain lines have been crossed, there's no going back.

God, forgive me. I hate myself. I didn't mean to.

Or did I?

That's the worst of it: I wanted it to happen; I've wanted it for a long time. That's what I can't stop thinking about, what I can't forgive myself for.

She's my cousin, my family. And I betrayed her. If my mama taught me anything, it was never to turn your back on family. That's why she sent me here, to Vivianne. Before I even knew she called herself that.

Mama told me: *Marta will look after you. We look after each other. Go to her. She'll help you.*

So I came here, and my cousin Marta had become Vivianne, and since then nothing has been as it should.

Oh God. How could I do such a thing?

I keep telling myself that it wasn't so bad—just a moment of weakness, just two lonely people. We have that in common, after all. We are both lonely, both concerned about Ma'am. She was all we talked about, so surely it can't be so bad? Is it really so unforgivable?

No one saw. No one needs to find out. No one needs to hear what I've done.

Yes, she has treated me badly; I can't deny that. I don't want to deny it. She can be a witch at times, but still, she doesn't deserve this. I didn't betray her six months ago when she was my tormentor; I betrayed the disconsolate woman who can barely get out of bed for grief. I waited until she was weak and vulnerable and then I took what belonged to her.

It wasn't me who leaned in. I didn't make the first move.

But I didn't pull away either.

After that first dinner, it didn't take long for it to happen again, and that time it wasn't because Sir asked me to. There's something so unbearably sad about a beautiful man dining alone at a grand table. So one day I just asked if I could eat with him, and then he smiled at me, a heart-wrenching smile, and said yes—he would love some company.

So I sat with him, and I ate. We didn't talk so much that night. But I saw that he ate more than usual, and that warmed me up inside.

It didn't happen every night. Not on the nights when Märit was with me in the kitchen. It was a tacit agreement that we had, that it would stay between him and me. Our little secret.

Oh God, how could I be so stupid?

I should have said no when he asked if I wanted to have a glass of wine with him in the drawing room. He saw my hesitation, I know he did, because he added, almost immediately:

"Ah, Annika, you don't have to. I know you have a lot to do. You might not even like wine. And you probably have better things to do than spend your evenings with me."

I should have said no. I should have gone out to Märit, and Kicki, and Mats. Or gone up to my room and read a book. I could have asked to borrow Märit's record player. If I played the music quietly enough then no one else would hear.

There is so much I could have done.

But I didn't do any of it.

I said:

"I like wine."

I didn't do it because I wanted the wine. I did it because I knew it would make him smile, and he did smile, and oh my God, all this because of that smile. What I wouldn't do to see that smile.

I sat down on the couch because Sir usually sits in one of the armchairs, and when he sat down next to me my heart was pitter-pattering so hard I thought it would burst out of my chest. The wine was dark and smelled strong, and it's been so long since I drank anything like it that I started to cough, and then he laughed, but not in the way that Ma'am would have done.

"Is it a little too full-bodied for you?" he asked. "Vivianne prefers white wines. She says the red stains her teeth. Perhaps I should have given you something else."

I thought it then—that there was nothing wrong with what we were doing, despite the tingling feeling in my fingers and toes. I thought there couldn't possibly be anything wrong with it, that it was just me being foolish, a conceited little girl with a conceited little crush. This was no fling. Because he was—is—married to my cousin, and because he's lonely, and because I'm lonely, and because I'm young and he's older, and because he took pity on me and I took pity on him.

I mean, we weren't even doing anything, really. We were just having a glass of wine. He's had wine with many other ladies before—I've seen it. And yes, it had always been in the company of others, and yes, Ma'am had always been there too, but she was only lying upstairs at the time. It wasn't like she was so very far away. And besides, she was on our lips all the time.

"No, I like red wine," I said. "We used to drink it back home."

As soon as I said it I bit my tongue. Was that the wrong thing to do, to talk about home? Whenever I did it around Ma'am she would pull my hair or pinch my arm to shut me up.

But he took a sip and looked at me with those still, blue eyes.

"Tell me more about 'home.'"

So I told him. About Mama, and how tired she always was, and how she was scrupulous about scrubbing under her nails every evening, to get rid of the dirt from the factory. And how much I missed her.

Sir listened attentively without taking his eyes off me, as though he was trying to memorize every word. It made me feel . . . bigger, like I grew a little bit with every question he asked. Like I got to exist. For the first time in so long.

Perhaps that was why I said it. Either that, or the wine had loosened my tongue.

I said:

"When she was Marta—" and he interrupted me, for the first time. "Marta?"

I could see that he had understood. I felt all the blood drain from my face.

"Please, don't say anything to Ma'am. Please, I didn't mean to; I don't know what she'll do if she finds out. . . ."

"Annika," he said, as he leaned in and placed his hand on my shoulder, "I won't say anything. I promise. This stays between us."

His hand felt very warm on my arm. The wine was coursing through my veins. My glass was already almost empty.

"Was that her name before she came here? Marta?" he asked.

All I dared do was nod.

He looked at me for a very long time, his hand still resting on my arm. His glass was empty, too. There was a softness to the light coming in from outside. It was blue and lovely, like the flowers at the forest's edge.

"Did you have another name, too? Before you came here?" he asked. His voice was quieter: I had to watch his lips to catch what he was saying.

"Yes," I said, and I was whispering, too.

Sir said nothing. I realized he was waiting.

I swallowed, and then I said:

"Anushka. My name is Anushka."

He nodded. So slowly.

"Anushka," he repeated.

Hearing Sir say my real name felt like nothing I have ever experienced before.

"Anushka, Anna. My grandmother was from Russia," I said. "She wanted me to have that name."

"It's beautiful," he said. "I like it better than 'Annika.'"

He moved his hand from my shoulder to my cheek, and it was as if I froze on the spot. I didn't dare breathe.

"Anushka," he said again.

And then he leaned in toward me, and I didn't pull back.

He kissed me.

It felt like dying.

It was only a kiss. It lasted no more than a second. Then he pulled back, and his eyes were wide, and I jumped up and said, "Sorry! Sorry!" and turned tail and ran. Out to the stable, to the horses, where it was just me and the animals.

I stayed there till long after nightfall. I have only just dared sneak back to my room.

Truth is, I didn't run because I was scared. Or because we had done something wrong.

I ran because I couldn't bear to see the regret in his eyes when he opened them.

Oh God. How can I stay here?

How will I ever look him in the eye tomorrow morning at breakfast?

· ELEANOR ·

T hat's enough, Eleanor," I hear Sebastian say. I quickly look up.
     He is on his feet, still holding the water glass. He's gripping it so
tightly his knuckles have gone white.

"Look at him," he says now, a little quieter. "He's badly hurt. We have
to get him out of here, to a hospital. Now."

Rickard's face is gray, the dark circles under his eyes like bruises, the
breaths coming in jolts.

"You're right," I say to Sebastian. "We have to get him back to the
house."

I look at Rickard.

"Can you stand?" I ask him. "If we both support you, do you think
you'll be able to walk?"

He gives a wan smile.

"I don't think I have any choice," he replies.

"Sebastian, if you get on the other side of him we can lift him from
both sides," I say.

But Sebastian doesn't seem to be listening to me. He's looking at the
cabinet in the corner.

"Sebastian?"

He walks over to it and opens it.

It's empty. When it was closed I thought it was your average corner cabinet, but I see now it's some sort of rack, with four spaces for some-thing long and thin.

He turns around and shakes his head.

"What is it?" I ask. "What are you doing?"

"It's a gun cabinet," he says. "My dad has one. I thought it might be good to take one."

He looks on edge as he says it. Sebastian has never so much as held a weapon in his life. I know he has gone out with his father's hunting team a few times, but, unlike his little brother, he has never had any interest in taking part in the shooting itself.

"Good idea," I say, and it seems to reassure him, "but come here—let's get Rickard to his feet."

You can't trust anyone but yourself, Victoria. Understand? No one's going to look out for you. You have to do that yourself.

I reach out and pick up Bengtsson's phone, check if it has any signal, just in case. Nothing. It must be coming and going here, just like in the house. I shove the phone in my pocket, just in case.

Sebastian sits down next to Rickard and puts his arm around his shoulders. Rickard drapes his other arm around my waist.

I look at his bare fingers, and can only imagine what the biting wind outside will do to them.

"Do you know where your other glove is, Rickard?" I ask. I look around us but see nothing.

Rickard shakes his head.

"OK," I say. "Then let's go. Now!"

Rickard lets out a long, involuntary groan when we both pull him up to his feet.

Once he's up, his face is deathly white, his eyes are wincing, and his lips are freshly flecked with blood.

Who could have done this to him?

The fear in my mouth tastes metallic. I swallow it down. It has no place here.

"Rickard, I'm going to zip up your jacket and pull the hood over your head now," I say. "For the cold. OK? Then we have to walk. It's going to hurt, but we can't stay here. We have to get you to the house so we can try to call an ambulance. If we can't get them to come here, we'll drive you to the hospital ourselves."

He nods weakly, his eyes still closed.

We stop by the door. I reach for the door handle.

What if someone is waiting outside?

Someone with a blank, white face and silver scissors in their hand?

I brace myself.

Then I open the door.

· ELEANOR ·

The wind whips against us like it has a will of its own, and I am temporarily blinded by the flurry of snowflakes.

It's so dim out here that it feels like dusk. The trees around us are nothing but towering shadows, and it's impossible to see more than ten feet ahead.

Our own footprints have already disappeared.

I crack my neck and start walking. The arm I have linked around Rickard's back has already started to ache. He's heavy, and he seems to be dragging his feet.

"Rickard!" I shout over the wind, and I can only hope that he hears me through his hood. "You have to try to lift your feet!"

I don't know if he hears me. If he replies, I don't hear it.

All I can hear is the wind and my own labored breaths. Sebastian and I are heading in the direction that I think—hope—leads to the edge of the forest. To the house. To safety and warmth.

If it can even be called safety.

Things are different now, worse. My very skin feels on edge, all of my senses alert. When I was running after Veronika last night I was scared, yes, but it was a different type of fear, shapeless and drunk.

It's another feeling to know for a fact that there is somebody out here with us. Someone strong enough to break Rickard's ribs. Someone fast and discreet, anonymous and motivated.

Someone who may have killed before. Who has seen my face. Who wants to hurt us.

We are clumsy, and slow, and oh so vulnerable. Whoever it was who did this, the storm will hide him until he's already too close.

We are defenseless. We had to leave our paltry weapons in the lodge, so that we could lug Rickard's full wounded weight through the forest.

We can only hope that the storm hides us long enough to reach safety.

My face is already numb, and my jacket feels hopelessly inadequate. The snow is sneaking in through all the cracks it can find. I'm out of breath, and my legs were shaky to begin with.

Are we even going the right way? Or are we already lost in the trees?

I have heard stories about people freezing to death, sometimes just a few hundred feet from safety, because the cold had made them tired and confused and they couldn't see where they had to go. Like us, now.

Whatever we do, we can't stop. If we stop, we're dead.

That's the mantra I'm repeating to myself.

If we stop, we're dead. If we stop, we're dead.

My foot catches on a root, and I stumble. I don't know if it's Rickard's groan I hear when he slumps heavily onto my shoulder, or my own.

"I'm OK!" I shout.

Then I bite my tongue.

Quiet. Must be quiet. So the murderer can't hear us if he's waiting out there.

Whoever it is, he could come from any direction. Maybe he's creeping his way behind us, biding his time, waiting for the exhaustion to take over and for us to let our guards down.

There. Something between the trees. A shadow.

The breath freezes in my throat. My feet refuse to move.

"Eleanor! What are you doing? We have to keep going!"

Sebastian. His voice pierces through the whirling snow and the screaming gale.

"There's someone there," I whisper.

Something tall, thin, and dark. Eyes staring at us.

"Eleanor!" Sebastian screams.

Rickard's head is lolling between his shoulders. I don't know if he's still conscious. I take a firmer grip around his waist, keeping my eyes on the shadow. When we start walking again it seems to pale and dissipate like smoke.

Or just back away, now that it's been seen. Back between the trunks, where it's invisible once again.

How much farther can it be now? Shouldn't we be there already?

Rickard pulls at me.

No, he isn't pulling me: his legs give way underneath him, and he drags me down with him into the snow. I can feel the frozen blueberry sprigs cracking beneath us.

"Rickard, you have to get up," I say. His arm is slack around my waist. "Come on, get up."

My lips have split in the cold. I can feel it with my tongue, but it doesn't hurt. My eyes are stinging from the wind and snow.

"Eleanor," I hear, like a whisper.

Somewhere in the trees.

There's no one there, I tell myself, my teeth chattering with cold and fear. *I'm seeing things.*

But then I hear it again, and now there's somebody tugging at my arm. Sebastian. He has let go of Rickard.

"He won't make it," he says. His voice sounds thick and distorted.

But then, when I look up, I see it—see the trees up ahead starting to thin out. And something, a silhouette like a mirage, there behind them.

"We're almost there," I say. "Look! Just a few hundred feet to go."

Sebastian looks small when I look at him. Alien.

"We'll have to carry him. Come on, Sebastian. You can do this. Link your arms with mine under his shoulders. Help me to lift him up."

I lock my eyes on Sebastian's. Try to give him the same steely look that Vivianne used to give me—as though his only option is to do what I say.

You can do this, Victoria.

Sebastian nods. He squats down on the other side of Rickard.

Well done, Victoria.

I tighten my grip even though the muscles in my back are screaming, stick my arm under Rickard's shoulders, and lift.

· ANUSHKA ·
JULY 16, 1966

Märit can sense that something is off.

I keep on telling myself I should just leave. Sir won't even look at me now, and he has been spending ever more time out in the hunting lodge. I should be grateful, but it just makes my stomach ache. I don't know what I want. I don't know what it is I hope he will do. Tell me that it was nothing. That it won't happen again.

This morning Märit asked me what was wrong. She asked if it was "that week" and I said it was, but I must have said it a little too hastily, or with the wrong tone of voice, because I could tell she didn't believe me.

"Aren't you happy out here? Are you feeling lonely? Do you miss your friends?"

To that I replied:

"I have no friends," and I didn't mean to, but my voice shook slightly. At this, Märit put down the pot she was washing, dried her hands on the tea towel on the counter, and wrapped her arms around me.

"That's not true," she said. "I'm your friend."

This made me start to cry. I hate crying. Mama always said that people like us can't afford to cry. We can't show any weakness.

I wish I could tell Märit what happened, but at the same time I don't want her to know. I don't want her to look at me with contempt when she finds out what kind of girl I am. The sort of girl who kisses her cousin's husband. The sort of girl my mama used to point at on the streets back home, and whisper about under her hot, contemptuous breath.

If she had known that this would happen, she would never have let me come here.

That might have been for the better.

I was supposed to go in and change Ma'am's bedsheets half an hour ago. I stood by the door for what felt like an eternity, trying to pluck up the courage to go in, but I couldn't. I was afraid I would break down and confess as soon as I saw her.

So now she's lying in there alone on dirty bedsheets, while I'm sitting here writing my shame in a book.

Märit has suggested we ask for some time off on Sunday and take Kicki to the nearest town to go to the movie theater. She said that I should ask, because "Sir likes you better," and she laughed when she said it. I felt like I was going to be sick.

But I can't tell her that I can't either.

Perhaps we should ask Mats if he wants to come with us. Mats, who is young and suitable and who likes me. And who isn't married.

I'll ask him tonight.

And then, if Mats says yes, I'll ask Sir if we can go.

· ELEANOR ·

Sebastian and I drag Rickard onto the rug in the hallway. After the subdued, dark grayness outside, the electric light from the ceiling seems unnaturally sharp, and the family portrait gazes down at us with flat, pitiless eyes.

"Rickard?" I say. "Can you hear me?" I roll him onto his back and try to find a pulse. Despite the thick gloves I have just taken off, my fingers are too cold to feel anything.

"He's breathing," says Sebastian, and I can see that he's right. Rickard's eyes are closed, but his chest is still rising and falling.

"We have to warm him up," I say. "He's way too cold."

"I'll get blankets," says Sebastian.

He runs up the stairs while I unbutton Rickard's coat. He lets out a quiet sound, which I take as a good sign. Any sign of life is a good sign right now.

When Sebastian returns, his arms are full of comforters. He spreads them out delicately over Rickard, and then takes a step back.

"What else can we do?" he asks. "We need some sort of heating pad, or . . . I don't know, anything. A fire?"

"I think we'd better try to call an ambulance," I say, "right away. Or drive him to the hospital."

Sebastian nods.

"I'll check my phone," he says.

He runs into the kitchen. I hear his heavy steps echoing off the floor-boards along the service passage.

My eyes are drawn back to the painting. To the woman who was Vivianne, and the man who was my grandfather.

Did you kill him?

I can't imagine that Vivianne would have murdered her husband for an inheritance. Not that she would be incapable of killing: I have seen her in the deepest depths of her rage, received slaps so forceful it felt like my head would fly off my neck. At her most angry it was like she wasn't even there at all—her eyes would blacken completely.

But she would never have killed anyone for money.

Of that I am sure.

Four people in the painting. Three of them dead, the fourth bed-bound upstairs with a head wound.

My mom, taken all too soon by breast cancer. My grandmother, murdered before my very eyes.

And my grandfather? Evert?

His expression in the portrait is so pared back he could be anyone.

I think of the body in the hunting lodge. Mats Bengtsson. Of his terrible, empty face.

Vivianne. Evert. Mats. All dead. For what?

Not for money. It can't have been for the money.

What did it say in the letter he left?

I have kept watch for them for half a century.

I have given all I could give.

Who are "they"?

When I close my eyes I see a photograph. Two women. One of them with a straight, dark braid.

The cousin. Anushka.

Is she one of the people he kept watch for?

Vivianne's voicemail messages, that last week.

"I can hear them in the walls."

I open my eyes again when I hear Sebastian's footsteps returning. He doesn't need to say anything: even before he opens his mouth I can tell from the look in his eyes and his stiff grip on his phone.

"Nothing at all."

I nod.

"Then we'll have to drive," I say. "It's our only choice."

Sebastian shakes his head.

"What if we get stuck?" he says.

"Better than staying here," I say, letting my eyes sweep up the stairs to the dark landing. "We have to get out of here."

Sebastian's arms are crossed. He looks so pale, so wiped out. It's as if all of his features—all those little features I have made an effort to memorize—have fragmented and dissolved.

I get up and walk over to him.

"There's something about this house, Sebastian," I say, quietly. "Don't tell me you don't feel it, too. There's someone out there. Someone who did that to Rickard." I nod at the bundle lying on the rug.

I raise my hand to Sebastian's cheek. It feels cold under my palm, scratchy with stubble.

"Let's get out of here. To safety. We'll drive carefully."

I kiss him, warm lips against his rigid, unmoving ones. I breathe in his smell, try to force something of the tension in my body to release.

"I'll go start the car," I say. "I'll try to heat it up a little before we get Rickard and Veronika and go."

"Not alone you're not," Sebastian says. "I'm going with you."

I know better than to argue. I just nod. I see Sebastian cast one last, long look at Rickard lying there unconscious on the floor, and then we head to the door.

unds more

as to work.

Veronika's

er, gasping,

asks. "What

id it was just
too. If it *was*

e gloom. In
He could be

dness," I say.
cognize him.

hing?"
istinguishing

make a sound.
vision.
ble to identify
ice . . . I might

n able to utter
le to articulate

ANOR ·

ack outside, but not much. I'm hold-
ve walk, and he is squeezing my finds lost in the woods. When we reach
jump into the passenger seat as fast

r as out, but at least there's no wind.
fs of vapor, and the car feels smaller
und with his keys before he finds the
on.

plutters, and for a single, crushing
me. But then the sound dies and

the key again.
r a few seconds, the silence is ear-

rth attempt he curses so loudly that
onto the wheel so hard it sends the
y.
er.

he battery. Or the oil." He shakes

his head. "I don't know," he adds, with a short chuckle that s[ounds]
like a snort. "I have no fucking clue. But it won't start."

"We'll just have to try the other cars," I say. "One of them [will]
Right?"

He doesn't reply. His silence says more than enough.

"We're getting out of here, Sebastian," I say. "Let's go ge[t the]
keys. Try her car."

In the compact car his hot-tempered breaths sound lou[der,]
like he isn't getting enough air.

"How does this all fit together, Eleanor?" he eventually [says. "What]
is this?"

I pause before answering.

"I never understood it," I say slowly. "When the police sa[id it was]
a break-in, I never understood why they didn't attack me, [if it was]
just a break-in, I mean."

I turn to look at him, see the contours of his face in t[he dark. In]
this dusky-gray storm light I can't make out his markers. [He could be]
anybody.

"I mean, the murderer didn't know about my face bli[ndness," I say.]
"He couldn't have. So he couldn't have known I wouldn't r[ecognize him.]
Right?"

Sebastian says nothing.

"So why did he just walk away? Why didn't he say anyt[hing?"]

In my memory, that shiny, white face has one lone [distinguishing]
feature.

Its silence.

Whoever it was who killed my grandmother, he didn't [say a word.]
From the moment he saw me to when he left my field of [vision.]

"He said nothing," I say. "As if he knew I wouldn't be a[ble to identify]
him by his face alone. As if he knew that if I heard his v[oice I would]
recognize it."

As I say it, I realize this is the thought I haven't bee[n able to think]
since the gap in my memory, the words I haven't been a[ble to say]
for fear of sounding paranoid or unhinged.

· ANUSHKA ·
JULY 21, 1966

Yesterday I took a walk in the forest with Mats.

Since asking if Märit, Mats, and I could go to the movies in town, I have tried to avoid Sir as much as possible. It was one of the most uncomfortable conversations I have ever had. I had braided my hair so tight it was pulling at my roots, and I kept my hands clasped in front of my apron. Meanwhile Sir cleared his throat after every other word and said that of course, naturally, quite all right, we could stay out as long as we wanted.

I hardly remember anything about the movie we saw. I think it was about cowboys. Kicki got scared by the pistols, but Märit kept on whispering that it was only pretend and wasn't it exciting to see them fight? She said that the pistols and weapons were just toys, and that no one was killed. After the film, Kicki would only talk about "baddies" and how she was going to "shoot all of them." Mats played cowboy with her all the way to the car, pretended to fall over when Kicki "shot" him again and again.

And so then, yesterday, when the three of us were eating our lunch by the lake and Märit nudged me and raised her eyebrow, then I thought: *Yes. This can work. This can help.*

So I asked Mats if he wanted to take a walk in the forest after our dinner, and he went bright red and nodded.

Once we were in the forest, we slowly strolled down one of the paths.

Mats didn't say very much but pointed out birds in the trees and told me where he usually takes the horses to ride them. I said I had never sat on a horse before, and he mumbled that he could show me, if I wanted.

I said I would love to.

It was so easy to be out there with him. There was no tension, no sense that I was doing something wrong. A housemaid and a stableboy— what could be more right? And he's not bad, looks-wise. Not that he's particularly handsome either, but there's nothing wrong with his face. When I almost stumbled on a root, he gave me his arm. It felt warm and safe under mine.

When we stopped in a little clearing, I stood on my tiptoes and kissed his cheek. It was smooth against my lips. He seemed to lose his footing completely, looked away, and then said to me, with a voice that wasn't quite steady:

"I like you so very much, Annika."

And I tilted my head a little to one side and said:

"I like you too, Mats."

It's true. I do like Mats. Like a little brother.

But perhaps I can come to like him another way, if I try. I can teach myself, with a little effort. I have taught myself so many other things. Lost so many other things.

Perhaps I can teach myself to like Mats that other way, just as I have taught myself to be Annika.

And perhaps I can teach myself to stop thinking about Sir, just as I have taught myself to stop being Anushka.

· ELEANOR ·

We try Veronika's car, but without any luck. The engine refuses to start. We dig through Rickard's pockets to try to find his keys, but when that fails I tell Sebastian to stay with him while I look upstairs.

I pull out all the drawers in his room, rifle through his bag, pick up his papers. Nothing. On the way to the study, I pass Veronika's room.

"What's going on?" she asks.

She is still lying on her side in bed, her long black fringe flopping over her face, her narrowed eyes watching the doorway, like a cat.

"I need Rickard's car keys," I say bluntly. "Our cars aren't starting. We have to get out of here."

"Perhaps we just have to wait out the cold," she murmurs.

"We can't!" I exclaim, feeling all the energy suddenly seeping out of me. I can't even keep myself together enough to check the rest of the rooms. I drop straight to the floor, my back against the chest of drawers beside Veronika's bed. The hard knobs dig into the sore, soft parts of my back, and I don't even have the energy to care.

I'm so tired.

I'm just so tired.

"What's happened to the lawyer?" Veronika asks, now with another type of sharpness.

When I open my eyes and turn my head, her face is only a few inches from mine. That distanced, sardonic look that seems to always reside there has disappeared.

It all comes flooding out. I tell her about the hunting lodge and what we found, about Bengtsson's dead body, about what Rickard told us, and the fact that he hasn't woken up since we got back to the house.

Veronika whistles when I'm done.

"Shit," she says. "I thought there was something fishy about him. But Aunt Pernilla . . ." She shakes her head.

"Do you know her?" I ask.

"No," says Veronika. "Daddy would talk about her sometimes. But we never met his family. He said they didn't like Mother." She shuts her eyes.

"So what do we do?" she asks when she opens them again.

"We can't wait out the storm," I say once I've caught my breath. "I don't know much about cars, but I'm starting to wonder if it really is the cold that's preventing them from starting."

Or if someone has sabotaged the engines. To make sure we're alone, and helpless, and cut off from the world.

"Ugh, I'm so fucking *angry!*" I shout, pounding the wooden bed frame so hard it claps. It hurts, more than I expected, and I curse and shake my hand.

To my surprise, Veronika lets out a soft, whinnying giggle.

"What's so funny?" I ask, throwing her a sideways glance.

"I've been waiting for that since you were a little kid," she says. "You never got angry as a kid. No matter what Vivianne did, it just didn't faze you. I thought it would come when you were a teenager, but it never did. So it's about time."

I can't help but smile, bitter as it is.

"Oh, I've been angry for a long time," I say, and it's true. Perhaps truer than I've realized. "A really long time."

"Good," says Veronika. "Good. We all need a little anger sometimes." She sits up and leans back against the headboard, then grimaces and raises a hand to the back of her head.

"That's what Mother said, at least," she adds. "After Daddy died."

I stare at her. The yellow light from the old bulbs saps the color out of the rest of us, but it seems to sharpen Veronika's features.

"Do you think it's true?" I ask. "That Vivianne could have killed Evert?"

"No," she says immediately. "But I can see why Pernilla might think that. I mean, I don't know the woman, but I could probably have thought so too, if I didn't know better."

"What do you mean?" I ask.

"Vivianne loved Daddy. She was crushed when he died. Worse than—look, don't take this the wrong way, but worse than when Vendela died. I don't know how much you remember of that time," she adds hastily, and I shake my head.

"Not much," I say.

All I have are fragments. The smell of hospitals, sterile and unpleasant. Faceless, interchangeable nurses.

A chair at a bedside, so high that my little legs didn't reach the floor. Closed eyes. A limp hand in mine.

The overwhelming taste of fear.

And then, suddenly, Vivianne.

Everything after my mom is only Vivianne.

"She was furious," says Veronika. "Furious at the doctors, at the drugs, Vendela. She would tell Vendela off for not fighting enough. For looking so sick. She was always telling Vendela she couldn't give up, that it was her duty to try. That Vendela couldn't do that to her." Veronika shakes her head—small movements, as though not to make the pain in her head any worse.

"When we were at the hospital, after Vendela had . . ." She trails off.

I see something that looks like tears glinting.

She closes her eyes.

When she opens them again, the tears are gone.

"We were all there," she says, "you too. We were saying good-bye. And Vivianne was incandescent. She screamed at Vendela. At . . . the body; she said she couldn't leave her like that. I told her to stop, to think of you. You were so small, and you seemed so confused. I tried to hug you, but you were completely limp. You wouldn't even look at Vendela."

Veronika stares at me. It's like she's looking at somebody who isn't there. The tenderness in her eyes is so unlike her it makes me uncomfortable—makes me want to pull away.

"I wanted to take you in, you know," she says, and that surprises me more than anything else. "I guess I never told you that, huh?"

"No." I shake my head.

"Well, your father had never been in the picture, so I thought I could raise you. Vendela and I were pretty close. She hadn't said anything about who should look after you when she was gone, because Vivianne refused to discuss it. And she was there all the time. Initially Vendela tried to raise the subject of a will, or something similar, but as soon as she even mentioned it Vivianne would blow up and start screaming at her. After a while she was too weak to try." Veronika takes a deep breath.

"But I thought I could take care of you. I . . . I loved you. I had an apartment, a job . . . I never imagined Vivianne would have wanted to. She never seemed all that interested in being a mother when we were kids. But when I suggested it after Vendela died, she completely lost it. She said I couldn't even take care of myself, let alone a child, and that I had no right to take you away from her. She said you were all she had left." Veronika's lips are a tight dash.

"That was one of the worst fights we ever had," she says, "and you know what she was like."

I nod.

"In the end I gave up," she says. "I regretted it for a long time, and tried to come and see you as much as I could. I was afraid Vivianne would treat you the way she treated us—that it would be like it was for us after Daddy died. But she kept it together better after Vendela. When you were a kid she actually tried."

"Not enough," I say, and the words leave a bad taste on my tongue.

"No," Veronika agrees, "never enough. I don't think she was capable of being a mother. I don't know what had happened to her in the past, but she was a broken woman. Just broken."

It's an insight I wouldn't have expected from Veronika. She has always seemed to have nothing but contempt for her mother. But I can hear that this is coming from somewhere deep-rooted. I can hear the pain in her voice.

The love.

"She actually tried," she repeats. "And after Daddy died she couldn't even do that. She just cried. We were so young—I was as young as you were when Vendela died—and she wanted us to console her. She drank herself to sleep on the floor every night, stopped washing, told—"

She cuts herself off.

When she goes on, her voice is quieter.

"I know my father took his own life," she says, her voice scratchy. "I've always known." She has pulled up her long, thin legs and linked her arms around her bent knees. Her dark gaze is fixed on the opposite wall.

"I'm the one who found him, you know," she says. "Here. In the study. With a half-drunk bottle of whisky and an empty pot of pills in front of him."

"Oh God," I say.

"He had locked the door. He never normally locked it, and I picked the lock. One of the servants had taught me how to just a few weeks before. I just wanted to show Daddy my new trick."

I want to reach out and touch her, but I can't bring myself to do it. Even in spite of it all, it's not how we do things in this family.

"You were so young," is all I can bring myself to say.

Veronika scrunches up her eyes.

"No one's ever old enough to see something like that," she says, a vulnerability in her voice.

"He left a letter. So I know Mother didn't do anything to him. I haven't read it in about thirty years, but I still have it. It's in his handwriting—he wrote it. My father died by his own hand. No one else's."

We are both quiet. Then she says:

"In the nights when she would lie curled up on the rug in the hall-way, in the months after he died, she kept on saying that she hated him for leaving her to bear the burden alone."

"What burden?" I ask.

"I always assumed she meant us girls," she says, slowly. "But now I'm wondering if it wasn't something else."

A silence falls between us.

When the door opens I jump to my feet. Sebastian is standing there, wild-eyed, with flecks of red on his cheeks.

"Rickard's awake. I have the keys. His car is new and he says it copes well with the cold. Come on, let's get out of here."

· ELEANOR ·

Sebastian sticks the key in the ignition. My heart is hammering so fast I can feel it in my fingers and toes.

Please. Please.

Let this work.

When he turns the key and the engine growls to life I hold my breath, just waiting for it to cut out again like the others did. It seems to have gotten even colder since the last time we were outside. It's hard to tell through the clouds, but I think the sun has started to set. Another day gone. If we don't get out of here now we might never.

It's the sort of weather I normally wouldn't want anyone to drive in—icy roads and poor visibility. Once darkness has fallen I'm not sure we can risk it at all.

But the sound doesn't die. Instead it gets stronger, and steadier.

"*Yes!*" cries Sebastian.

He turns around, beaming.

"What a car, Rickard! You're a fucking hero!"

We have loaded Rickard into the back seat. He is lying with his feet on Veronika's lap, and seems to be drifting in and out of consciousness.

I'm not sure if Rickard hears him. His eyes are closed, and there's a little furrow between his eyebrows. His chest hardly moves when he breathes.

At first I don't dare believe it—can't believe we're on our way out of here. All I want is to put this goddamn place behind me, but the adrenaline is still pulsing through my veins. My hands are knotted in my lap, and I'm squeezing my fingers, as though trying to find strength in something. I'm expecting the car to give up at any second, to stop just a few feet from the house and force us all back inside.

We're safe now, I try to convince myself. Try to force myself to feel the same confidence that Sebastian seems to have.

But I can't shake the feeling that Solhöga isn't done with us yet.

In my mind it has taken the shape of something animate, a slumbering presence. It feels like more than a house. It has been waiting for me for over forty years, for us to return and discover its secrets.

It feels like it's alive.

As though everything that happened here, everything we still don't know, has seeped into the walls and taken hold like mold, growing and expanding over the many long, quiet years, clawing its bony fingers behind the wallpapers and under the floorboards.

It doesn't want to let go of us. It wants to squeeze the life from our very bodies.

My eyes are fixed on the road ahead as Sebastian slowly pulls out of the drive.

Please, let us go, I beg the house. *Let us leave.*

I don't care what happened here. I don't need to know. I don't need to know who Vivianne was before she was Vivianne, or why my grandfather killed himself, or why Mats Bengtsson followed in his footsteps after all those years. I don't need the answers.

Vivianne's secrets can stay dead with her.

Secrets don't die, Vivianne whispers in my head. *Nothing truly dies, Victoria. I'm still here, aren't I?*

"Shut up," I mutter to myself, so quietly my lips barely move.

We are now on the forest road. I separate my hands, stretch out my fingers.

The car has started to warm up. The numbness has started to leave my feet.

Sebastian is still driving slowly. Part of me wants to tell him to speed up, to drive as fast as he can.

Get us out of here before the house changes its mind.

The trees stand tall and dense on either side of us. The road is narrow and uneven and I can feel every root we drive over, but I can also start to feel the hope budding in my stomach.

"Stop! *Stop!*"

Veronika is the one who shouts, her voice hoarse and immediate, and I flinch.

"What the fuck is that?" Sebastian says as he brakes.

I tear my eyes from him and look at the road.

The shadow ahead of us isn't a person.

Even though it's crumpled and half covered in snow, I can still see what it is.

It's a car. And it's blocking our only road out of here.

· ANUSHKA ·
JULY 25, 1966

I only left her alone a few minutes, but that was all it took!

I should have known better, really, but Kicki is normally so sweet and obedient that I didn't think. I know that in theory she shouldn't even be in the main house, but Märit had to take the car into town to stock up the pantry and Mats was on his way out to the forest to deal with a tree that needed felling, so she asked me to keep an eye on Kicki while she was gone.

I didn't feel like I could turn her down. Märit is always so kind to me, and Kicki's so small and easily amused. It couldn't do any harm, I thought. Neither Sir nor Ma'am ever come into the kitchen, and Kicki keeps herself occupied so long as she has a toy. I sat her down in the kitchen, gave her a glass of milk and one of Märit's rhubarb buns, and told her to stay there. She nodded at me sweetly.

I was gone two minutes, definitely no more than three. I was polishing the silver, and all I had to do was fetch the big silver tray from the dining room. We haven't used it all summer, seeing as we only get it out when they have guests, but I thought it could be good to give it a once-over while I was already doing the rest. So I went into the dining room to take it from the big cabinet. The key got stuck in the lock, so I had to jiggle it a little—but that was it.

When I got back to the kitchen, Kicki had disappeared without a trace.

My heart leapt into my throat. I looked around and said her name, quietly, so that they wouldn't hear it in the rest of the house: "Kicki? Kicki?" I thought she was probably just hiding under the table, or in one of the cupboards.

But there wasn't a sound to be heard.

The kitchen door was locked, and the door into the service passage was shut. It was like she had vanished into thin air.

It was only when I saw her doll on the floor by the dumbwaiter that I realized the hatch was open a crack.

Now, Kicki likes the dumbwaiter. She has even climbed into it a few times, when Märit takes her down to the wine cellar. She's so small that she can fit inside it easily, and once she's inside she has learned that she can pull at the chains. Märit always scolds her and tells her it isn't allowed, and every time Kicki bursts into tears and promises never to do it again. I don't know what got into her. Perhaps she was bored, or thought I wouldn't be as strict as her mother—or perhaps she didn't think at all, seeing as she's five years old.

I ran out and down to the wine cellar, my heart pounding in my chest, hoping against hope to see that fair little head sticking out of the shaft. The ticking off was already on the tip of my tongue.

But the wine cellar was dark and empty, and there was no one there.

Oh no, I thought. *Oh no. Oh God.*

My steps thundered up the staircase. I didn't care about the noise; I just wanted to get my hands on Kicki before anyone saw her.

I don't know if I have ever felt as scared as I did when I cracked open the door to Ma'am's bedroom and caught sight of the two of them.

Ma'am was sitting on the floor in front of Kicki, her hands on the girl's shoulders. Kicki was standing stock-still, her back to me. The room was sunk in shadow since the curtains were closed, but enough of the blazing summer sun was peeping through the cracks for me to be able to see them properly.

She was mumbling something to Kicki, but I couldn't hear what. Then she let go of her shoulders and ran her long, bony fingers through one of her blond locks.

This broke my paralysis. I said:

"I am so sorry, Ma'am; I will take her downstairs."

My voice was trembling, and I could hear my accent was stronger that it had been in a long time. Chatting to Märit and Mats all day has given me lots of practice and my Swedish is normally much better than it was before, but now my words felt clumsy and inadequate.

Ma'am didn't even look at me.

When I was just a few steps from them I could hear what she was saying.

"Aren't you lovely. I knew you would come. I knew I hadn't lost you, that if I just waited long enough you would come back."

It was only then that I heard that she was speaking our language.

"Ma'am," I said, but she didn't react. She just kept on mumbling softly under her breath to Kicki. She let go of her hair and started stroking her soft, chubby little cheek.

"You do look a little like Evert, now, but soon enough you'll look like me, I can tell. I can take you out and buy you some nice clothes. Won't that be fun?"

"Marta."

It just slipped out of me. On hearing that she looked up and saw me, but there was no hint of recognition in her eyes.

She has lost so much weight that she looked like a ghost. Her cheekbones seemed to be pressing against her skin, and her eyes were huge in her thin face.

I said:

"Marta, she's Märit's daughter. I'm sorry. I'll take her back downstairs."

But she said:

"See? Here she is. You told me she was dead, but I knew she would come. Vendela. My Vendela's here now."

My armpits were clammy from the fear. The only thought running through my head was:

She's insane. She's sick. She doesn't know who I am.

"No, she isn't your daughter. She's Märit's daughter."

At this Ma'am grabbed Kicki and clasped her tightly to her chest. Kicki let out a little squeal—like a cat taken too roughly.

"No," Ma'am said, and the flash of desperation in her eyes felt like a punch in the gut. "No, this is my Vendela. She's come back to me."

I didn't know what to do. I had to get Kicki out of her clutches and away from her, but I didn't dare step any closer: it felt as though at any moment that desperation could turn to wrath. And then what would happen to the child in her arms?

"Vivianne," I heard a voice behind me. "Let go of the girl."

I turned around, and there was Sir. His shirt was creased, and his eyes were fixed on Ma'am and Kicki.

His voice was endlessly soft.

"Evert," she said. "Look at her; isn't she beautiful? Didn't I tell you how beautiful she would be?"

He took a step closer.

"You're scaring her, Vivianne," he said. "You don't want that now, do you?"

He was moving cautiously, and as though in complete calm. But I could see the tension in his shoulders through the fabric of his shirt. He was just as scared as I was.

Just as crushed by what he was seeing.

"Come, let's let go of Kicki so she can go back to her mother," he said. Ma'am shook her head.

"She's with her mother. *I'm* her mother."

She looked so happy as she said it, a sort of manic joy. That was the worst of it.

I saw his hesitation. But then he said:

"Yes, you're right, Vivianne."

My eyes widened and he must have seen it, because he discreetly shook his head, a movement so subtle I thought I was imagining it. But then he went on:

"Let me look at her. I want to look at our—our daughter," he said, his voice faltering as he said those last words.

Ma'am didn't notice.

She just lit up—a big, beautiful smile. One I have never seen before.

"I knew you would understand. I knew you would recognize her."

As he walked over to Ma'am, she let go of Kicki, and he swept her up so quickly that the whole room seemed to shift. He handed her to me.

"Get her out of here."

"Evert, what are you doing?"

Kicki clung on to me with both hands and feet, her whole compact body tense and stiff, and I turned on my heels and ran. Out of the room and down the stairs.

Behind me I heard Ma'am ask:

"What's she doing? Where's she taking her? Annika, come back! *Come back with my daughter! You can't take her! You can't take my daughter, not again; you can't. Come back with her; come back. . . .*"

I didn't look back until I had carried her all the way out to the field in front of the house. Kicki didn't make a sound. Her face was buried deep in my neck.

In the distance I could hear the sound of Märit approaching in the car, back from town.

I'm still shaking as I write this.

I haven't seen Ma'am since then. When I finally dared set foot back in the house, Sir was gone.

But the image of Ma'am's blissful face and Kicki trapped in her hard grip remains etched on my mind.

· ELEANOR ·

Our full beams light up the vehicle in sharp relief. It's a red car, and there's enough snow on the roof to see it had been there at least a few hours.

The car has crashed into one of the trees by the side of the road, but it's now angled diagonally across it, leaving less than a foot between its rear bumper and the pine trees on the other side. It must have hit the tree pretty hard: the car's front bumper is completely crumpled, and the door on the driver's side is hanging open.

"No," Sebastian whispers.

I unbuckle my seat belt and get out. The wind catches me and tries to knock me over, and I almost lose my footing. Beneath the snow the road is completely covered in ice. It isn't hard to see why the car crashed.

I walk over to the car. The wind isn't as biting here as it is by the house. The trees envelop me, huddle in as close as they can around me.

There's something familiar about the car.

Or am I just losing it? Am I seeing things?

I can't shake the feeling that I've seen this car before. Not as it is now, with its crumpled metal and dimmed lights, half buried in snow. But that bright red color, the curve of the windows, the soft contours . . .

The memory is partly submerged, and no matter how hard I try I can't force it to the surface.

Now, standing by the car, I place my hand on its body. My mouth is dry. I have to brace myself for a second before I bend over and look inside.

It's dark; of course it is. Snow has blown in over the seats.

I listen for breaths, someone hiding in the back. Lying in wait, ready to pounce from the darkness.

But no. There's no one here. The car has been empty for a while.

I brush the snow off the front seat, climb in, and open the glove compartment. All I find inside it are a half-empty packet of tissues and a windshield scraper.

I stare at the tissues.

There's nothing special about them—a packet of pharmacy own-brand tissues.

Still, it rings the same vague bell as the car, deep down in my consciousness.

"Eleanor," I hear Sebastian's voice behind me.

I climb out and see him standing a few feet away from me, his hair flapping over his forehead in the puffs of wind.

"Are the keys in the ignition?" he asks me flatly.

I bend over to look.

When my face is right by the wheel, I see it. It has frozen in the cold, but when I pull off my glove and rub it with my finger it leaves a reddish-brown mark.

I straighten up and shake my head.

"No keys," I say. "But there's blood on the wheel."

"I'll have to try and hot-wire it," he says straightaway.

"Sebastian—" I start, but he cuts me off.

"Do you have a better idea? We have to move it. Otherwise we're not getting out of here."

I step aside without a word. Sebastian sits down in the driver's seat.

He won't be able to hot-wire it. I know that, and he does, too. He's just so close to hysteria that he can't accept it. Even if he did know how to hot-wire a car, this one is completely totaled.

We aren't getting out of here on this road.

I take a few steps back, still staring at the blood on my finger. It has already started to dry. I wipe it on my jeans and then rub it with snow, until I'm sure it's clean.

The snow.

I take a few more steps back. Sweep the surface layer with my foot.

The car's headlights pick up every last detail. The thin, frozen layer of snow over the gnarled roots underneath, the dark flecks on the ice.

And there. A shape, half buried. Small and discrete, just a few feet from the car.

I bend over to pick it up, but I already know what it is.

"Sebastian, I'll go check on the others," I say to him.

He doesn't reply.

I walk back to Rickard's car, temporarily dazzled by the headlights. I'm still seeing spots in my eyes when I open the passenger-seat door.

It's warm and steamy inside. Veronika gives me a fixed look when I climb in.

"You aren't going to be able to move it, are you?" she asks.

I shake my head.

I look at Rickard, at his bare hands hanging limp at his sides. He has short, stubby hands that don't match the rest of his elegant appearance.

"Rickard," I say.

When I don't get any response I say to Veronika:

"Shake him."

She looks at me as though she's wondering what I have in mind, but she does as I say. He groans faintly.

"Rickard," I say. "Look at me."

He opens his eyes slightly. His pupils are big and feverish under his heavy eyelids.

"You said you saw lights in the snowstorm," I say.

He nods weakly.

I squeeze his missing leather glove in my hand.

"Could it have been car lights?" I ask him.

His eyes flit around.

I think of the bruises on his torso, of the broken ribs, the blood, and his confusion. My first thought wasn't that he had been beaten up. When we saw his black-and-blue torso, my initial reaction was that he had been run over by a train.

What if that's really what happened?

"Try to remember," I say. "Do you know how far you followed the person you saw? Could you have followed them here?"

Could he have stood in the way of the car when it was trying to drive away?

I can see it all now: Rickard, the private eye, sees someone who shouldn't be there. Confident and cocksure, he chases the person all the way to a small, red car parked a little way up the road, out of sight.

I see that person trying to drive off, see Rickard standing in the road to stop them.

See them stepping on the gas in desperation, hitting him head-on, and then losing control of the car. Crashing into a tree. Slamming their head against the wheel.

Staggering out of the car. Dragging Rickard to the hunting lodge to hide him. Getting caught by Veronika in the storm on the way back, hitting her in the back of the head so as not to be seen.

And now? Where is that person hiding now?

And how did they know the hunting lodge was there?

"I'll be right back," I say to Veronika.

Sebastian is still sitting in the car, looking pale and focused, fiddling with something under the wheel. I crouch down by the open door.

"Hey," I say, and put my hand on his thigh. "Sebastian. Stop."

He shakes his head.

"I think I can get it to work," he says. "If you just give me a few minutes, I can . . ."

"Sebastian," I say, with more weight to my voice. "You aren't going to get it started. You know that. Stop."

He sits completely still for a few seconds. Then he looks at me.

"If we don't get this engine started we'll never move the car," he says.

"No, we won't. We aren't getting out on this road."

I keep my eyes on his until his gaze folds.

When he speaks again, his voice is almost a sob.

"I just want to go home, Eleanor," he says.

"I know," I reply. "We just have to wait out the storm. Let's take Veronika and Rickard back to the house. We have enough food to last us the weekend, no problem. You were going to have lunch with your dad on Sunday, right? He knows we're here. When you don't show up and he can't reach you by phone he'll call the police."

Sebastian doesn't say anything.

"It's just a few days, Sebastian."

"I don't think Rickard will make it that long."

I have no good answer to that.

I have no good answer to anything.

Instead I just say:

"We have no choice."

"We could try to walk . . . ," he begins, but I shake my head.

"Not in this," I say. "Not in a blizzard. It's too far. And what about Veronika and Rickard? Are we really going to leave them here? Rickard can't even stand up, and Veronika's hurt, too." I pause.

When Sebastian looks at me I see something flicker in his eye.

"I don't think we should go back to that house," he says. "It's like you said. There's something about this place. I think bad things have happened in that house and bad things will happen to us if we go back. I think it's best if we leave Veronika and Rickard in the car and walk. I think that's safer than going back."

"We aren't dressed warmly enough," I counter. "And it's about to get dark. It's way too cold, and way too windy."

He shakes his head. The look on his face reads both resignation and desperation.

"I know," he says. "You're right, but I just . . . please, Eleanor, please listen to me. Just this once. You never have to listen to me again. I've never said anything like this before. But we can't go back."

What he's saying is true. He has never said anything like this before. He's stable, rational Sebastian. My rock.

But he's wrong. And I'm not about to let us freeze to death in the forest.

· ANUSHKA ·
JULY 26, 1966

I haven't seen Ma'am since yesterday.

I should have told Märit what happened, but I didn't dare. Instead I gave her a part-truth. I handed Kicki over to her and told her she sneaked off and Ma'am had found her. Märit scolded Kicki for being badly behaved, and apologized profusely. She seemed worried that Sir and Ma'am would be angry, seeing as Sir had said Kicki couldn't be in the main house.

I said she needn't worry about that. That I would take care of it.

She thanked me and told me I was an amazing person. She held me and looked me in the eye and said, "You're a good friend, Annika. I really mean that."

I felt so rotten when she said that.

It was all my fault, after all.

I wasn't even sure if Sir would want dinner. I was all thumbs as I prepared it, jumping at the slightest noise. I didn't dare go look for him, because I was so afraid of the moment I would find him, but I knew I had to speak to him nonetheless. So I boiled potatoes and cut them up, added mayonnaise and garlic and parsley just as Märit has shown me, and made a potato salad with red onion and capers. I cleaned one of the perch that Märit bought in town, and fried the thin, white fillets, my stomach squirming restlessly as the scent rose up my nostrils.

I tried to eat too, but I couldn't get anything down.

The bell rang from the drawing room at six thirty-seven.

I smoothed out my hair before I walked through with the tray.

He was sitting in one of the armchairs. His shirt was buttoned up to his neck, and it looked uncomfortable. I could feel my fingers itching to undo that top button so he could breathe.

He didn't look at me.

I could hear my voice shaking as I said:

"Would Sir like dinner in the dining room or in here?"

It was only then that he looked at me.

He looked completely sober. There was no anger in his face.

He seemed weary.

I heard myself whisper:

"I'm so sorry. I didn't mean to upset Ma'am. I know Kicki shouldn't be in the house, but Märit had to go into town and I said I could watch her. She got upstairs in the dumbwaiter. It was my fault, not Märit's; she didn't do anything wrong; it was me who . . ."

Sir shook his head, and I fell silent.

"My wife . . ." he started to say, but then trailed off.

"I don't know what to do, Annika," he said. "She's sick. I thought things would get better out here. She used to love this house. But now I'm starting to wonder if she can ever get better."

"Perhaps she needs a doctor," I said.

I was still standing as Ma'am had taught me to stand, with my back straight and my hands clasped over my apron. But when Sir shook his head and buried his face in his hands I could only sit down beside him.

"You saw her, Annika," he said. "You heard what she said. She's not herself." He looked at me. The whites of his eyes were bloodshot, and from here I could see that they were swollen. As though he had been crying.

"I tried to get her to see a doctor at the start, but she just screamed at them. She refused to speak to them, or let them examine her. And if I bring anyone here now I'm afraid they'll . . . take her away. Take my Vivianne and lock her up somewhere."

"No," I said. It just slipped out, in my language, and I clapped my hand to my mouth. "She isn't dangerous," I said afterwards, in Swedish. "She hasn't hurt anyone, so why should they lock her up?"

But as I said it I saw her before me again. Those long, spindly, white arms latching onto Kicki and not letting go. Those frantic, staring eyes.

No, Ma'am hasn't hurt anyone, not yet. But what would have happened if I said the wrong thing? If he hadn't come in in the nick of time?

"I could never do that to Vivianne. She won't get better in a place like that. She'll only waste away," he said.

She's already wasting away, I thought. *She's disappearing, bit by bit. Day by day. Soon there'll be nothing of her left.*

It's impossible for me to get my head around how somebody like her could have shrunk so much. When I came here she seemed so strong. I was so afraid of her, and so jealous of her, and so dazzled by her. She seemed to be drawn with sharper contours than everyone else, seemed to take up more space than any of those garish, twittering women who passed through their homes and lives.

She's a ghost now. No more than a ghost.

A shiver ran through me at the thought.

Sir looked up at me.

"I'm glad you're here, Annika," he said. "I've wanted to say—ever since that night, I've wanted to apologize. I'm sorry. It was inappropriate. I shouldn't have done that. It won't happen again, I promise."

I just shook my head. I couldn't find the words, because if I spoke I would risk him hearing the shameful sting of disappointment I felt within me.

"I don't know what got into me," he went on. "I've been so confused these past few months, and you've been such good company. I don't know what I would have done without you here." He smiled, but there was no joy to it.

"Pretty sad, huh? That I have no one else to talk to?"

"No," I said. "I like talking to you, Evert." Realizing my mistake, I shook my head and added:

"Sir, I mean. Sorry."

"You can call me Evert, Annika," he said. This time that little smile looked a touch more genuine.

Neither of us said anything for a few seconds. Then he said:

"If I have dinner in the dining room, would you join me?"

He said it hesitantly, as though he knew it was wrong.

How I wish I had hesitated. I should have thought of Mats, who I kissed on the lips yesterday—a quick peck that turned his face bright red.

I should have thought of Ma'am, asleep upstairs.

I should have done so much.

But I didn't think at all. I answered, far too quickly:

"Yes. I would love to."

· ELEANOR ·

We carry Rickard upstairs, then lock the doors and check all the windows. I pull the heavy, black, iron key out of the lock in the kitchen door and place it on the counter.

The house is as shut and sealed as it can be.

When I walk back into the living room, Sebastian is standing in front of the bookcase. He is looking at a leather-bound book, turning it and flipping it in a way that suggests he isn't really looking at it at all.

He puts it back on the shelf.

"I've checked the kitchen," I say. "Everything's locked."

Sebastian just nods.

My stomach is tied up in knots. I want to say something, but I don't know what. I want to fix this, but I don't have the words.

You can't go taking responsibility for every little feeling the men in your life have, Victoria, I hear Vivianne's voice in my head. *It's just the way they are, you know. Overemotional. They think they're so strong, but we're the ones who have to keep them in check.*

I wish, just this once, that I could listen to her.

"He doesn't want any water," Sebastian says. He still isn't looking at me.

"Maybe he just needs to rest," I try. I can hear the grating neediness in my voice.

Look at me, I think inwardly. *Please. Take my hand. Hold me. Tell me I'm doing the right thing.*

But I can't ask that of him, and I know he wouldn't do it. There's a cleft between us.

"Sebastian . . . ," I start, but he takes a step back.

"I'll go check on Rickard," he says.

Once he's gone I sink down onto the couch and press my hands against my eyes.

I don't want to cry. I have no right to cry.

If I had just checked that Rickard was who he said he was, we wouldn't be here. If I had just called the firm, or googled him.

But I wanted to come here. Truth is, I wanted to see Solhöga.

I wanted to see what Vivianne had hidden from me.

I wanted to know the secrets she had taken to the grave.

Well, in that case you got what you wanted, didn't you, Victoria?

When I open my eyes, they land on the coffee table. The diary is still lying where I left it. "Couldn't *you* have kept a diary, Vivianne?" I say to no one.

I open the diary and flick through the pages. I have translated more than half of it, but without Google Translate I can't understand what I'm reading. Still, there is the odd sentence in Swedish—presumably quoting what someone has said.

I give a start.

Her name has caught my eye.

Vivianne.

All I want is for Vivianne to be happy, it says.

The handwriting is neat but faded, and I have to squint a little at the words. Even so, I can read what's written below it without any issues.

If my wife needs to believe that I believe she's the daughter of a wealthy Swede who grew up in France, then I'll let her believe it. If my wife wants to maintain that our maid, who looks just like her, is just some poor kid without family or prospects who turned up on our doorstep, then I'll let it be true so long as that's what she needs.

I look for a name but find nothing.

Still, surely it must have been Evert who said it? It can't have been anyone else. It must have been my grandfather.

So Evert knew.

He knew Vivianne wasn't who she said she was.

I carry on flicking through the diary. Here and there the pages are too water damaged to be decipherable, and toward the end of the diary the text is less clear, the handwriting less neat. It's jerkier, looks stressed and fitful, dotted with exclamation points and marks that look like the remnants of droplets of water. Like tears.

It was an accident. A terrible, terrible accident.

Was it really an accident, Vivianne? Or did it have something to do with Grandfather Evert's death? And with Mats'?

And with yours?

On the penultimate page I can make out something else. It's the last entry in the diary.

The pen has leaked, leaving streaks of blue ink across the page, but the text is still legible.

Did she see us? Goddammit, did she see us?

Then, something a few lines below it. It's written in Polish, so I can't read it all.

But I do recognize one of the words from the translations I did yesterday.

Zabić.

To kill.

Then suddenly all of the lights around me go out, and I'm plunged into darkness.

· ANUSHKA ·
AUGUST 2, 1966

It happened again.

This time I was the one who leaned in.

I hadn't even had anything to drink, but I still feel drunk from the touch of his lips.

This time I didn't run. I stayed, and I looked him in the eye. There was no regret.

I know it'll happen again tomorrow.

I have to stop. I should leave this place. Tonight, before this goes any further than it already has. Before I do anything more, anything worse; anything I can never take back.

I can still smell his aftershave in my nose.

I won't stop.

I hate myself.

· ELEANOR ·

I jump up from the couch, my heart pounding in my chest, and try to listen as closely as I can. All I can hear is silence. There isn't a sound in the house.

I put the diary down on the couch—quietly, so no one will hear—and turn on the flashlight on my phone. The meagre light is enough for me to see where I'm going, but it's not enough to light up the corners.

I walk slowly into the hallway, look around me.

"Hello?" I call up the stairs.

"Eleanor?" I hear Veronika reply. "Why are you shouting? Some of us are trying to sleep."

She sounds more angry than scared, which does a lot to calm my nerves. The doors are locked. We have nothing to worry about.

"The power's out," I say. "It must be the blizzard. Or the fuse box. I'm sure it's old. Nothing weird there."

Try to believe what I'm saying.

Try not to imagine a dark figure cutting cables to shroud us all in darkness.

The doors are locked. We're safe here.

Once upstairs, I head for Rickard's room. I point my flashlight through the doorway but am surprised to find Rickard alone.

I walk over to the bed and lean over him, taking care not to point the flashlight at his eyes or wake him up. I'm not even sure I could wake him up if I tried. He looks so lifeless that I check for a pulse. When I find it, it doesn't really set my mind at ease; it's so weak it barely feels like a fluttering under his skin.

He groans faintly but doesn't wake up. I pull away and turn around.

I shine the light through the next doorway.

"Where's Sebastian?" I ask Veronika.

Veronika grimaces and closes her eyes at the bright light.

"I don't know," she says. "He's not here. I was asleep—I only woke up when you called."

"Do you have any painkillers or anything that we can give Rickard?" I ask Veronika.

She shakes her head.

"I don't think he can feel so much now, anyway," she says, with a tone of voice that makes me gulp.

"Just a few days," I say. "He just has to hang in there till Sunday."

Veronika shakes her head.

"There's no better option," I snap, forgetting to keep my voice down. "What else can we do? There's no way out of here; the road is blocked. We can't walk in this blizzard."

"I'm not saying it's the wrong decision," says Veronika, her face unexpectedly stiff. "But I want you to be prepared that he might not make it."

The words pile up in my throat until I can't hold them in anymore. All my anxiety, my rage and fear, splutters out of me:

"Fuck you, Veronika!"

I turn and walk out of the room, the light dancing along the walls and the floor from my tightly clenched hand.

I stop on the landing. I don't know why I'm expecting her to call after me. It's not like Vivianne ever did. In her view, if the other person stormed out it meant Vivianne had won the discussion.

Come to think of it, she thought she had won it if she stormed out, too.

I turn off the flashlight on my phone.

For one second I stand completely still in the darkness.

Listening.

I hear a movement that must be Veronika back in the bedroom. The whistle of the wind outside. The sound of the floorboards creaking under me as I shift weight.

The rest of the house is silent.

The power cut out in the storm, I say to myself. *Nothing weird there. It would be weirder if it didn't cut out. It's an old house.*

I hear Sebastian's words echoing in my head.

I think bad things have happened in that house.

I can't deny it. Not to myself. It feels like there's something embedded within these walls, something lurking between the floorboards, watching me.

I know it isn't true. In spite of everything, it's just a house. No matter what happened here, it's just a house.

A person did this. A person attacked Veronika and Rickard, and killed Vivianne. A person. Not a house.

But why? Is all of this really related to Evert's death? Would anyone in his family really be so desperate for the truth, after all this time, that they would be willing to kill for it?

Would I be desperate enough to kill to find out what's really going on here? Or who killed Vivianne?

I want to say no. I want to believe I wouldn't be capable of that.

But I'm not so sure if it's true.

I still can't stop thinking about that red car. I have seen it before; I'm sure of it. Not a car like it, not the same color: *that* car.

And those tissues in the glove compartment. A small, green, half-empty packet, a pharmacy brand. Nothing special there. Nothing special about the car either.

Except for the fact that together they ring a bell so loud I can't get it out of my head.

There—a sound. Just a faint little creak, but it's unmistakable. A footstep, coming from the master bedroom.

I turn the flashlight back on, walk up to the door, and pull it open.

Sebastian is sitting on the bed. He gives a start and raises his hand to block the sudden light.

"Hi," I say. It comes out quieter than intended.

"Hi."

I hesitate before I take another step into the room.

"Power cut," I say, and he nods.

"I noticed. The storm must have taken down the power lines."

See? I reproach myself internally. *Even Sebastian knows it's just the storm. Not even he's worried.*

"We can light a fire." I walk over and sit down next to him on the bed.

"It could be the fuse box." Sebastian is holding something, studies it in the dim light of my phone. "The fuses always used to blow in our summer house when there was a lot of wind. There the fuse box is outside the house. It's probably outside here, too."

"Could be," I say.

I look at what he's holding. It looks like a photograph.

"What's that?" I ask.

"It was on the bed."

I lean in to take a better look, but then he starts talking again, and this time his voice is louder, kind of shrill.

"I never liked Vivianne," he says. "You know that. Not because she didn't like me—she would have hated anyone you brought home so long as they made you happy; you and I both know she couldn't stand to see you happy—but because of what she did to you. I hated her for that. I really did."

The photograph creases slightly in his hand.

"I don't care if she came here as a maid or whatever, and worked her way up, or if she was unhappy, OK? It's her fault we're here. If it turns out she killed your grandfather it wouldn't surprise me. I . . ."

Now he's clenching the picture so hard his hand is shaking.

"I hate her for bringing us here," he says. "Eleanor, why couldn't you just let go of her?"

The realization hits me so hard it almost feels audible: something muffled, fleshy.

"You aren't angry at Vivianne," I say. "Just say it. You're angry at me. You're angry at me for bringing you here. It's my fault we're here. You said that maybe we should just leave the lawyer to it, but I refused and here we are."

Sebastian stares at me for a few seconds. Something vibrates between us.

Then he looks away and shakes his head.

Something breaks.

I feel it just as clearly as I feel my own heartbeats.

The hand holding the photograph drops down to his lap. I so dearly want to put my hand on his, but I'm scared he'll just pull away.

So instead we sit in silence, all the words I want to say stinging in my windpipe.

I clear my throat.

"What's that photo?" I ask eventually, when I can't take the silence anymore.

He laughs bitterly and hands me the photo.

"Vivianne. She's inescapable."

I pick up the photo and look at it in the light of Sebastian's phone but raise my eyebrows when I recognize it. It's the picture I found in the red dress, the one of the two young women in black-and-white maids' outfits, and the little girl with the blond curls.

"No. it isn't," I say. "That's the girl who wrote the diary. Annika. And someone else called Märit, who worked here, too. She's mentioned in the diary. And that's Märit's daughter, Kicki."

Sebastian shakes his head.

"No," he says, "that's definitely Vivianne."

"But it says 'Annika' on the back of the photo," I say. "And why would Vivianne be wearing a maid's uniform?"

"I don't know why, but the woman in the photo is definitely your grandmother," he says. "She looks exactly like the painting, only without the makeup and with her hair tied back. Look, she even has that little scar on her chin."

I look at the photo, and see the familiar scar he is pointing at.

"But that . . . ," I begin, then shake my head again.

"Do you mind if I take the photo downstairs and compare?" I say. "It has to be a coincidence."

Sebastian looks away.

"Do whatever you want," he says wearily.

I hang back a second, the lump in my belly weighing my whole body down.

"I'll see if I can find a fuse box," I say. "Maybe we can get the power going again."

"Sounds good," says Sebastian, his eyes still on his lap. "I'll ask Veronika to help me move Rickard in here, and we can try to get the masonry heater going. We'll need a little heat in one of the rooms to get us through the night."

I pause on the top step, almost thinking I can hear something.

But I push it aside. I'm tired of hearing things. No one knows better than me that my senses can't be trusted.

Instead I go downstairs to the hallway.

· ANUSHKA ·
AUGUST 9, 1966

Märit can tell that something has changed. This morning she asked me how things are going with Mats. She asked the question in the same conspiratorial way as usual, with a nudge and a smile, but there was something watchful in her eyes. As though she knew more than I wanted her to.

"It's going well," I said. "He's a nice guy."

"Nice guys are always the best option," said Märit. "Nice guys become good men. That's the sort of man you want. They step up when they need to."

I noticed that she glanced at Kicki as she said it. This was after lunch and Kicki always gets sleepy after she eats, so she was lying with her little blond head on her arm.

"I just don't want you to make the same mistakes I did, Annika," Märit added. "Kicki's father promised me the world, but in the end that meant nothing. I knew what he was like, deep down, but he was so good-looking and exciting I didn't care. You're smart, Annika, but you're young. It's easy to do stupid things when you're young and in love. Don't make the same mistakes I did."

I could feel my heart pounding in my chest. I did my best to play dumb and not let it show—play the naïve little girl listening to her older, wiser friend.

"I won't, Märit," I said, and she gave me a wan smile.

"Good. I'm happy to hear it, Annika." She went back to scrubbing the kitchen floor. "Stick with Mats. He worships the ground you walk on. He'll never hurt you."

It's true; I know it is. I'm not blind, I can see the way Mats looks at me, and his caring attentiveness toward me, and it makes me feel so bad it leaves a sour taste in my mouth. Yesterday I went for another walk with him. He told me he wants to have a farm out here one day, a farm of his own where he can keep his own horses, and he looked at me as though he was willing me to say I wanted to live on that farm with him. It almost made me want to scream.

It feels like I'm being ground down by everything I want and don't want.

I want to leave this place and never come back. I want to stay here forever.

I want to throw myself at Ma'am's feet and beg for forgiveness. I want to confess everything. I desperately want to keep the secret.

I want to stop.

But I can't.

Yesterday Sir took me out to the hunting lodge. Märit had helped me to make and serve the dinner, so he and I couldn't eat together. But I told her I could take care of the dishes myself. She looked at me as though she suspected something then too, but she just smiled that usual, sunny smile of hers and thanked me, which made me think I must have been imagining it—that my bad conscience was making me anxious.

Sir came into the kitchen when I was doing the washing up, and when he asked me if I would have a glass of wine with him in the drawing room I jumped. I said that we couldn't, that we couldn't carry on this way, that someone could walk in on us at any moment.

He nodded and said I was right, and that it was wrong, and that he was so very sorry to have dragged me into all of this.

"I want to stop, too, Annika," he said, his eyes glinting in the last of the sunlight. "If I could, I would."

I wanted to be strong. I wanted to tell him to go away, to go upstairs to his wife, my cousin, to tell him that I would leave the next morning and never come back.

But I was too weak.

I couldn't do it.

When he said we didn't have to do anything—that he just wanted to talk—I chose to believe him even though I knew neither he nor I really meant it. He said we could go out to the hunting lodge and sit there and just be, that all he wanted was to spend a little time with me.

He said I make him feel a little less alone.

My back is red and sore from the rug in the lodge. Things went so much further this time around, because no one was nearby and we were all alone. This time I didn't stop him when his fingers found their way up my skirt, or when he pulled up my blouse to kiss the places no one has seen before.

I didn't stop him, because I wanted him to do it. I felt like I would die if he didn't.

When we're in that moment it feels so right. In that moment it feels like I'm alive again, like the two of us are the only two people in the whole wide world.

So is it not worth the hate I feel for myself afterwards? Worth those sleepless nights when I lie awake wishing I was dead, so I wouldn't have to live with what I've done?

So many people could get hurt.

I have always thought myself a good person. Mama always told me I was. She said I have a good heart, and that that would get me a long way in this world.

But as it turns out, I'm black and rotten on the inside. I'll do anything to get what I want, and I don't care who I hurt. I pretend I care—even to myself—but if I really cared I would stop.

I know I'll go with him to the lodge again tonight.

I know it'll go even further this time.

Oh God, let something break. Give me the strength to stop. Give us both the strength.

Something has to break.

I just hope it isn't me.

· ELEANOR ·

The oil paints in the portrait glisten in the light of my phone. Black and blue and red. From this close I can see the brushstrokes, the slight bumpiness on the surface.

I am not looking at the girls. Or at Evert.

I only have eyes for Vivianne.

Always Vivianne.

Her eyelashes are long and dark, the pearls in her earlobes half obscured by her elegantly curled hair. Her face is haughty, her gaze steady. She has been sitting here, staring into thin air, for half a century.

It can't be the same person.

When my eyes move from the small, black-and-white photo to the saturated canvas, at first all I can see are the differences. These have to be two different people. They were relatives, after all. It wouldn't be strange if there were similarities—if Sebastian mistook Anushka for a young Vivianne.

Veronika said I looked like Vivianne when I was wearing her dress. It would be an easy mistake to make.

But . . .

I see the scar on her chin in both images, on both the young girl in the photo and the woman in the portrait. Barely more than a line—a pale dash, but unmistakable.

It has to be a coincidence. An accident. Weirder things have happened.

The thing is, over the years I have taught myself to memorize individual features, to see and compare shapes.

And now that I study the two faces in front of me, the lines start to fall into place.

That same sharp chin. The same high forehead—exposed in one image, with the hair tied back in a tight braid, and covered in the other, by a sweeping fringe. The same soft, pronounced Cupid's bow on the upper lip. The same thick, dark hair, the same intense, forthright gaze that refuses to bend for the camera or the artist.

Oh God.

The same fingers.

Those same long, thin fingers. In the photograph with short, neat nails, in the portrait with long, red talons. But the same nonetheless.

I feel sick.

They can't be the same person. Vivianne and Anushka can't be the same. I have read the diary, and Anushka writes about Vivianne in the third person. As Evert's wife. Her boss. Her tormentor.

Two women with the same face. Two men who died by their own hand, more than forty years apart.

A terrible, terrible accident.

I have kept watch for them for half a century.

If not Anushka, then who?

It feels like the pieces of the puzzle want to fall into place, but that half of them are missing. My mind is struggling to put it all together.

I look at Evert.

He knew.

He, if anyone, knew who Vivianne really was. Her children didn't know, her grandchild doesn't know, but he knew. He was in on it.

He cut off contact with his family for her. This goddamn house belonged to him. Whatever happened here—whatever it was that made him hate this place, and made Vivianne shut it up and refuse to sell it or even let his relatives visit, whatever it was that made Mats Bengtsson watch it until the day Vivianne died—Evert knew.

I can't help but wonder if that's what made him do what he did.

If he couldn't bear it any longer, couldn't live with himself

I think about what Veronika said.

He left a letter.

Could it be one of the letters that Rickard took? Is that why Veronika blew up so resoundingly?

They are still in his car.

I throw a glance up the stairs. I can't hear a sound from up there.

None of them will miss me.

If I'm fast they won't even know I'm gone.

They're safe up there. I'm not putting anyone at risk but myself. I have the keys to the house, and the car is a matter of feet away, on the drive. I can lock the door behind me so no one can get in, not even if they wanted to.

But I have to find out.

Is that selfish, Vivianne? I ask inwardly. *Is that what you would have done? I just want to try to understand, to know why all of this is happening. It feels like I have a right to know.*

This has ruined my life. You ruined my life. Perhaps long before I was even born.

What the hell did you do, Vivianne?

No response. Not even in my head.

Her shiny, two-dimensional eyes carry on staring out of the portrait, into nothing.

I pull on my jacket and step out of the door before I can change my mind.

· ANUSHKA ·
AUGUST 16, 1966

It happened.

It should never have been allowed to happen, but it did. It hurt and I knew it would, but I wanted it. I wanted it more than I have ever wanted anything before.

I cried afterwards. Not because I regretted it, but because I could never undo it.

That was four nights ago now, and it has happened again every night since.

It has been so hot and humid this last week, like a lid sank over the whole estate. Kicki runs around by the lake in no more than a pair of underpants, and Märit has stopped wearing her uniform, opting for a blouse and cut-off men's trousers instead. But I can't bring myself to do the same. I don't want to see any more of my own skin than I have to. When I wash myself, I scrub my skin so hard it goes all red and blotchy, as though I was trying to wash away the shame. Wash away his touch.

So I walk around sweating in our heavy woolen uniform and initially Märit teased me cautiously about it, but as the days wore on she stopped. She follows me with her eyes, watches me when she thinks I don't see.

I know she knows that something has happened. I told her I'm just tired and have a summer cold, but I know she doesn't believe me.

I can barely even speak to Mats anymore. I have given him the same excuse of a cold to avoid taking my evening walks with him. Unlike Märit, he doesn't even question it. He just takes what I give him, never asks for more.

Mats isn't like Sir. Sir doesn't even have to voice it anymore, doesn't even have to ask. He knows I'll meet him in the lodge after sundown every night—even though my steps are heavy as I leave the house, even though I try to stop myself, even though my skin is dry from being scrubbed frenetically multiple times a day, and even though I haven't slept properly since it started.

Today Märit asked me if I wanted to sleep with her and Kicki tonight. She said I look so pale and tired, and that it must be uncomfortable sleeping in here with the bosses. She suggested I might sleep better if I bunked up with her and Kicki in the guesthouse for a few nights instead.

I don't know if she meant what she said, or if she knows—has realized. If she is trying to stop me from doing it again, from making a mistake I can't put right.

It's already too late for that.

I am already longing for nightfall. For the sun to sink below the horizon and the wind to die down, and for me to be able to feel him again.

Every time I leave the house it feels like I'm walking into a catastrophe. Toward something inescapable.

Something that will crush every last one of us, sooner or later.

And if it happens—when it happens—it will all be my fault.

· ELEANOR ·

I jump into the driver's seat and shut the door behind me. In my haste I haven't brought any gloves or a hat, and my hands are already cold. I pull my jacket tighter around me.

Twenty-four hours ago I was in this car. With Veronika.

Had Rickard already been hit by then? Was that faceless other already dragging him out to the hunting lodge to hide him?

I look around the car. I was the last person to have the letters, wasn't I? I picked them up when Veronika ran off. And I didn't take them with me into the storm.

I must have left them in here. But where?

I bend forward and feel around under the seat for them. The folder is scuffed and a little muddy when I pull it up, wet in one corner from snow that has melted off our shoes. But when I pull out the letters they are unscathed, untouched by the water.

Evert's handwriting is elaborate and old-fashioned, strangely feminine in my eyes. He alternates between blue and black ink. Some of the letters are written to both Veronika and my mom, and they are all simple in style, clearly written with a child's eyes in mind. But the odd thing still shines through.

In a letter dated February 6, 1974, he writes:

I am very sad to be away from you kids & I miss you a lot! I hope you & your sister are being good as gold. Mommy works hard to look after you while I am away, & you know how she can be. We don't want to make her more stressed now, do we?

From a letter dated April 13 of the same year:

You know that you & your sister are my princesses! I love you more than anything, & I think that you are the sweetest little girls in the whole wide world. Deep down Mommy feels the same. Look after your sister, give her a kiss from me & tell her I will be home soon.

. . . it isn't that Mommy doesn't think you are both lovely. Sometimes grown-ups find it difficult to be reminded of certain things. You will grow up to be a handsome woman, Vendela, but sometimes from some angles you look a little like one of Mommy's relatives, & she doesn't like to be reminded of her. Please understand that this is nothing to do with you. I shall have a word with her when I get home.

September 19:

I know you are keen to celebrate Christmas at Solhöga, but it will be difficult. To be quite honest with you, this old man of yours is very tired and would really rather stay home. Couldn't it be just as festive to celebrate Christmas in town? All your friends are here, & we can go ice-skating in Kungsträdgården Park together. Wouldn't that be nice?

And, finally, November 12:

I love you both so much. You know that, don't you? You & your sister mean everything to me. And Mommy, too, of course.

. . . I will always love you. Sometimes grown-ups have to make difficult decisions. But you & Veronika have to know that I love you more than anything in this world. Be a dear and remind her of that tonight. I will try to call, but Mommy is a little sad right now & might not let me talk to you if I do. Tuck your sister in & give her a kiss on her forehead from me.

That's the last letter.

But there's an envelope in the folder, too.

It's undated and written on unlined paper, and I know what it is straightaway. I know as soon as I touch it.

Vivianne,

I'm sorry. I'm so sorry, for all of this. And I'm sorry to leave you this way. You're stronger than I am, you always have been, & I know you'll get through this.

I know you'll hate me when you find out. I can't blame you for that. It's what I deserve. All of this is my fault, & we both know that.

Solhöga haunts me.

Look after our girls.

I love you. I know you don't believe me, but I have loved you as well as I could.

I love you. I love you. I love you.

I must go now.

Evert

· ANUSHKA ·
AUGUST 19, 1966

Oh God, we almost made it. We were almost careful enough. But almost is never enough, and we were thoughtless.

I can't stop sweating as I write this, even though the first winds of autumn have already started to draw in in the evenings. I can smell the approaching clouds, the cold yet to come.

I'm expecting Ma'am to open my door at any second. To stand there like a ghost, an apparition, and then it will all be over.

We're supposed to go back to the city next week. We had only a week to go, and we got careless.

Last night Sir walked me back from the lodge. Before then we have always come back separately—he would wait while I walked back alone—but yesterday he came with me. He took my hand in the forest and at first I pulled away, but then I saw that he was hurt.

"Someone might see," I said, to which he replied:

"Who would see us out here?"

I allowed myself to relent, even though I knew better.

Anushka would have known better, but I'm not Anushka anymore. I'm stupid little Annika. It's Annika who is doing this with her cousin's husband.

It was Annika who reached out for his hand and squeezed it.

But there's still something of Anushka left in me. Anushka said to him:

"We'll be going back to town soon."

I don't know if he heard something in my voice, or if he had been thinking the same thought, but he said:

"Annika, please."

"No," I said; Anushka said. "This has to end when we go back. This has to stay out here."

He went quiet for a long time, and I could feel the softness of his fingers against mine. Not like Mats'. Mats' hands are rough and callused from his work, just as mine are red and raw from the dishes and the cleaning and the laundry. But Sir's hands are just as soft as the skin on my inner thighs. He tends to linger there with his fingers, slowly caressing me until I'm begging him, please, please, don't keep me waiting anymore: Touch me. Touch me there.

"I know," he said. "But I . . ." He didn't say anything more.

We walked on in silence. Like two children, hand in hand. I couldn't bring myself to say what I knew I had to say.

That I'm leaving them. Leaving him.

It was only when we reached the house that I turned to him. The night was clear, and out here the stars are so much brighter than they are in town. The sky feels higher here, the air much easier to breathe. I'll miss it.

The moon was almost full. I could see him clearly in its white light. In the last few weeks I've memorized every feature and detail in his face: the fine lines around his mouth, the coarse hairs in his eyebrows, the shadows under his eyes.

"I've . . . ," I started to say, but he leaned in and kissed me, and I let him, because I didn't want to say what I had to say. Because I wanted to feel his lips on mine.

He kissed me for a long time, and I could feel my eyes starting to sting.

One week, I thought. We can have one week more. That will have to be enough. It's stolen, what we have. I have stolen it from her.

After this week it'll all be over, and I'll never think about it again. I'll undo it, wipe it from my memory.

When he pulled back all of a sudden I felt strong. My head was humming, and I thought that I could say it.

I opened my mouth again, but then he looked up at the house and suddenly tore his hand from mine.

"Did she see us? Goddammit, did she see us?"

When I looked up I already knew what I would see. A black silhouette, in a faintly lit upstairs window.

There was only one week left. We just had to get through one more week. It was so stupid.

Perhaps she didn't understand what she saw? Or perhaps she didn't even see us in the darkness?

That or she saw it all. And she'll come sneaking into my room tonight and hold a pillow over my face until I stop breathing.

I can't stop thinking about the look in her eyes when she was holding Kicki. She hardly looked like a person anymore.

It's what I deserve, really, but dear God, I'm afraid she's going to kill me.

· ELEANOR ·

Veronika was right. Evert took his own life.

But this letter tells me nothing.

Something happened here, something Evert couldn't live with. There was one woman called Vivianne, and one called Anushka. And somewhere along the way the one must have become the other.

I can't get my head around it, but it's the only explanation that might fit. The only thing that can explain why Vivianne and Anushka have the same face.

I can hear them in the walls; they're whispering to me.

"Who, Vivianne?"

I so desperately wish she could answer me. It feels like a physical thirst.

But the voice in my head isn't really there.

It exists only on my voicemail. That last message, the one I still can't bring myself to delete.

Vivianne called me seventeen times that week.

"I hear them when I'm asleep. They refuse to stop."

"There's something I have to tell you, Victoria. Call me."

"Stop pretending I don't exist, Victoria!"

Could she have called Mats Bengtsson, too?

I put his phone in my jacket pocket in the lodge. I rummage around for it: still there. Nine percent battery.

It has no pin code.

I pull up the calls log. It has no names, only phone numbers.

The second-to-last call came from Vivianne's phone. A missed call. She left a voicemail. Forty-seven seconds long.

I press the phone to my ear, having to remind myself to breathe.

The sound of Vivianne's voice makes my stomach contract. I raise my hand to my mouth, feel my eyes tearing up.

"Mats, it's . . . ," she begins. There's a slight pause. I had forgotten how raspy her voice was, gravelly and whisky gruff. That little speech impediment that was never a speech impediment.

"It's Vivianne . . . Annika, I mean," she corrects herself. Her voice sounds a little quieter when she says it.

"Mats, she's been calling me nonstop lately," she goes on. At first I think Vivianne is talking about me, but it can't be. I only called her once a week. On Wednesdays. That was our agreement: I was to call her on Wednesdays, and have dinner with her on Sundays.

"She won't stop," Vivianne goes on. "I think she knows something. Or perhaps she's remembered something. I'm starting to think . . . Mats, perhaps it's time I told her. Perhaps she has a right to know." She goes quiet. Her breaths sound a little strained. They did in all of the messages she left me, too.

"I don't know how long I have left, Mats," she says after a pause, even quieter now. "I don't know when I got so old. It feels unfair."

She exhales into the receiver. It sounds like a hiss.

"I'm going to tell her," she says, as though she has just made the decision mid-sentence. Typical Vivianne. Her mood could flip like a switch, from a "maybe" to a "no" in the blink of an eye.

"I'll invite her over this weekend," she goes on. "Before Eleanor comes for dinner. That way it won't drag on too long. I can't bear to hash it out for hours, but she has a right to know. I've always told myself she had a good life, that we could give her that, at least. That she had a better life than she would have had otherwise. But sometimes I wonder . . . ah well. It's no use wondering anything anymore."

Vivianne sighs.

"She may call you. Tell her as much as you can bear to."

Another short pause. As though she is pulling herself together.

"You've been a good friend, Mats. A better friend than I've deserved. Thank you."

Click.

The message is over.

I lower the phone from my ear. Realize vaguely that my cheeks are wet with tears.

The longing is like a force of nature; it swells within me. I don't even feel the cold anymore; I'm just clinging on to the little black phone like a lifeline.

Who is "she"?

Who was Vivianne planning to tell?

And what did Vivianne think she had a right to know?

"I'll invite her over this weekend."

I have to get back to the house now, or else they'll realize I'm gone and worry. I still have the little phone in my hand when I step out of the car and close the door with a clap.

As I start walking back to the house I click on the last number that called Mats Bengtsson and press the phone to my ear. It must be the person who told him Vivianne was dead. The only one who could have known.

It's ringing.

I wait with a knot in my belly to hear someone pick up and say their name. To finally put a name to the faceless figure in the doorway.

Still ringing. I use my own phone to light the way back to the house but stop and frown when my eye is caught by something that doesn't fit. Something flapping out of the corner of my eye.

I take a step to the right. See the shadow whipping back and forth in the wind.

Why is the door to the wine cellar open?

It's hanging open, moving back and forth in the storm.

A beep on the line. A recorded message. The voice I hear is horribly, intimately familiar.

"Hi, I'm afraid I can't come to the phone right now, but you can reach me by email or through my website. . . ."

Suddenly it all falls into place. The red car. The half-empty packet of tissues.

It can't be. This has to be some sort of strange mistake, a misconnection.

But why is the door to the wine cellar open? It can't have blown open by itself, and it was shut—I remember it was shut. I checked all the doors. All the windows and all the doors were locked.

But I didn't check the door to the wine cellar.

And the dumbwaiter goes straight from the wine cellar into the house.

I start running to the front door, my feet slipping around on the ice lurking treacherously under the snow. I struggle to get the key in the lock; I have to get in, have to get them out, have to warn them.

I open the door just as I hear a gunshot upstairs.

· ANUSHKA ·
THEN

It's late afternoon. We go back to the city in two days.

The past few days I have felt like I can smell thunder in the air. Twice I have asked Märit if she can smell it too, the smell of moisture and cold and electricity on the breeze. She just laughed at me. *Look, the sky's clear*, she said. *You're imagining things. Summer isn't over yet.*

But I know she's wrong.

The heat today is heavy and oppressive. I'm sweating under my thick woolen uniform. We're busy cleaning out the house before we close it for summer, so everything is being pulled out of the closets and drawers for dusting and washing and drying, to have it all in perfect condition for next year.

I saved the lodge till last.

I haven't been here since Ma'am saw us. Nor has he. He has been pacing around the main house, restless and irritable, and we have hardly set eyes on each other since it happened.

My body aches for him, but it's for the best.

I have taken food up to her room three times, and she hasn't said a thing, hasn't even looked at me. I hope that means she didn't see anything, or that she forgot what she saw, or that she thought it was a dream.

I hope Sir takes her to see a doctor when all of this is over. That she feels herself again.

The sounds of the forest calm me, and when I reach the lodge I feel ready. I brace myself and open the door, leave it open behind me as I step inside.

The place smells of Sir.

I have to blink a few times to stop my eyes from welling up, and scold myself inwardly as I set the pail of rags and soap down on the floor. *Pull yourself together, Anushka. Do your job and lock up behind you and never come back.*

I open all the windows to air the place out and start dusting, quickly and efficiently, not caring about the sweat beading on my face. Good. All of this is good. All of this will be over, soon.

Perhaps I'll go back home.

Sweden has never suited me. I have never felt at home here. I know we're poor back home, and that every day would be a toil, but Mama's still there. Mama, and my aunts and my cousins. Aunt Maria, Ma'am's mother, was my favorite aunt as a child. She used to give me candy when Mama wasn't looking.

I could go home. Speak my own language again. Hear people call me by my name. I could tell Aunt Maria that Ma'am's sick and needs her mother. Sir already knows she isn't who she claims to be, so he wouldn't care. Surely if her mother came here he would only be grateful.

Maybe then she would get better again.

And I would be far away. No one would find out.

Yes, I can go home. I have saved almost all of my earnings here. It's no fortune, but enough for a train ticket, with a little left over to give Mama when I get there. Then perhaps she won't be so angry at me for coming back. She might even be happy to see me, might hug me and squeeze me like she did when I was little, briskly and brusquely and so intensely it almost hurt.

I never thought I would miss that.

When I hear the footsteps running outside I stop. I am just rolling up the rug to scrub the floor, and I feel a twinge in my back as I turn to look at the open door.

Märit has flown in on the breeze. She is standing on the front step, panting and red in the face. Her short blond hair is all ruffled, and the downy hairs around her hairline are stuck to her forehead with sweat.

"Märit, what is it?" I ask. She has started wearing her uniform again in the past few days to clean, so that the bosses wouldn't see her in her normal clothes, but she looks in complete disarray.

"She . . . She . . ." Märit gasps. I suddenly find it hard to swallow.

"Märit, what's happened?" I ask. I should walk over and help her, put my arm around her, but I can't bring myself to do it. It's like I'm rooted to the spot.

Märit steps inside. Her eyes are enormous in her red, blotchy face.

"Annika, you have to get out of here," she says. "Now, right now. Here, I took the car keys. Take them and drive."

She presses Sir's car keys into my palm.

"Why?" I ask. It feels like the room is suddenly airless. I'm shaking with fear.

Now Märit gives me a serious look. For a second I see a flash of anger in her eyes.

"I told you not to do this, Annika," she says. "I told you not to make a mess of things. I thought you were smart enough not to get involved with somebody like him. I've seen his type before—his wife gets sick and his head is turned by the first pretty girl he sees. Do you think he loves you? Is that why you don't want to go? He doesn't care about you, Annika. You mean nothing to him! You have to go, now! Right this second."

A drop of sweat trickles down her forehead. Her gaze is steady, but my vision is blurring. I shake my head.

"I didn't mean to, Märit; I didn't mean for this to happen. No one was supposed to find out."

"She knows. Ma'am knows. And she's after you. That's why you have to go. I don't know what she'll do if she gets her hands on you."

"Did she say that?" I ask. "Did she tell you she knew?"

"She didn't say anything to me," Märit says. "She didn't see me, thank God. I heard her mumbling to herself. She said she had to find the little whore."

She lowers her voice on the last word, as though she can hardly bring herself to say it. Suddenly I feel so light-headed I have to grab one of the armchairs next to me for support.

He kissed me in it, I remember, two weeks ago. Slow kisses that burned my lips.

I tear my hand away.

"Just drive," Märit says. "I'll take care of the rest. I'll tell Sir you got sick. He won't ask any questions. He'll just assume you got scared and ran away, or that you're pregnant. Believe me when I say that either way he won't care."

"Where can I go?" I ask, my voice shrill and unsure, like a child's. "I have nowhere to go."

"Go to my sister," says Märit. "It's not far. I'll write down her address for you. Tell her I said you could stay in my room for a few days. We'll figure something out with the car. Then the next day I'll get another lift with them back to town, and we can arrange everything else."

My knees are shaking. Märit walks over to the desk, tears a piece of thick, creamy letter paper from the pile, and scribbles down an address.

"This is where my sister lives," she says. "Third floor. It's small, but it's somewhere. Help her out with the kids and she'll be happy to have you there."

She hands me the sheet of paper. I take it, but she doesn't let go.

"Annika, tell me the truth," she says. "Are you pregnant?"

"No!" I exclaim in shock, and shake my head.

"Are you sure?" she asks. "When did you last get your period?"

I try to think, but my mind won't stop whirring.

"Two weeks ago, I think," I say.

"Good," says Märit. "Have you had sex since?"

My cheeks flush. I close my eyes and nod.

"If you're pregnant, Annika, we'll take care of it," she says. "There are people who can help. It'll cost you, but it's worth it, I promise."

I open my eyes and look at Märit.

"It'll be OK," she tells me, slightly calmer now. "In a few months' time it'll be like this never happened. I promise. I'll help you."

"Why are you being so kind to me?" I whisper.

Her gaze is straight, but endlessly sad.

"Because I wish somebody had been kind to me."

There is so much in those words.

My eyes are stinging and my throat is smarting, like there's something caught in it. I say:

"Thank you."

"Thank me later," she says. "Just go, now, before she finds you."

I leap over and hug her, long and tight. She smells of sweat and soap, and she hugs me back.

"It's going to be OK," she whispers in my ear. Then she lets go and gives a faint smile as she adjusts a wisp of hair that has fallen out of my braid.

"Now off you go."

I nod and turn to the door.

But I freeze on the spot.

Ma'am isn't wearing any shoes. Her feet are pale and dirty, her toenails unclipped. Blood is dripping from a scratch running down one of her skinny calves. She must have caught it on a branch in the forest.

Her hair is tangled and greasy; it lies dark and flat against her skull. Her white nightgown is so thin I can see the contours of her body through the fabric. Her mouth is pursed in a small, condescending smile, one so familiar and characteristic that she would almost look like herself, if it weren't for the eyes.

Her eyes are blazing.

"So this is where you're hiding," she says.

But she isn't looking at me.

She's looking at Märit.

· ELEANOR ·

Sebastian!" I scream as I storm through the hallway, up the stairs, and into the master bedroom.

Then stop, as though paralyzed, in the doorway.

My eyes haven't had time to adjust to the darkness, but Sebastian's phone is lying on the floor with the flashlight on, and that's enough for me to be able to orient myself in the room.

My eyes find Sebastian, but at first I can't tell if he's hurt. He's sitting on the bed, Veronika next to him. Behind them I think I can make out Rickard's shape, tucked in under thick covers.

The rifle is pointed at Veronika. When I take another step inside the room, the barrel swings around slowly and then stops when it's pointed at me.

She has her finger on the trigger.

The dumbwaiter hatch is open behind her, gaping like a hole in the darkness. It matches the hole on the wall by the bed—the one the bullet has just made.

She is holding the weapon with sure hands. Her eyes are steady, despite the dried blood on her split eyebrow.

The room smells of terror and gunpowder.

I don't dare say a word, don't dare breathe. No one has ever pointed a weapon at me before. I've seen it in movies and on TV hundreds of times, but it's another thing entirely to know that my own life could be snuffed out in a split second.

Part of me can't take it in, can't believe this is real. It brings out animalistic impulses I never knew I had. I've never felt such electricity in my body before, such undivided desperation.

"I'm so sorry, Eleanor," she says, her voice impossibly calm.

If I hadn't just heard her voice on the recorded greeting, I would never have recognized her. She's too far removed from her usual environment; all of her markers are wrong. Her nose is swollen, her neat, grayish-blond hair unbrushed, and she is wearing a thick, knitted sweater instead of her usual soft cardigans. There are no reading glasses hanging on a thin silver chain around her neck. She is so far out of her usual context that I want to believe I'm wrong, to believe this has to be some sort of misunderstanding. She can't be here. She doesn't belong here.

But her steady hands are the ones holding the rifle. And there's a flicker of determined sorrow in her eyes.

"What are you doing here?" I ask, hearing the hopelessness in my own voice. "What are *you* doing here?"

She shakes her head. Her usually so well-combed bob swings as she moves. The rifle does not.

"I really wish it didn't have to be this way."

I think:

I have to get them out of here.

I think:

Where did that rifle come from?

I think:

The gun cabinet. The lodge.

It was empty when we were there, but that doesn't mean it was empty when she was.

I lick my lips. My tongue feels dry.

"You don't have to do this," I say, but the words ring hollow.

She smiles. A small, compassionate smile. As though she wished she could agree.

Veronika moves slightly, shifts her weight, and the barrel swings straight back to her.

"Sit still, Veronika," she says. "I don't want to shoot you. But if I have to, I will."

There is no hesitation in her voice, no suggestion of fear or uncertainty. How I have relied on that voice. How I have followed it over the years. She has been my security.

"How could you?" I ask, feeling a sting in my throat.

I have never trusted anyone like I trusted her.

She saved me.

I thought that she, in her own way, loved me.

"You helped me!" I manage to splutter out. "After everything. After Vivianne. All those afternoons I talked about it and cried about it and you . . ."

Now, for the first time, I see a shift in her face. Behind her eyes. Something behind that decisive calm.

"You needed help," she says. "I tried. I wanted you to feel better. I didn't want it to destroy your life."

"But you're the one who killed her," I whisper. "No one knew better than you that I wouldn't be able to identify you. You're the one who told Mats Bengtsson what had happened."

She doesn't reply.

"Isn't that so, Carina?"

· ANUSHKA ·
THEN

M̈ärit is more quick on her feet than me. She smiles and picks up the pail from the floor.

"Yes, here we are, Ma'am!" she says cheerily, as though Ma'am has just come out to find us to tell us to get started on dinner. As though she is clean and immaculate and dressed to the nines, scolding the help before a dinner party.

"We were just cleaning the lodge for the winter. I asked Annika to help me so we could get it done faster."

Ma'am steps over the threshold and the floorboard creaks, even though she doesn't look like she could possibly weigh anything anymore, as emaciated as she is.

But her fingers are bent, her nails are long and sharp, and the veins in her forearms are pressing through the skin.

She is thin, and she is sick. But standing there with that little smile on her face, she still looks awfully strong. Her eyes see only Märit.

"I've been looking for you," she says. "I've been looking for you everywhere. Did you think you could hide out here?" She looks around. Her eyes pass over me as though I'm not even there.

"Is this where you do it?" she spits, and her smile contorts even more, until it looks like a mask.

"Do what, Ma'am?" Märit asks, but she doesn't sound quite as chirpy anymore. The top of her arm brushes against mine, and I can feel that she's completely tensed up.

My mouth is dry.

"I know," Ma'am says slowly, running her finger along the cabinet by the door. It's a beautiful, mahogany cabinet, with a big, heavy key in the lock. I have never seen it open before, and never wondered what was inside. But something about the way the edges of Ma'am's mouth curl sends alarm bells ringing through my head.

I don't like the way she is looking at Märit. I have to get her to look at me instead.

"Marta," I say in our language. "You aren't well. Let me get you back to the house."

Now Ma'am turns her gaze on me, swift and sharp. I want to recoil but steel myself.

"Anushka," she says, and her voice is soft and pliable as a caress. She moistens her thin, chapped lips with her shockingly red tongue. "I'm so happy you're here, Cousin. You're going to help me, no? You do want to help me, don't you?"

"Of course," I say, and for a second I can fool myself into relief. Because her voice is as smooth as cream and she isn't staring Märit down with that horrible look anymore, and she's saying she's happy I'm here. Surely that has to be a good thing?

"You're going to help me deal with the whore who tried to steal my husband."

Then Ma'am moves, so quickly and so suddenly that a scream escapes me.

The key turns soundlessly in the lock, the door swings open, and she grabs the lone slim rifle hanging inside.

Her hands are all too steady as she points it at Märit.

Märit lets out a little sound. Just one. It isn't even a word.

"Marta—Vivianne—please, stop! Put it down!" I exclaim, so scared I hardly know what I'm saying. I'm speaking a mixture of Swedish and Polish.

"Put it down. Please, Ma'am, she hasn't done anything. I don't know what you think she's done, but she—please, Cousin, put the gun down. We can talk about this."

I can hear myself babbling. My palms feel completely cold.

Ma'am's face is blank. Still pointing the gun at Märit, she whispers coolly:

"You tried to steal my husband, you little whore, but he doesn't want you. You're just an ugly, worthless little hussy. All you know to do is spread your legs."

The tears are streaming silently down Märit's face, down over her cheeks. Her eyes are so wide that her eyelids appear to have vanished. She doesn't even blink. Her lips are trembling.

"Ma'am, Märit hasn't done anything with Sir," I say. I'm struggling to keep my voice even, not to shout, not to scare her.

"Ma'am's made a mistake; Märit hasn't touched him, I swear!"

My voice is trembling.

Märit opens her mouth. She says:

"It's true, Ma'am. I've never touched Ma'am's husband. Not once."

I can hear her teeth chattering.

When Ma'am cocks the trigger all it makes is a small click, but the sound still rings in my ears.

I can't breathe.

"You took my daughter, you whore," she says quietly. She is whispering in Polish, as though Märit understood, as though she doesn't remember where she is.

"Where have you taken her? Where have you taken my Vendela?"

Her eyes are glistening with tears.

Märit is white as a sheet. She doesn't move a muscle.

I crack. I scream:

"Marta, it was me; I'm the one who slept with your husband!"

When she bends her finger and pulls the trigger, the sound of the shot seems to fill the whole world.

· ELEANOR ·

Carina has been my therapist for eight years. She started treating me when I moved out of Vivianne's apartment and into my little student room in Gärdet, my first home of my own.

Carina and her husband were part of Vivianne's social circle when I was growing up, a regular feature at Vivianne's dinners, lunches, and cocktail parties. She was twenty years or so younger than Vivianne, but that wasn't unusual; many of the people in Vivianne's set were younger than her.

Carina was always kind to me. She liked playing with me when I was small, and could sit with me and my dolls for hours without losing her patience. Vivianne didn't like that. Whenever she found us together she would shoo Carina away, tell her there was someone she was dying to introduce her to, and leave me alone. Carina always did as she was told. She seemed to look up to Vivianne.

Carina was the first person who noticed my prosopagnosia when I was a teenager. She was the one who suggested I get checked. Vivianne went through the roof when Carina suggested it, so Carina dropped it, but later she pulled me aside when Vivianne was in the kitchen and whispered that she could help me, if I wanted.

I started seeing her in secret. She was the one who helped me to set boundaries with Vivianne. She was the one who made sure I got a diagnosis.

No one knows me better than Carina.

When I knocked on the door after she had slit my grandmother's throat, she must have had to think fast. She knew it was me, that Vivianne and I had a standing Sunday night dinner. And she knew that if she pulled on a hat and kept her mouth shut I would never be able to place her—however well I knew her features, her walk, her voice, or her mannerisms.

I'm used to seeing her in a small, well-lit therapy room in Karlaplan, wearing soft knits with expensive price tags and a warm look in her eyes. Always with the same horn-rimmed reading glasses on a chain around her neck. Creating a safe, consistent context is important for people like me.

Of course I didn't recognize her in Vivianne's hallway, with blood on her hands.

The corners of her mouth sag slightly, so that the parenthesis-shaped wrinkles around it deepen. So familiar. I have always liked those wrinkles. The softness in her face. It looks human in a way that Vivianne never allowed herself to look. Everything that Vivianne paid to slice off and tighten up is to be found in Carina.

Carina, who is standing there with a gun in her hands.

"I didn't mean for things to go this way, Eleanor," she says, patiently, like this is some sort of misunderstanding. I so wish it were.

I let out a sudden, harsh laugh that shocks me so much I clap my hand to my mouth.

"What?" I say. "Was it an accident? Did you trip while carrying the scissors in your hand?"

"Please, Eleanor, don't act out," says Carina. "We've talked about this, remember? Your feelings don't control you. Feelings are behaviors."

It's so surreal that I actually start seeing double. She sounds so calm and rational, and I'm so close to hysteria that I want to give in to her voice. I feel an impulse to listen to her, to calm down, to let her take control.

Stop, Victoria, I hear Vivianne's sharp, venomous voice in my head.

You have more backbone than that; I know you do. You know what you have to do. You have to get your boy and Veronika out of here. Or get them away from her. She may sound calm, but she's out of her mind. Look at her. You know better than to let yourself be fooled by a calm, collected exterior.

Vivianne's voice makes everything shift back into sharper focus. I stand up straighter. See past the voice, the hypnotic calm, the barrel. The authority.

See through to the eyes of the dangerous animal behind them all.

Yes. Yes, I can see them.

"You killed my grandmother," I say coldly. "I think this is what you would call a 'functional response.'"

She gives a wry, fickle smile, her eyes narrowed. I see a flash of uncertainty behind them, a spark so fleeting it's almost impossible to catch.

"You always were a good patient, Eleanor," she says. "A complex case, but you always worked hard. I appreciated that. Not everyone works for it, you know—not everyone wants to get better. It takes a lot of effort to find strategies that work. Most people don't get that. You understood. You're stronger than you think."

"Are you seriously trying to give me therapy before you shoot me?" I snap. I hear a trace of Vivianne's haughty irritation in my own voice, an echo that feels strangely comforting.

Don't get her worked up, Victoria.

Show her you aren't going to give in to her, but don't provoke her.

You know how to do that.

You did it with me, remember?

Oh, I remember.

I can see Carina's knuckles whitening as she grips the rifle even tighter. She has fired one shot. I remember Sebastian's father's speeches on hunting rifles. I'm pretty sure she only has one shot left until she has to reload.

Still, one is more than enough for her to blow my brains out.

Or Sebastian's, or Veronika's.

I can't stop my eyes from wandering over to them, for a second. She sees it, and lets the rifle swing back until it's pointed at Sebastian.

"I don't want to hurt him, Eleanor," she says.

The breath catches in my chest.

"On the bed," she says. "Sit down."

If I sit down she will never let me stand up again; if I sit down then everything is lost.

The seconds tick past in slow motion. One. Two. I have to buy myself some time, say the right thing. I know that's what I have to do.

But it isn't me who breaks the silence. It's Veronika.

"Please," she says, her voice breaking in a way I've never heard it do before. Suddenly she sounds so young.

"You don't have to do this, Kicki."

· ANUSHKA ·
THEN

I want to scream, but it just comes out as a breath.

"Märit."

She has slumped to the floor, and I kneel down beside her not knowing what to do, my hands heavy and useless in my lap. The seconds seem to tick past one by one, endless, marking the rhythm of my pulse. I can hear them in my ears.

With every beat of my heart, the blood spreads across the floor.

Märit is staring at me with a child's eyes. Never has she looked so much like her daughter as now.

When she opens her mouth, her lips are flecked with blood.

She looks like she's trying to say something, but not a word crosses her lips, just a single, strained breath.

The hole in her uniform has rough edges. Beneath it I see flesh, flesh and bone and blood, a mess of white and pink and red.

She tries to inhale but coughs, and I realize that the small, hot prickles on my face are blood. She is coughing up blood onto me.

"Märit," I say, and then: "Please."

As though asking her not to die.

As though asking her to be whole.

I don't know what to do.

I pick up a rag from the floor and it's dirty and it's damp and it's wrong—it should be a clean bandage—but I have nothing else. I press the rag against the hole in her chest, but it doesn't help because the blood is flowing out the other side, beneath her, seeping down between the floorboards, and I have to make it stop, but I don't know how.

My knees are warm and wet from her, and it smells of raw meat, and Märit moans when I try to press the rag against the wound, and that must be a good thing—any sound has to be a good sign; it means she's alive, right? She isn't dead yet. It's just a wound. Wounds heal. That's what she says to Kicki: wounds heal, and they hurt to make us learn to be careful. She's going to be OK; everything is going to be OK; she said everything would be OK.

She parts her lips. Her eyes are searching for something in my face. Her pupils are very small.

"Kicki?" she says to me. Like a challenge. A question.

"Yes," I say. "Think of Kicki. You have to think of Kicki. You're going to be OK."

But she doesn't reply.

Her eyes are staring at the ceiling.

And then she exhales, and doesn't inhale again, and her eyes don't see anything anymore. And I want to say her name again, but I know she won't respond.

I lean away from her and vomit in the pool of blood.

Outside I hear the twittering of a bird.

When I turn to face Ma'am I'm not surprised to find the rifle pointed at me.

I already know I'm going to die in here.

· ELEANOR ·

Carina purses her bare lips, so that her mouth is no more than a thin line.

"Don't call me that," she says to Veronika, her voice jarringly chipper, in stark contrast to the look on her face.

"Kicki?" I say, confused. "Märit's daughter—*that* Kicki?"

Veronika doesn't look at me. Her eyes are fixed on Carina.

"Let them go," she says to Carina. "Eleanor hasn't done anything. Nor her boyfriend. This isn't about them."

Veronika's body is tensed, like she's about to stand up, and I want to shout at her not to move. To sit still.

The rifle is old. How reliable is it? How much would it take for it to go off by mistake?

"You want to punish Vivianne, don't you?" Veronika says, a naked desperation visible in the deep shadows under her eyes. The white glare of Sebastian's cell phone paints her in black ink.

"You won't do that through Eleanor. Vivianne didn't give a shit about her. Eleanor was just a plaything for her."

My eyes start to sting.

Quiet, I want to say. *Be quiet. This isn't going to help, Veronika. You can't fool her.*

Carina pulls a melancholy smile.

"It's lovely to see you love your niece so much, Veronika," she says.

"And you're wrong. I don't want to punish anybody. I never wanted anybody to get hurt. I didn't want to hit you, Veronika. I saw you there in the storm, and I was scared you'd see me, recognize me. . . . I'm glad you made it. Really, I am."

She shakes her head and says, slightly quieter:

"I don't want anyone to have to come to harm unnecessarily."

Unnecessarily.

"In that case," says Veronika, her voice curdling, "no one needs to come to any harm. Let us go. We don't have to say anything. No one gets it more than I do. I know what she was like. I get why you wanted to do it. She was a fucking bitch. Vendela tried to persuade her not to send you away when Daddy died, did you know that? She begged and pleaded until Mother slapped her across the face. Vendela loved you. I loved you." Veronika swallows, loudly, and her slender neck contracts.

There. Something peering out from behind Carina's mask.

"You were only children," she says gruffly.

"So were you," Veronika says.

Everything goes quiet.

"Mother loved you, too," says Veronika. "She did, I promise. She wanted you to be taken care of. She just didn't think she could do that herself. Sometimes I wish she'd sent me away, too. She loved you like a daughter. In the only way she could."

That was the wrong thing to say.

I feel it like a sudden gasp of wind.

See the muscles in Carina's jaws tense up.

"Vivianne didn't love me," she says, spitting out the words.

"Vivianne," she repeats, raising the gun a little higher so that it is pointed straight at Veronika. "Vivianne took everything from me."

· ANUSHKA ·
THEN

M a'am stands there giggling to herself. Then she breaks off and turns her nose up when the smell of Märit's body hits her.

"You have to clean that up, Anushka," she says, her voice back to normal. "It smells terrible. Isn't it your job to keep this place clean?"

She eyes my vomit with loathing.

"God, you can't do anything right, can you?"

I shut my eyes. I can't even look at her.

"She didn't do anything," I say. "She didn't do anything, Marta. It was me, you hear? I slept with your husband. It wasn't Märit. She's . . ." My throat knots up, and I can't get another word out.

I open my eyes. Ma'am is staring at me in mild confusion, as though I've said something that only vaguely interests her.

"Just do it," I say to her. "Shoot me. I'm tired of waiting. Do it already."

"Why would I do that?" she asks. She looks hurt. As though I've said something cruel.

"You're my cousin. You're family. I would never hurt you, Anushka. I know you love me. You even helped me to take care of the whore who slept with my husband, see?" she says, pointing the rifle at the body next to me.

The body that was Märit.

"Now help me clear this up, so Evert won't see," she goes on. "He hates it when it's dirty in here."

When I don't move, a faint crease appears between her eyebrows, still beautiful and dark and arched under her smooth forehead.

"Well then," she says in Swedish. "Clean this up, now. Look, there's a rag. Start wiping."

The barrel of the rifle is still staring right at me.

I have never hated myself as much as I do when I lift the bloody rag from Märit's cooling chest and start to wipe the floor. My vomit mixes with the blood, but nothing gets absorbed. My arms are shaking beneath me.

"See, that's better," she says. "Everything will be fine now, Anushka. We're going to be a family. Me and Evert and Vendela and you. You'll get to help me with her; won't that be nice? I want her to get to know her family."

I stop. My chest is heaving. With every passing breath I take in, it feels like the smell from Märit's body is getting stronger.

"You're right," Ma'am says, as though I said something. "Let's go get Vendela first. I don't want her to be afraid. Poor little girl, she's been away from her mommy so long."

"She isn't your daughter, Marta," I say. I drop the rag. My hand is stiff, and the liquid on it feels disgusting, cold and sticky.

She stares at me blankly, a puzzled little smile on her lips.

"Her name isn't Vendela; it's Kicki. And she isn't yours. She's Märit's. You have no daughter."

She shakes her head.

"No," she says. "Stop saying that."

"Her name isn't Vendela; it's Kicki," I repeat, the tears welling up in my eyes, and I scream:

"Her name is Kicki and you're not her mother, you killed her mother, and I'll kill you myself before I let you take her! Understand? Do you understand me, Marta?"

"*Stop!*" she screams. "*Stop lying! Don't call me that!*"

She raises the rifle and points it straight at me.

"My name isn't Marta," she says, now calm again. "My name is Vivianne."

I want to close my eyes but can't.

I see her cock the trigger again.

See her face: relaxed, assured, content.

And then I see her jerk and fall forward, see the gun slip out of her hand and fire into the floor on its way down, and I scream and cover my ears and close my eyes.

When I open them again Ma'am is lying facedown on the rug, the back of her head a bloody mass of hair and bone. Mats is standing behind her in the doorway, still as a statue, a big, heavy, bloody stone raised in one of his hands.

· ELEANOR ·

What do you mean?" I ask. My mouth is dry, and it feels like all of my senses have sharpened.

"Vivianne took my mother from me," Carina says.

"Märit?" I ask, and I see her face twitch. She gives a quick nod.

"She knew," she says. "She knew the whole time. She let me believe my mother abandoned me, let me believe she didn't want me." Her arms are shaking—whether that's from tension or exertion, I don't know.

But I'm still standing. She seems to have forgotten that she ordered me to sit down.

Keep her talking, Victoria, Vivianne whispers in my head.

Keep her talking, but don't make her so angry she shoots.

Listen to her. Coax it out of her. Ask the right questions.

Don't let her realize what you're doing.

You know what to do. I know you remember.

I have been going to therapy with Carina for eight years. I know the way she asks her soft, encouraging questions, and the way she repeats what I have said, clarifying what I'm feeling even when I can't put my finger on it myself.

I must have learned something from that.

"Vivianne deceived you," I say. "She betrayed you."

"I had no one else!" she splutters. "I was just a child. I trusted her. I was only five years old."

"There was nothing you could have done," I say.

"No. . . ." For a second her voice falters. "I was helpless. She said she would look after me. She said my mother had abandoned me, just upped and left me. She said she wouldn't let anything happen to me."

"But she abandoned you."

"After Evert died. She shipped me off to live with strangers. First she took my mother, then she took my security. She took Solhöga from me."

"She had no right to do that," I say. "It wasn't even her house."

Carina gnashes her teeth.

"No. She had no *right*."

"I know how it feels," I say. "I had no mother either. All I had was Vivianne. And she couldn't give me what I needed. She didn't even try."

Her eyes narrow, almost imperceptibly. Another person might not have noticed it, but I'm used to paying attention to every little detail, every muscle twinge. With Vivianne, even the slightest movement could mean a false step.

I go completely still.

"Oh, well done, Eleanor," she says slowly. "Clever girl. But you should never say you know how it feels. Because no one ever knows how another person feels. You don't know how it feels. Vivianne loved you. She never loved me. To her I was just a liability, I remembered too much. I was five years old when my mother died, twelve when Vivianne sent me away. I was too dangerous to keep close, too dangerous to let go of. So she would send me away and then reel me back in, constantly reminding me how much I owed her. Just to keep me in my place. To stop me from giving it too much thought. From remembering. Asking questions."

My throat feels tight. I'm finding it hard to swallow.

My mind is racing.

I can feel every part of me contracting, bit by bit. Nearing the inevitable end point.

"What didn't she want you to ask about?" I ask.

Carina opens her mouth. Then she shuts it again and smiles with closed lips.

"That doesn't matter, Eleanor."

She raises the rifle.

· ANUSHKA ·
THEN

Mats is still standing on the threshold. The stone drops from his hand. He's staring into space, his breaths short and shallow and gasping.

I get to my feet, slipping in the blood, and run over to Ma'am. I roll her onto her back. Her eyelids twitch, which gives me a foolish, raging hope.

"Marta?" I say to her quietly.

My eyes are stinging, and there's a sour taste in my mouth. I give her smooth cheek a few gentle slaps.

"Marta, wake up," I say.

Her chest is still rising and falling. But it's a jerky, fluttering movement, one that's getting weaker and more irregular with every breath she takes in.

I know it's too late. I saw the back of her head. That sort of thing doesn't heal. Everything she was has already fled her body.

"Annika?" I hear a cry. I jump and get to my feet.

Mats has stumbled into the room. And behind him Sir is coming.

Sir stops in the doorway and looks into the room. I see him gulp. That neck I know so well. I have kissed the skin under his jaw more times than I can count.

We have done this. We are to blame. No one else.

The smell in the lodge is almost unbearable. There's nothing left in my stomach, but I can still feel the acid rising.

"Vivianne," he whispers hollowly. Like a statement. Not a question.

She is the one he's looking at. Not Märit. As though Märit wasn't even there.

"She was going to shoot Annika," says Mats, his face wan and blankly expressionless. "I didn't know what to do. I couldn't let her shoot Annika. I didn't think I hit her so hard."

Mats stares at the bloody stone on the ground.

"She killed Märit," I say. The very name hurts my lips. "She killed Märit, Evert. She knew. But she got it wrong. She thought it was Märit, not me."

He doesn't look at me, but Mats does. I'm expecting to see it dawn on him in some way, the pieces of the puzzle falling into place. But all I see is anxiety. His hands are shaking.

I get up. Take a step toward him.

But it isn't Mats who comes toward me. It's Sir.

I shrink back, half a step, as though expecting him to hit me. But instead he throws his arms around me.

He clings to me desperately, as though I'm the only thing keeping him up, digs his nails into my back so I feel them through the fabric of my uniform. He starts to cry onto my shoulder.

The blood on my knees has started to harden. My eyes are completely dry.

Mats stares at me mutely over his shoulder. Not a word passes his lips. He looks so helpless, like he's already lost.

"What do we do?" Sir asks, again and again into my shoulder. "What do we do?"

His tears and mumblings are the only sound in the room, beyond my own, rasping breaths.

"I don't know," I whisper. In my own language.

"We have to call the police," he says, and then I pull away and step back, shaking my head.

"No," I say. "They'll put Mats in prison. It wasn't his fault."

He did this for me.

Him. Märit. Marta.

All dead or lost. Because of me.

I can't let Mats go to prison because of me.

"They'll never believe us," I say. "They'll never believe Ma'am shot Märit and was going to shoot me, too. They'll put Mats in prison. They won't listen."

I've seen what happens when the police arrive. Back home prison is a place of no return.

Mats is innocent. He's the only person in this who is. If anyone should end up in prison it's me, or Sir. The guilt is ours.

But I can't bring myself to say it out loud, voice the words, make it real.

"I can talk to them," Sir says. "They'll listen to me." But his certainty wanes with every syllable.

He looks over at Mats, who is by now so pale that his eyes look black in the failing light.

"I didn't mean to," he says, and his thin voice makes my heart break.

"I know," I say, stepping toward him.

I want to hug Mats, but Sir grabs my arm.

"Annika," he says, and I want to scream that my name isn't Annika. I'm not Annika. I'm Anushka.

But I find I don't have the words.

"Mats doesn't have to go to prison," he says. "No one has to go to prison. Kicki doesn't have to end up in an orphanage."

Kicki. It feels like someone is sitting on my chest.

"She can't," I say. "We can't let her end up in an orphanage. We have to look after her."

"She doesn't have to," he says, a strangely intense look in his eyes. "This never has to have happened."

"What do you mean?" I ask.

"We say she disappeared," he says. "We say Märit couldn't cope and ran away. And she left Kicki here with us because we would look after her, make sure she had a good upbringing. It happens all the time. No one would question it."

I shake my head.

"We can't," I say.

"We can," he replies, squeezing my upper arms with both hands. He isn't even looking at Mats. It's as though we are the only two people in the room.

"And her?" I whisper, forcing myself to say the name: "Vivianne?"

He fixes his feverish eyes on mine.

"You can be Vivianne, Annika," he says.

· ELEANOR ·

want to know," I say, my heart pounding hard in my chest. "I want to understand."

"You don't need to understand, Eleanor," says Carina. "You can't understand. This will all be over soon."

The silence that follows is deafening, broken only by the whine of the wind outside.

"What do you mean?" I ask.

Something resembling sorrow comes over her face.

"I didn't want it to be like this," she says. For the first time she sounds tired. And sincere.

"It wasn't supposed to be like this. This was never my intention. I didn't want to hurt anybody. I meant what I said—I wanted to help you, after Vivianne. I didn't mean for it to go the way it did. I lost my head. It's not something I'm proud of." She swallows, and I see her neck contract.

"I just wanted her to stop talking," she says quietly.

Then she shakes her head.

"I shouldn't have done it. But I thought I could try to make it up to you, by helping you. I thought that . . . that it didn't have to destroy your life. You know I care about you. I wanted to help you get your life back. Be free of her."

All those afternoons after Vivianne. All the tears I shed in Carina's calm, safe therapy room. All the tissues she handed me from cheap, small packets. A basic, pharmacy brand.

The rage is threatening to take over, but I force it back down.

"You don't have to hurt anyone."

"I wish that were true," she says. "If I had been able to keep away from here, then maybe things wouldn't have had to be this way. I acknowledge my responsibility there. But when you said you were coming here I couldn't resist. I really tried to. It's important that you know I did try to keep away. But I had to know." She shakes her head.

"I called Mats afterwards. Told him Vivianne was dead. Not how it happened, of course—I just said there had been an accident. I asked him to let me come here, for closure. But he refused. Vivianne had ordered him not to let anyone in the house, and he would never go against her wishes, not even with her dead. I thought about coming out here, picking the locks or opening a window, but I tried to let it go. I was scared of what might happen if Mats saw me. I tried to move on, let it go. With Vivianne gone, it had seemed possible." She sighs.

"But I knew Mats couldn't stop you from coming in. You're the heirs, after all. It was all I could think about, night and day. If I could just find something—anything—that could show me what had happened to my mother." Another fragment of genuine emotion makes her lips tremble.

"I just want to know where she is," says Carina. "I want to know where they buried her."

"Your mother," I say, and she nods.

"They left her here," says Carina. "I had to see this place again, to see if it could jog my memory." She smiles at me.

"I did help you, didn't I? When you were stuck in the dumbwaiter? I didn't mean for you to get stuck—I just wanted to give you a little nudge so I could get out. So that no one would see me. When I saw what had happened I tried to help you get out."

Lie still.

The open bathroom door.

That strangely familiar voice.

"I loved that dumbwaiter when I was little," she says with a short laugh, so inappropriate in the situation that it makes my knees start to quake.

"I used to play with it. Mommy would always get angry at me. She said it wasn't a toy. But I thought it was a magic closet, that it could take me wherever I wanted to go."

She sounds lost in thought.

"Carina . . ." I try to step toward her, but she immediately jumps to attention and clenches the rifle even tighter.

"Not another step. Stand still, Eleanor."

Her frustration is breaking through.

"What are you going to do?" I say.

"I don't want to shoot any of you." That little streak of sorrow in her voice again.

"But none of you are leaving here."

· CARINA ·
THAT AFTERNOON

Carina looked at herself in the elevator mirror, picked away a piece of fluff from her blazer, and leaned in to check her lipstick wasn't smudged. Vivianne would find something to comment on, regardless. She always did. Carina took a deep breath, counted to four, and then breathed out slowly through her mouth: one, two, three, four.

She was nervous.

Nervousness was no weakness. It was a normal response. Not only to the situation, but to Vivianne.

Vivianne had been a source of both love and a context. Despite being hurt by her time and time again, Carina had been unable to keep away—not even after Vivianne sent her away after Evert's death. She had kept on trying to build bridges, in spite of the scant fragments of affection Vivianne offered. When Vivianne refused to see Carina after she started treating Eleanor, the rejection had hurt just as much as it did when she was thirteen.

The truth—when she could admit it to herself—was that she missed Vivianne.

Sometimes Carina still had the occasional urge to pick up the phone and call her. Hear her dry, husky voice, that little speech impediment, her waspish comments on mutual acquaintances, and her rare, always equally unexpected compliments.

Carina knew that compliments didn't mean more because they came from someone who gave them so rarely. She knew that better than most. Over the years she had treated many patients with similar issues to her own—attachment difficulties, a troubled relationship with parental figures, a tendency to get drawn to emotionally unavailable partners—and had seen her own dysfunctional behaviors reflected in dozens of others.

But none more so than Eleanor.

So, yes, she knew better than anyone else that those little crumbs of affection Vivianne was capable of doling out weren't worth all that much. But she longed for them all the same. Even after all this time.

She would soon be turning sixty. Shouldn't she have gotten over this by now?

Perhaps.

The elevator stopped. She smoothed her hair one last time before stepping out and across the hallway, and ringing the doorbell.

Vivianne took her time to come to the door. Carina had made sure to be punctual. She knew she could never win, not really: if she arrived early she would get her head bitten off for being so badly brought up that she didn't know ten minutes late was the only acceptable arrival time; but if she did arrive ten minutes after the appointed time she would be dragged over the coals for her lack of respect for others' time. Being there precisely on time was the safest option, even if that too wasn't without its risks. Carina didn't want to give Vivianne any excuse to blow up.

When Vivianne eventually opened the door, Carina felt her back straighten automatically. The sight of Vivianne came as something of a shock: she didn't appear to have aged a day since Carina had last seen her, eight years previously. Carina felt her own wrinkles embed themselves that bit deeper and her skin hang a little more slack with every passing day, but Vivianne appeared to have been frozen in time.

Up close it was possible to see the traces of expensive surgeries—the taut skin over her forehead, the way it pulled over her cheekbones—but there was still no mistaking her beauty. The beauty that had once been there. It still haunted her boot-polish-black hair, her dark-red lipstick, her elegant fingers and arching, painted-on eyebrows.

"Kicki," Vivianne greeted her, and Carina swallowed and shrank.

"Vivianne," she replied. "So nice to see you."

Vivianne stood unmoving on the threshold, relishing Carina's discomfort, but then she leaned in and kissed the air next to Carina's cheeks.

"Come in," she said. "I don't have much time. Victoria's coming over for dinner in an hour or so. It's the only time I get with her now, thanks to you."

Of course she has no time for her. Of course something else is more important.

Vivianne must have suggested this time deliberately, just to have the chance to throw it in Carina's face.

Carina followed her into the hallway, took off her boots, and hung up her jacket on a hanger. Vivianne observed her with raised eyebrows and compressed lips.

"Didn't you bring any indoor shoes?" she asked.

Carina stiffened and opened her mouth to say no but was cut off by Vivianne:

"You can use a pair of mine. Your feet are bigger, but you'll just have to make do. I won't have you running around in here in stocking feet."

Sixty, Carina said to herself. *I'm almost sixty. I own a lakeside house and have a successful practice. I don't have to do as she tells me.*

Then, without a murmur, she squeezed her feet into a pair of black indoor shoes that were at least two sizes too small. Her toes were already throbbing in pain as she followed Vivianne into the living room.

Vivianne was wearing a simple yellow blouse and slim black trousers. Unusually underdressed for Vivianne.

There was probably some thought behind it—perhaps to make Carina relax and let her guard down. Carina knew better than to believe Vivianne didn't have a plan. Vivianne never did anything rashly. It was part of her appeal.

"Sherry?" Vivianne asked, pouring a glass before Carina had a chance to say anything.

"No, thanks," Carina uttered, and Vivianne rolled her eyes and handed her the glass.

"Oh, don't be so ridiculous. It's a Sunday."

Carina held firm.

"No, I really don't want any."

Vivianne looked at her intently for a few drawn-out seconds before shrugging and taking a gulp from the glass herself. Something about the motion made Carina wonder if it was her first glass of the day. She suspected it wasn't.

Not that it was unusual for Vivianne to drink, but it was unusual for it to be noticeable—at this time of day, at the very least.

Could it be that she was nervous, too?

Vivianne sat down on a firmly stuffed embroidered chair, while Carina sank down uncomfortably far into the soft couch beside it. Vivianne was still holding the sherry glass in one hand, her little finger standing to attention. The scintillating crystal twinkled in the light of the chandelier.

The apartment had, if it was possible, grown even more cluttered since Carina had last been there, with paintings big and small lining the walls like a patchwork quilt. Each one was probably worth a tidy sum. Vivianne had good taste. She just didn't know when it was time to stop.

"So," said Vivianne, a venomous bite to her voice. "Thanks to you Victoria doesn't want to pick up the phone when I call her anymore. How is my granddaughter?"

"I can't say anything about my patients . . . ," said Carina, but then relented: "Eleanor is doing fine."

Vivianne rolled her eyes.

"I can't understand why she still persists with that. I thought it was just a phase. I told Vendela when she was pregnant that 'Eleanor' was a dreadful name. But 'Victoria'—now that's a name."

Carina said nothing. She wanted to cut to the chase. But she knew how Vivianne worked. You couldn't force her to talk. You had to let her get to the point in her own sweet time.

They made small talk for a while, Vivianne dishing out short, snappy remarks that were probably intended to sound sharp but mainly sounded tetchy and a little drunk. Carina kept herself to herself. Waited.

Eventually Vivianne leaned forward.

"Well, I haven't asked you here to chitchat," she said. "Though it might be nice if you cared to pay a visit to the woman who raised you every now and then."

You're the one who cut me off, thought Carina. *You're the one who abandoned me.*

"I know you're still wondering about your mother," said Vivianne. "Well, I'm no spring chicken anymore, and . . . it's time we talked."

The breath caught in Carina's chest.

"Do you know something?" she asked, hearing the words tumble desperately from her lips. "I've been wondering so long, Vivianne. She might still be alive. She would be old, but maybe . . ."

Vivianne shook her head abruptly. A sharp, irritated flick, as though she were swatting away a fly.

"Look, I've told you she isn't coming back," she said. "You were always like this. Whining on about when Mommy's coming home. She's gone. What about that don't you understand?"

Carina's throat was stinging. Suddenly she was five years old again, there in the forest at Solhöga, crying and calling out for her mother in the trees until she lost her voice. She had kicked and screamed when Mats came to get her.

"But she worked for you," Carina pressed. "You must have documents, right? An employment contract? Something with an address on it? Maybe she went home. I think she had a sister—maybe she knows something?"

Vivianne stood up abruptly from the chair and took a few steps into the center of the room. Standing there she looked like a tall, straight pillar.

"Eleanor will be here soon," she said, as if to herself. "Perhaps this was a bad idea. We should probably do this another day."

Carina stood up, too.

"You know something, don't you?" she said. "If you don't want to tell me then can't you at least tell Mats to do it? He refuses to say anything, says he can't break his promise to you. But you know where she went, don't you? She told you before she left."

Her whole life Carina had been looking for her mother—in Vivianne, in her foster mother, in her college professors, and then in her husband—always searching for some explanation as to why her mother had left her. What it was about her that had meant her mother didn't want her. What her mother had seen in her that was so repellent or ugly or wrong that she couldn't cope.

Vivianne said nothing.

Carina took a step toward her, put her hand on her thin shoulder.

"Vivianne," she said, feeling raw despair in her throat. "You have to tell me."

Vivianne yanked herself free and shook her head.

"This was a bad idea," she said again, and her speech impediment sounded stronger now, the words rounder.

"No!" Carina exclaimed. "No. You have to tell me. You have no right, Vivianne. If you know where my mother is you have to tell me. I want to meet her. I want to ask her why she left. If you know, you have to tell me."

"Sometimes it's better not to know, Kicki," Vivianne said over her shoulder, throwing Carina an unexpectedly dark, melancholy look. "We did it for your sake. Don't you understand? We wanted to give you the best life we could."

It felt like there was a pressure on Carina's chest. As though someone had taken a seat on her rib cage and was refusing to let her inhale.

"You gave me no life at all," she said. "None. Evert was the only one who cared about me, and when he died you packed me off before his body was even cold. You never willingly looked after me, Vivianne, but still you were always telling me how grateful I should be—grateful that you wanted me even though my mother didn't. Do you know how that feels? Can you even understand? To have to live with that?"

"You have no idea what I have had to live with," Vivianne snapped. "You have no idea what I have borne so that you wouldn't have to. None of the others could hack it. Understand? I've carried the guilt alone. Mats holed himself up in that house, and Evert swallowed a handful of pills. I was the only one who looked after you, the only one who could. No one else. I had no one, but I found the strength. I did it for you."

"What?" said Carina. "What have you 'borne'?"

"The truth," said Vivianne. "Do you think Evert actually cared about you? Evert used you to torture himself. He looked after you because every day you reminded him of what we had done. It was nothing but masochism, Kicki. You were never any more than a whip he could lash himself with."

The pressure in Carina's chest and head was starting to build. It felt like her skull was going to explode.

"What did you do?" she whispered.

Vivianne shook her head and started to walk into the hall.

"It's time for you to go, Kicki," she said. "Put your boots on and get out. Out of my apartment. I don't have the strength."

Carina ran up to her and took hold of her arm.

"No!" she exclaimed. "Not until you tell me what happened. I have a right to know. Tell me! Tell me what you did!"

Vivianne spun around, her eyes blazing in her pale face. Her red lipstick had smudged a little around the corners of her mouth.

"Your mother's dead, Kicki," she spat. "Is that what you want to hear? She's been dead for over fifty years. She never left Solhöga. She's dead, you hear? We killed her!"

The blood was roaring through Carina's ears. Her hand had stiffened to a claw around Vivianne's arm.

"Let me go!" she heard Vivianne cry, though it sounded like barely a whisper through the storm in Carina's own head. "You're hurting me."

Carina didn't hear her. She groped around blindly with her free hand, trying to find the wall, something to steady herself against, to hold her up.

Her hand landed on the dresser, and her fingers closed around the thin, antique silver scissors.

· ELEANOR ·

"All I wanted was to get out of here," says Carina. "I tried to get out of here. Even after the crash. I couldn't bring your lawyer into the house, because then you would see me. So I dragged him to the hunting lodge. At least there he would be out of the snow until you found him, but then I saw . . ." Her jaw clenches. "Then I saw Mats."

When she says his name there is an audible tremor in her voice.

"Just like she said," she says, seemingly more to herself than us. "He couldn't live with it. None of them could live with what she did."

I don't dare say anything. I hardly dare breathe.

She turns to Veronika.

"I didn't want to hurt you," Carina says. "I just panicked. All I wanted was to get out of here. I didn't want you to see me. I had already tried to go back to town, and then I hit that man, and I didn't know how to get out of this place. All I knew was that nobody could see me. I didn't mean to hurt you. It wasn't supposed to be like this."

She sighs. "But it's too late now."

"It's not too late," I say. "You can go. We won't tell anyone. Rickard doesn't remember anything."

Carina looks at me. I keep on babbling.

"I know what she was like, Carina," I say. "She said something, didn't she? She provoked you. Maybe she even wanted you to do it. It wasn't your fault. Vivianne knew which buttons to press. At times I've wanted to kill her myself. She made you do it. It was her own fault."

I hold my breath. Carina shakes her head.

"I wish I could believe you, Eleanor," she says. "But that's a risk I can't take. Vivianne took everything from me. She took my whole life. If I end up in prison now, she's won."

I have no words left.

"I'm not going to shoot you, Eleanor," she says. "I don't want any of you to feel pain. If I could have gotten out of here without coming back into the house I would have. This has all been so humiliating. This was my home, and here I am having to sneak around like a trespasser. Like a shadow." She shakes her head.

"But I needed Mats' car keys. His car is parked on the logging road. They used to use it for transportation. It's further out in the forest, just past the hunting lodge. You would have seen it if you had gone another few hundred feet. He wrote in his good-bye letter that the keys were in the kitchen, and I couldn't get out of here without them. I knew that you would be on your guard. I wanted to try to get in and out and away from here without you seeing me. I knew that if you saw me I wouldn't be able to let you leave."

Her eyes are sad.

"If you hadn't locked the door I could have just sneaked in, taken the keys, and gone, but the only way in was through the dumbwaiter. I've known since I was a child that you could pull the chains to travel up and down. I tried to get out in the kitchen, but the hatch was stuck. I really did my best to prevent things from turning out this way, Eleanor. . . ." She shakes her head and sighs.

"The power's out. The temperature will soon start to fall. I'll open the doors when I go. I'm going to take your shoes and jackets and tie you up. Not hard—I don't want it to hurt—just tight enough so you won't be able to free yourselves. It'll get colder and colder and . . . it'll just be like a dream. You'll hardly notice what's happening. You'll drift off to sleep and never wake up."

"You can't do this, Carina," I whisper. "You can't."

"I don't want to," she says, her eyes glistening with tears. "You don't deserve this, Eleanor. I know. But I don't either. I can't let her win. She killed my mother."

Silence falls. She looks at me.

A single tear escapes me and runs down my cheek.

"Please," I whisper.

She swallows, shakes her head.

"I can't," she says.

The time seems to draw out, thin down.

Sebastian's phone bleeps. Then there's a flash of light, and everything goes black. Out of battery. The room is plunged into darkness.

"What . . . ," says Carina.

There is an explosion of activity.

I hear Sebastian scream: "*Run, Eleanor!*" followed by a heavy thud and a hard crack, and Sebastian groaning in pain.

I turn around and run, blind.

Down the dark steps.

Out into the blizzard.

· ELEANOR ·

The adrenaline is pumping through my veins, my heart pounding in my ears. I can't see where I'm going, I just run. Out. Away.

My boots slip on the icy snow. I never took them off when I ran inside. But I did take off my jacket. The cold wants to choke me, the snow swirls around me, and the darkness envelops me. I can't see where I'm heading.

I have to get away. Have to run. Have to save them.

She's going to follow you, Victoria, says Vivianne in my head.

You have to make sure she can't find you.

I don't even know where I am. Where can I run? There's nowhere to go. No one to ask for help.

I'm alone.

"Eleanor!" I hear a cry somewhere behind me.

I don't turn around. I keep on running.

"Eleanor!"

Her roars blend with the wind behind me.

I'm younger than her, much younger. But she's in good shape, and my thighs are already burning. I feel the chilled skin under my trousers tightening and rubbing as I run. My legs already want to give up.

She has a gun. I have nothing.

If you stop now, you die, Victoria.

You can't stop.

"If you don't stop I'll shoot!" she cries behind me.

She can't shoot me if she can't see me.

The ground beneath me slopes downward, and the snow turns into a mix of ice and gravel. The lake.

I don't hesitate. I run out onto the lake. Onto the ice.

How deep is the lake? How thick is the ice? I don't know. I have no time to think. Maybe I can hide out here. Maybe she won't follow me out here.

There is only a thin layer of snow on the shiny ice, and the soles of my boots are worn. I slip, try to keep myself upright. It isn't the biggest of lakes. I'm almost at the middle.

"Eleanor," I hear again.

Closer now. Too close.

The ice has slowed me down.

Don't stop.

I stop.

I turn around.

The shadow in the blizzard is standing by the shore. I don't need to see her clearly to know the rifle is pointed at me.

She starts walking toward me.

Run.

If I run, she'll shoot me. The rifle in her hands is a hunting rifle: it must be accurate, even at a distance. And even if she doesn't hit me in the chest, she could catch an arm or a leg. Do I want to lie here and bleed out on the ice?

No, in that case I'd prefer a clean hit.

I'd rather that.

My pulse has slowed. I have never felt as alive as I do now. Is this how it feels, knowing you're about to die?

Was this how you felt, Vivianne? I ask myself silently.

Was this what you tried to tell me when you were lying there on the hallway floor?

She doesn't respond.

Carina is walking toward me with calm, sure steps. She doesn't slip on the ice. She doesn't need to run. She has time.

I didn't mean what I said up there, I say to Vivianne, to the voice in my head. *I was just saying anything I could to get her to let us go. You could be pretty awful. But you didn't deserve to die. I miss you. Every day.*

I know, Eleanor, she replies softly.

I love you, I say to her.

I know, says the voice that was never Vivianne. The voice that was always me.

Carina stops just a few steps from me. The wind is whipping her hair up around her head. The rifle is just a dark shadow.

Neither of us says anything.

"Do it," I say. "Shoot me."

Her arms are shaking.

"It didn't have to be like this," says Carina. "You could have just drifted off to sleep. You could all have just drifted off to sleep. I didn't want to hurt you."

"You want to kill us. So do it! Look me in the eye and shoot me!" I roar. My words are caught by the wind and hurled up over our heads. "You slit Vivianne's throat, didn't you?"

"Vivianne deserved it!" she screams, her shadowy face contorted. "Vivianne never cared who she hurt. Why should I care about her pain? She never cared about mine! She killed my mother!"

"This isn't about your mother," I whisper.

I see that she can't hear me. My lips are numb, my tongue frozen stiff in my mouth. I want to scream but can't.

She takes one step closer.

"What did you say?" she asks.

"This isn't about your mother," I repeat.

"Quiet."

"Your mother's been dead for more than fifty years. This isn't going to bring her back. But you don't care about that, not really. You just want revenge."

"Shut up," Carina says. The rifle floats like a specter before me, but I go on.

"You're in pain, and you want that pain to stop, so you want revenge," I say. "But that isn't how it works. 'An eye for an eye makes the world blind,' wasn't it you who told me that? 'The only one who can heal you is you.' *You* said that, Carina."

"It isn't fair!" she screams. "I never even got a chance. I deserve a chance!"

With Vivianne's voice on my lips, I say:

"You had your chance, Kicki."

I jump at her just as the shot fires.

It all happens so fast I don't feel anything—not the jolt of my shoulder slamming into her chest, nor me landing heavily on top of her as she falls onto the ice, winding myself in the process. There's no time to think, no time to breathe. I punch her in the face, surprised at my own force, then grab the rifle and pull it, hard—so hard my arms scream and ache—while pinning her down. Suddenly she lets go.

I hold the butt in one hand, the barrel in the other. Carina is writhing and kicking under me, trying to slip away, but I bend forward and press the barrel of the gun across her neck so that her head is pushed down onto the ice.

She coughs, and I press a little harder.

Her eyes are wide, and her face is red. Snowflakes are landing and melting on her cheeks.

"Please," she chokes. "Can't breathe."

I press even harder. Put more weight on the barrel.

Her hands flap.

All I want is to keep on pressing. Until she breaks through the ice and sinks. Until she closes her eyes.

"You killed my grandmother," I say to her.

The tears run down my cheeks, mixing with the snow.

Her feet are scrabbling behind me, searching for a foothold. There is nothing.

"Victoria," she says, "please."

Let go.

It's a soft whisper in my head: the voice that she would use back when I was a little girl, when it was dark and quiet and we were alone and she was sober, tucking me in bed.

Let go.

"My name is Eleanor," I say, then pull away the rifle and punch her in the face with my clenched fist.

FOUR MONTHS LATER

· ELEANOR ·

I had to part with my cell phone and keys. I feel naked without them. Ever since Solhöga I've felt a constant need to have my phone at hand. If the battery drops below 50 percent or the signal is poor it sends my pulse racing.

The room is small and bare. There are two squat, red armchairs and a table.

They said it wouldn't be long.

Twice I have stood up and told myself this is a bad idea, that I should just go home. But both times I have sat back down.

The door opens. I don't move.

In the anonymous, shapeless clothes she looks different. Smaller. The white glare of the tube lights washes her out. Her hair is longer, almost down to her shoulders, and she is wearing a pair of glasses that I don't recognize. All of the markers are wrong, but I know it has to be her.

The guard nods at me and then leaves.

Carina lingers by the door. Her lips are pale.

I gesture to the empty chair.

"You can take a seat," I say, struck by a sudden, intense memory of another time. Another Carina.

Of walking into her practice that first time, so nervous that I had almost thrown up in a trash can at the metro station. Of her opening the door and smiling at me.

Eleanor. I'm so glad you're here. Come in.

She sits down with what look like shaky knees. I don't see any new marks on her face. When I asked the police officer if I had hurt her very badly, they told me they couldn't disclose private medical information, but at the trial she seemed to have some difficulty talking. Veronika said I must have fractured her cheekbone. She said it with palpable relish, but it mostly just made me feel sick inside.

I fractured two of my knuckles from the blow. That felt fair. My hand had swollen to double the size by the time we reached the nearest hospital, half an hour after finding Mats' car on the logging road.

"You look well."

Carina breaks the silence and then quickly looks at the floor, as though surprised at her own words.

"As well as I can be," I say, "under the circumstances."

She clears her throat.

Then she says:

"Thank you for coming. I wasn't sure if you would respond to my letters."

"I didn't intend to," I say.

She looks up.

"So why did you?" she asks, with what sounds like genuine curiosity.

I shake my head.

Sebastian didn't want me to come here. We fought about it, twice. When I left home this morning he wasn't speaking to me. He didn't sleep so well last night. It's rare that a whole night passes without him waking up from the nightmares. Last night it happened three times.

"I don't know," I say eventually. "I wanted to hear what you had to say."

Carina's hands are clasped in her lap. It's hard for me to look at them, knowing they are the same hands that killed Vivianne. The same hands that pointed the rifle at us. That dragged Rickard through the snow and smacked a stone into the back of Veronika's head.

They just look like hands. Small and pale and veiny.

Carina takes a deep, hacking breath and looks up at me with glistening eyes.

"I wanted to ask for forgiveness."

I can't help myself. I laugh.

"You want to ask me for forgiveness? Are you insane?"

"Not for that," says Carina. "That I can't ask for."

"No. You can't."

"I wasn't myself. I was desperate. I wasn't thinking straight. I would do anything to undo it."

"You can't," I cut her off.

She looks away.

For a few seconds we both sit in silence. In the end I can't hold it in anymore.

"So if not that, then what did you want to ask forgiveness for?"

She still won't look at me.

"I should have done something. When you were younger. We all saw how Vivianne treated you. I know that a few of Vivianne's . . . acquaintances . . . talked about it, including me. I knew better than anyone how Vivianne could be. How badly she could hurt a child. I should have made sure you got out of there."

I swallow.

She goes on.

"I tried to make up for it later, helping you to manage your prosopagnosia, and teaching you to stand on your own two feet. I couldn't help you when you were a child, but I know . . . I know what it's like to grow up without a mother. I tried to be more than a therapist to you. Later. Some kind of mother figure."

When she does eventually look at me, her eyes are big and elusive. Imploring.

It's like something is caught in my throat.

"I want you to know that that was sincere," she says.

I rub my throat.

"I didn't need a mother," I say. "Vivianne was my mother. She wasn't a very good one. But she loved me." I can't stop my voice from shaking. "And you took her from me."

She clenches her eyes shut.

"Yes," she says.

Silence.

"Was there anything else?" I ask her after a while.

Carina looks at me. When she speaks I can hear traces of her old voice.

"You're stronger than you think, Eleanor," she says. "I want you to know that I'm proud of you."

I stand up.

"I don't hate you, Carina," I say. "But I don't forgive you. I don't owe you that. And you have no right to be proud of me. I don't need your approval."

I walk to the door and signal to the guard outside that the visit is over.

When I step through the door, with my keys back in my pocket and my cell phone safely in my hand, the sky is blue. For a moment I allow myself to stop, close my eyes, and tilt my face up to the sun. It draws fine, veiny patterns on the inside of my eyelids.

I listen for Vivianne's voice in my head. Something taunting, something angry, something loving.

But it's completely, completely silent.

· VIVIANNE ·
THEN

I have already vomited twice. If it were up to me I would cancel tonight. But we can't. Everything is riding on this dinner.

We haven't seen anyone in months. We stayed out here. He took time off work, said he had to care for his sick wife, and we worked and worked until every last crumb of Anushka had disappeared from my body and Vivianne was all that remained.

Every movement I make is studied, every word meticulously pronounced.

I look at myself in the mirror. The face that stares back at me doesn't look like my own. My hair is shiny and thick and brushed, styled in an intricate updo by one of the new girls. The blonde.

I can't bring myself to look at her. I find that I'm short and aggressive with her, the grief and guilt poisoning every word I say.

I hate her because she isn't Märit.

It feels so strange to see those two girls bustling around in the kitchen, shrinking under my gaze, flinching when I order them to do something. And I just fall into Vivianne's tone of voice, for if I let that mask slip, even just for a second, it feels as though I might crumble. Or give myself away. That would be worse.

We have come too far for that now.

He has stopped seeing his family. He claims they knew her too well, that they would know. All of those lovely, lively, colorful cousins they

· 325 ·

used to have over for dinner can never come here again. Instead just superficial acquaintances. This little shindig tonight is for his colleagues and their wives. We are calling it a country Christmas dinner.

I hear, rather than see, him step into the bedroom behind me. I ask over my shoulder:

"Could you do me up?"

His steps are heavy. I see him stand behind me, place his hand on my bare shoulder for a second before pulling up the zipper.

The thick, red silk of the dress shimmers in the light of the candles. I asked one of the girls to light them. It reminds me of home.

"It's a beautiful dress," he says quietly. His hand is still heavy on my shoulder.

I remember the last time I saw this dress. She wore it two summers ago. It was one of the last parties of the summer, and she called it the August red.

"Will this be suitable for the dinner?" I ask without meeting his eyes.

"Yes," he says. "You are very beautiful."

He squeezes my shoulder, soft fingertips, then pulls his hand away.

"Could you go downstairs and check the wine?" I ask.

"Of course," he says, and turns on his heels. I don't think it's just my imagination that he's relieved to leave the room.

The silences between us have started to get longer and longer. I wonder how long it will be before we start to hate each other. The worst of it is, I love him. Foolishly and desperately, like a giddy little schoolgirl. I had nothing else to do in all those months out here.

I long for the day I can hate him. Then it will be easier. Then it won't hurt to see him pull away, see him drown his sorrows more each day, see him fade and wither under the weight of what happened.

My stomach lurches again. I run into the bathroom and throw up water into the toilet, careful not to ruin my lipstick when I pat my mouth dry.

Once I've washed my hands I sink back down to the floor, rest my head against the cold porcelain basin, and close my eyes. I place one hand on my belly and the other one in my pocket.

It was inevitable, I suppose. By day we don't speak, but by night we tear each other apart, grab each other with such force it leaves bruises in the dawn. As though we are trying to punish each other for the lie we are living. For the secret we will both have to carry for the rest of our lives.

It has been three months since I last had my period. I haven't started to show yet, but I know that day will come soon.

I have never been as scared of anything as I am of what is growing inside me. A new human. One I will have to look after and raise.

But maybe, just maybe, it can be a good thing. Maybe this can be the start of something new. Maybe we can redeem the terrible thing we did.

A sibling for Kicki. Then we can all be together here at Solhöga. Mats can teach them to ride the horses in the stable. Mats, who is now so quiet. Who helped us to sink the bodies into the lake that night.

An accident. It was an accident.

If I say it enough, perhaps it will make it true.

It's how I became Vivianne, after all.

I pull out the photograph I hid in the thin, invisible pocket at my hip. I can now almost look at it without getting tears in my eyes. It's of me and Märit, half a lifetime ago. In the photo she is squinting into the sun. She looks happy.

"Kicki lives with us now," I tell her. "I want to give her a family. I'm going to raise her the way you would have wanted. And we'll bring her out here every summer and winter, so she can be near you. Doesn't that sound nice?"

She doesn't reply. I have tried to hear her voice in my head many times, but always without success.

I don't even remember how it sounds.

Perhaps it's because she knows I'm lying.

I would like nothing more than to send Kicki away. So I don't have to see her, or that little face of hers that seems to resemble Märit's more and more each day. Or hear her ask after her mother, time and again.

But I don't dare send her away.

I don't know what she remembers.

Does she remember Marta? Does she remember that I once had another name?

Did she notice Mats' shifty eyes and trembling hands when he came to carry her into the house that night?

It's a risk we can't take.

I put the photo back in my pocket. That last little crumb of the person I was.

Annika is dead. Anushka is dead.

I buried her in that little maid's cubby and had the door wallpapered over, so I would never again have to see who I once was.

I hear the doorbell downstairs ringing and stand up. Smooth my dress out over my hips. Look in the mirror to see the ghost of my cousin staring back at me.

She is smiling. Bloodred lips over white teeth.

I don't allow myself to feel anything.

I just walk down the stairs with a hand on the bannister and greet them with a little wave, like she would have done, like I have seen her do a thousand times:

"Welcome! Welcome to our home!"

The woman in the couple that has just arrived is in her early forties, with fluffy gold hair. When I take her coat she stares at me, and the anxiety makes my stomach turn again.

Then she breaks into a smile.

"Oh, Vivianne, it's so nice to see you again! You look dazzling."

I smile and feel nothing. Nothing at all.

· THANK YOU ·

Writing a book can be hell sometimes, but it makes it easier if you have snus, spirits, and coffee at hand. No, wait—that should be "supportive friends and a fantastic team." Damn autocorrect!

(I will also be blaming autocorrect if I forget anyone.)

Thank you to Anna, my eternal first reader and Friend Extraordinaire, who listened to me patiently as I went on about how hard it is to finish a draft—and who inspired Alexia, a character who unfortunately didn't make it all the way through the edits. The problem was that she, like you, was way too funny and interesting and charismatic. She completely stole the show.

Thanks to Saga, who has known me since before I got braces and who always reminds me of the importance of taking breaks. Both the book and me are much, much better off than we would have been if I hadn't listened to you.

Thank you to my family, who put up with me for nine days over Christmas when I was in a manic writing frenzy to finish the second half of this book. Special thanks to my brothers, Alexander and Leo, whose memes, puns, and general charm kept me somewhat anchored to reality.

Thank you to Erika, my fantastic publisher. It is truly a gift to get to work with you. I become a better writer with every point you make. (Author's note: Erika messaged me after the edits and wrote so many kind things about the book. I am considering having that message tattooed on my lower back.)

Thank you to my editor, Eva, who has almost a better feel for my text than I do, and who somehow manages the near-impossible feat of giving the text a really good once-over while also making the world's nicest, most peppy comments. Keeping a writer both motivated and engaged is the toughest balancing act. You are a gem.

Thank you to my agent, Anna, who once told me I should write what I want to write, not what I think the market wants. That's the best advice anyone has ever given me, and it's so nice to know that I can place my book in your hands.

Thank you to Mark, my amazing boyfriend. I have never known anyone who is as proud of me as you. And yet that's just a fraction of how proud I am of you. I am so immensely lucky to have you in my life.

Thank you to Rasmus the Cat. You were my little editing assistant, and it pains me to think that this is the last book I will get to write with you purring away at my feet.

You were a very, very special cat. I didn't know it was possible to miss a pet this much.

And finally, thank you to my grandmother Lisbeth, who inspired this book. I started to write *The Resting Place* after you passed away, in an attempt to both understand you better and get to spend a little more time with you.

You were a fantastic, difficult, funny, driven, colorful woman who taught me about everything from the perfect crispbread toppings to how you can never over-coordinate your clothes. I know you were proud of me when you read my first book. I hope you would have been proud of this one, too.

CAMILLA STEN, FALL 2020